CARTWRIGHT'S CAVALIERS: DESCENT

BOOK FOURTEEN OF THE GUILD WARS

Mark Wandrey with Kacey Ezell

Seventh Seal Press
Coinjock, NC

Chris Kennedy/Seventh Seal Press
1097 Waterlily Rd.
Coinjock, NC 27923
https://chriskennedypublishing.com/

Publisher's Note: This is a work of fiction. Names, characters, places, and incidents are a product of the author's imagination. Locales and public names are sometimes used for atmospheric purposes. Any resemblance to actual people, living or dead, or to businesses, companies, events, institutions, or locales is completely coincidental.

Cover Design by Brenda Mihalko.
Original Art by Ricky Ryan.

Ordering Information:
Quantity sales. Special discounts are available on quantity purchases by corporations, associations, and others. For details, contact the "Special Sales Department" at the address above.

Cartwright's Cavaliers: Descent/Mark Wandrey & Kacey Ezell -- 1st ed.
ISBN: 978-1648551987

To all those who've fought for a cause,
especially the ones who knew it might be a lost cause.

Chapter One

Jim barely managed not to slam the conference room door with all his might as he exited, instead letting it close on its hydraulic mechanism. "Fucking assholes," he growled under his breath as he walked into the bustling hallway. A few of the functionaries glanced at him as they rushed by on their own business. Some might have actually recognized him. None dared say anything to the minister of war. His face was a mask of fury. He didn't care.

The last three hours of what he'd thought would be a situational meeting with his fellow ministers in the Terran Federation had ended up being anything but. Instead, they'd basically ambushed him.

"Minister Cartwright, can you explain the logic of the minister of war being directly involved in an assault on a Science Guild facility?" Jim had been caught completely flatfooted. So, he'd responded as he'd learned was best; he went right in, guns blazing.

"I would think 'minister of war' implies combat. It's in the title."

There had been a few chuckles among the other ministers in the closed-door meeting. The Federation prime minister hadn't been quite as amused.

"The United States is finally giving in to the inevitable," she said. "In six months, maybe a year, we might have reunification, something we thought impossible only a few months ago. Brazil has been

5

welcomed into the fold. Minister Cartwright, we don't need you tilting at alien windmills just now."

"The Science Guild was at the center of the plot to sabotage humanity's technological ability," Jim said. "I've provided the evidence to this end. Federation citizens—mercs—were abducted, duplicated, and used as *weapons* against us. I've also provided the tech needed to neutralize the computer virus they released."

"Though not the source of this retro-virus," the minister of technology said. "You've said it wasn't from the Dusman."

Jim nodded. "My source is confidential, and I have complete faith in their ability, as should you." He had no intention of making that knowledge public. He'd rescued a small group of survivors of a race from slavery, years ago, and considered the matter closed. That is, until they turned up in the Sol system, squatted on an old asteroid mine, and began inventing stuff. The Aku looked a lot like turtles but were possessed of technical acumen rivaling the Dusman, maybe even better. They were humanity's ally, and Jim intended to keep that alliance a secret if possible.

"So are you firing me?" Jim had growled.

"No," the prime minister said. "The lack of details regarding the minister of war participating directly in armed conflict was an oversight in the governing language. We've fixed it. You're officially forbidden from purposely putting yourself in harm's way, Minister Cartwright. This meeting is concluded."

He continued to mumble to himself all the way to his office. He'd been feeling pretty good about himself, too, until he'd been summoned to the meeting. "More like an official spanking," he grumbled as he passed his executive assistant.

"I'm sorry, Minister?" the man asked as Jim passed him.

"Nothing," Jim snapped back over his shoulder. "Hold all calls." He didn't wait for a response. *This* door he could slam as hard as he wanted. His assistant barked in alarm as the heavy door thundered closed. It didn't provide the satisfaction he'd hoped it would.

Jim plopped into his chair and stared out the window for a while. He fantasized about just quitting, calling them out over their hypocrisy in the press, or even just ignoring their new edict entirely. Ultimately, it was his father's words from many years ago that made him do nothing.

"Jim, the Cartwright family has a reputation to uphold. Generations before you have worked hard to make this family what it is today. Never forget that."

"What would Dad think if I made a hash of this?" he wondered aloud. Yeah, he already knew. With a sigh, he turned his office Tri-V on and looked over spreadsheets and reports, which was what took up most of his days, anyway.

After the battle on Morgoth against the ultra-powerful, synthetic intelligence Minerva, the last thing he'd thought he'd be doing was being berated for doing his job and spending day after day going over spreadsheets.

Amazingly, despite his level of distraction, he got through the mountain of spreadsheets and signed off on an equally large list of reports, and well before dark, which was becoming increasingly unusual.

Through the huge, armored glass window of his office in the Ministry Building, close to old downtown Houston, Jim could see a pair of Raknar walking stiffly out of the partially completed Raknar facility. The Cavaliers owned many thousands of acres on the outskirts of Houston, part of a trust his father had left for him. That and the 'museum' grade equipment stored at the Cavaliers' exhibits had allowed him to rebuild from the ashes of Peepo's plot to destroy him. He'd carved off a good-sized chunk for the Dusman to use for setting up the Raknar base.

One of the things yet to be worked out was how the Raknar and their Dusman manufacturers fit within the force structure of the Terran Federation. They were officially allies now, but the Dusman weren't mercs. The latter had been made quite clear to Jim. They wouldn't respond to assist in some contract for credits. They weren't interested in money.

"We're here for the coming war with the Kahraman," Sly had said shortly after their declaration of alliance with humanity.

"You're sure there'll be a war?" Alexis had asked.

"I've dreamed as much," Seldia had said. A Dusman *k'apo*, or far talker, also sometimes had prophetic dreams. Splunk should have been one, too, but didn't have all the gifts. She had, however, had one powerful vision; humanity and the Dusman would be allies one day. If you considered this dream had occurred years before any Dusman even laid eyes on a Human, it was doubly prophetic.

"When will this war go hot?" Nigel had persisted.

"We don't know," Sly had said. "Only that it draws ever closer. The mayhem your Union has fallen into, the reemergence of synthetic intelligences, all of this bears witness to what is to come. We have scouts searching for the Kahraman in an attempt to ascertain their plan of attack. One has been following their fleet elements after they recently retreated."

Jim had met with them several times in the weeks since the alliance began and discussed the Dusman's efforts on the other colonies.

"Your own race's lack of governmental cohesion led us to contact your surviving colonies. We needed recruits for Raknar drivers." Sly gave an all-too-Human shrug. "You would have eventually been informed."

"Eventually," Jim echoed. Nigel rolled his eyes, and Alexis shook her head. Sansar merely observed, as she had since the meetings began.

With his paperwork finished, Jim turned his attention to his monthly agenda. The brief conflict with the Science Guild had thrown a big, carbon-steel wrench into his plans. He'd been trying to get Earth ready to defend against another attack by the Mercenary Guild, not against SIs. Especially SIs with weapons like that near-C slug-thrower.

Sitting in his inbox was a recently updated analysis of the weapon from Chiss, the leader of the Aku, whom Jim considered a friend. Chiss reported he'd found an obscure reference to a weapon called a "Mobius Gun," which bore a significant resemblance to what they'd faced in Morgoth. The GalNet said the weapon had never been built, due to material sciences issues. Since they'd faced it in battle, it seemed once again that Minerva, the Science Guild SI, had simply plucked the invention out of existence and kept it for itself. He shivered as he considered there might be dozens, even hundreds of the weapons hidden throughout the galaxy. Apparently they were really hard to detect when they were just sitting there, hidden inside an asteroid crust, spinning like Satan's own gyroscope, waiting to destroy entire fleets.

In the short term, there wasn't much he could do. At least with the Dusman alliance, he no longer had to worry about an invasion.

Splunk had informed him shortly after the formal alliance began that they'd stationed a battlegroup around the emergence point.

Naturally, there were protests all over Earth within hours of the announcement. He left that to the Ministry of Information. When the press asked him, his response had been, "No comment." Thankfully, the Federation leadership had approved the alliance with almost no debate. Sometimes making friends with a vastly powerful alien race had its advantages. Jim still suspected there would be more talks. The United States had lodged a formal complaint with the Galactic Union. That made Jim grin; good luck with that.

On his list of to-do items was an upcoming trip to São Paulo for a dedication, then an off-world trip to the surviving Human colonies. He'd been inclined to put the latter off for some time, but after the day's meeting, he kept it there. He decided to get some sleep; the trip to São Paulo wasn't something he was looking forward to.

* * *

Dusman Cruiser *P'Ka*, Lunar Orbit, Sol

"*Vok'tor?*"

J'asa took a second to look up from the slate. She wasn't used to her new rank; that would probably take some time. "Yes, *Ske'i?*"

"Courier just brought in this communique from *Ch'to.*" The young naval officer held out a datachip, one of the highly-secured types, DNA coded and impossible to break.

J'asa—or Splunk, as she was known by her Human friends— took the chip and looked at it curiously. "Thank you," she said. The male officer looked at the chip curiously. "Is there something more?"

"I was hoping…"

"Dismissed, *Ske'i*," she said and turned back to her slate. She couldn't hear the officer leave in zero G, but she did hear the door close as confirmation. She grinned a little, her ears curving upward in amusement. The young officer was only curious, and likely excited. They were among the first to come back to normal space in eons, returning in anticipation of completing a war begun eons ago. A war J'asa had dreamed about while still in her creche.

Alone, she touched a finger to the datachip's sensor, changing it from blue to clear, then inserted it into her slate. It was a detailed report from As'bak, the *ske'ii* of scout frigate *Ch'to*. She'd last visited the Krrkow system and found evidence of the Kahraman, just as the intel from the so-called Mercenary Guild had said.

Thanks to their new servitors, the KzSha, they'd gained considerable information from the guild. Though the KzSha were not held in favor, they had channels and proxy to a seat on the council. The Kahraman had been trying to invade for an exceptionally long time, and a quiet war of resistance had been fought against them. Considering the pathetic level of technology the Dusman had found upon their return, it was amazing they'd managed to hold them at bay for so long.

J'asa had been reviewing all the details at her disposal. Though the Dusman had maintained listening posts in normal space, they weren't truly spies. It was far too risky to actively gather intelligence. Instead, they let it come to them, slowly, over centuries. Understanding the situation in the current day was complicated by what had been lost so long ago. If the Humans understood how limited their new allies' knowledge was…

The Tri-V behind her enveloped most of the compartment she used for her work. The entire galaxy was represented there, all 100 billion stars. Though it would take considerable enhancement to see them, the data was all there, including files behind each of the explored/known stars. Further, each of the composite arms had metadata attached to them. The Cygnus and Scatum arms, compositely known as the Fourth Arm, was full of blue dots representing unknown information.

"More than 20,000 years ago, you ran there," she said to the map. "Ran and slammed the door behind you." How, she didn't know. The method used to keep them from coming back was familiar to her, of course. The Dusman had ships equipped with interdiction field generators; all stargates were capable of it, too. Who had originally gone to the effort of interdicting an entire arm of the galaxy was unknown, though she suspected she knew the answer. Furthermore, though many ships in the galaxy had hyperspace shunts, none seemed to have figured out how to use them as interdictors. Their use certainly would alter the face of warfare as it currently existed. Interesting.

Ske'ii As'bak had been working her way along the edge of the front, the closest the enemy had thus far managed to penetrate from their formerly self-imposed prison. There was too much that didn't make sense. The addition of the SIs to the equation was both disturbing, and potentially game changing. But she lacked enough information, and needed answers to other mysterious questions. There was only one place to go to get them.

She activated the internship comms. "*Ske'ii?*"

"Yes, *Vok'tor?*" the ship's master replied immediately.

"Prepare to transition to 2nd level hyperspace. I need to visit the archives back home."

"Understood, *Vok'tor.* I will make the preparations."

She cut the circuit and quickly composed a message to Jim. He wouldn't understand, but he needed to know she'd be gone for weeks, or even months. The sooner she got this over, the sooner she'd be back. Hopefully with answers.

* * * * *

Chapter Two

Jim tried to pay attention to the speeches given by the various officials, celebrities, and community leaders. He wouldn't have been there at all, on the second anniversary of the end of the Omega War, if it weren't for a very recent event; Brazil had finally been accepted into the Terran Federation.

He'd gone on record as dead set against allowing Brazil to join so soon after the end of the war. The evidence of the old Earth Republic's complicity in Peepo's invasion, just like the United States', was unavoidable and incontrovertible. So much so that in recent elections large numbers of leaders in both countries were summarily shown the door. Jim still wanted to see prosecutions, and, with luck, he'd get them. Later.

The speaker drew the crowd's attention to the monument behind him. Jim looked at it. A kilometer long, it was made of a conglomeration of materials. Concrete and steel from ruined buildings, armor and guns from alien invaders, and the remains of destroyed CASPers. To finish it, Jim had donated parts of Sergeant Mays and Aura's Raknar, and the monument had been constructed on the spot where they'd died. He knew parts of Hargrave's burned and shredded armor were in there as well. They'd all bled for this memorial.

Finally, it was his turn to speak. There were almost more people on the VIP stands than in the crowd. Part of the reason was the radiation, of course. The assault he'd led on São Paulo—then the head-quarters of Peepo's armies—had utilized Raknar dropping from orbit. Their fusion-powered descent engines poured out massive amounts of radioactive waste. He hadn't fully understood the ramifications of this during the attack.

In intervening years since the attack, Dusman robots had worked hard to reduce the radiation. There were no more hot spots you would die from visiting, though the entire area was still well above background. The same robotic systems had built hundreds of new housing projects, all of this without cost to São Paulo or its people.

He moved to the podium, dressed in a dark gray business suit, with no sign of his mercenary rank or ministry position. None of that had felt appropriate.

"Two years ago, we fought a war to free our planet, our very people, from enslavement by Peepo and the Mercenary Guild. They wanted us to fight a war for them, to die for them, and sacrifice our freedom in exchange for this *privilege.*"

He looked out at the crowd and saw sadness, regret, some anger, and many other emotions. Memories of the battle there, their defeat, his imprisonment and eventual rescue, followed by the final defeat of Peepo flooded back. He stared at the speech in his pinplants for a long moment, the one his assistant had helped him write, then ignored it.

"People died," he said, quieter than he might have if he'd been reading from the speech. "Humans, aliens, men, women, and children. The numbers are inconceivable. We did what we felt needed to be done to liberate our planet. Historians will be dissecting the events of the Omega War for centuries to come, just like all previous wars. All we can hope to do is learn from our mistakes, and keep from repeating them."

He left the podium to polite applause he didn't even hear. He was already thinking ahead to the flight back to Houston, then to space. Instead, he waited as the last of the dignitaries spoke meaningless platitudes while he stared across the war-torn wastes, which had been a combined industrial/residential area before his fist of Raknar had turned it into the beachhead of the invasion of Earth. Much of it would remain like this for years, partly to honor the lost, and partly because it was too dangerous for long-term exposure.

His vision felt like it was blurred, as if he was looking through a murky tank of green algae. The energy bolt lanced down from space, spearing Mays and Aura's Raknar, and Doom roared in rage, crying for a tidal wave of blood in revenge.

"Are you okay, Minister Cartwright?"

Jim shook his head slightly and looked down at the functionary, who was starting at him in concern.

"Fine," Jim mumbled, and made a dismissive gesture. "Just the heat."

It was indeed hot, though since it was fall in the southern hemisphere, it was no real comparison to spring in Houston. The functionary nodded and turned his attention back to the speeches.

Finally the blathering was over, and the new president of Brazil, along with the Terran Federation prime minister, officially dedicated the monument to those who'd died in the war. They pressed the activation button, and the monument came to life.

Not just a sculpture wrought from the remains of war, it was a living testament as well. A surviving fusion powerplant from a destroyed Zuul tank provided the relatively small power necessary, and—carefully managed—would do so for millennia. Two eternal flames lit, composed of live plasma. One tinted blue at the peak of the long monument made to simulate Sau Paolo's skyline before the war, the other red and at the base. The blue was to commemorate the fighters who fell, and the red the innocent caught between aggressors. Along the left side was a Tri-V display that scrolled the names of all those known dead, along with their total number.

It currently displayed 173,009, which was the best known worldwide total. But as they watched, it went up by one, then another, then by three. The numerical value was dynamic, and would be constantly updated as new casualties were confirmed, or someone who'd been wounded during the war died.

The number didn't include the aliens who'd died, though Jim had fought for that as well. How many alien mercs fought willingly, and how many did so because they had no choice? He felt it left the monument ambiguous at best, and a lie at worst. But it was what it was. Anti-alien sentiment was pretty strong in São Paulo, which was currently trying to decide who they blamed more for their decimated city: Peepo, or Jim Cartwright.

There was a brief reception after the ceremony was complete. Some refreshments were offered, of which he didn't partake. Instead, Jim merely moved around the function space inside a newly constructed 5-star hotel, built against the hope of returned tourist trade to Brazil.

Once he decided he'd spent a sufficient amount of time speaking platitudes to the guests, Jim signaled his security detail and headed for the exit. A few reporters attempted to breach the gauntlet of six burly mercs, all Cavaliers, Jim's personal guard. Maybe they should have been Terran Federation soldiers. He didn't really care. He'd fought and bled with these men and women, and trusted them with his life.

"Minister Cartwright, do you feel remorse for what you did to São Paulo?"

The shouted question was in Portuguese, automatically translated by his pinplants. He didn't answer. They wouldn't like his answer.

A few minutes later he was in the dropship which had brought him down to São Paolo, its rockets roaring as it climbed into the afternoon sky. He had a last glimpse of the monument, now displaying 173,055. Just before they climbed out of view, it advanced again.

* * *

Cartwright's Cavaliers' HQ, Houston, Texas, Earth

Just over 100 years earlier, prior to first contact and major importations of galactic tech, the flight from São Paolo to Houston would have taken the better part of a day. Thanks to his dropship's suborbital hop, Jim was taxiing at the Cavaliers' runway 29 minutes after liftoff. While suborbital flights weren't yet as common as jets, they were commonplace.

"Thanks, men," he said as he unbuckled and tossed the guards a salute. The woman in his security team gave him a wry smile as she returned the salute. "I didn't forget you, Corporal Boscue."

"You better not, sir!"

Despite the rest of the day, he smiled as he exited the dropship. Since he was on his own base, they didn't accompany him back to the headquarters building. Instead, they waited until he was clear, raised the ramp, and the pilot taxied to the hangar, where they'd unass and debrief. Lieutenant Tony Sullivan, the platoon commander, would expect a full report, then that report would be forwarded to Lieutenant Colonel "Buddha" Kalawai.

Back in his office, he took a minute to upload his notes from the event out of pinplant storage to his office computer. They were a combination of written notes and a video transcript, encoded directly from his eyes to his pinplants. He'd made it a habit since taking the job. "Never trust politicians," his father had said. He'd said it often, too.

A knock sounded on the door. "In there, Colonel?" a familiar feminine voice said.

"Ziva!" he said and got up. She opened the door, a stern look on her face. "Sorry, Lieutenant Ziva. I was looking forward to seeing you tonight."

"That's why I came by. I'm going to have to take a raincheck."

"Oh, what's up?"

"Fssik and I are going to Azure."

"Part of the Depik project?"

"Yup," she said, walking over and sitting on the edge of his desk.

Their friendship had him in a confused place. Partly because she felt like more than just a friend, and partly because he'd doggedly refused to take even a fractional step past that well-defined friendship. At least he didn't have to worry about dealing with company scuttlebutt. That's all he needed—the press getting wind that Colonel/Minster Cartwright was having a relationship with a junior officer, not to mention a woman raised off Earth who was partner to a Depik.

"You know how long you'll be gone?"

"Months, at least." She saw the disappointed look on his face. "Less than a year, I promise. They need Fssik there, and she wants me nearby."

"A year with nothing but scientists and Wrogul to keep you company? Ugh," he said in mock disgust.

"There will be other Humans, both scientists and bonded members of clans. We haven't had many opportunities to get together as a community." She looked at him, her expression turning serious. "We're going to talk about Khatash, too."

Jim was instantly focused. "Are there still survivors there?"

"Unlikely," she said, shaking her head. "I mean, maybe in a few places, yeah." She looked at him, seemingly calculating. "When I get back, we can talk more. You've got a lot to do; you won't even know I'm gone."

"That's not true," he said. "I'll miss you."

"Thanks. I'll miss you, too." Then she leaned in and kissed him lightly on the lips.

Jim felt his cheeks growing hot. "Good thing it's after hours, or I'd have to put you on report."

She snorted and smiled. He loved her smile. "Call it a leave of absence?"

"Sure," he agreed. "No problem."

They chatted for another minute or two, then she was gone. He still didn't know how he felt about her. The saying might be overused, but he still considered it complicated.

After a time, he sat back at his desk, shaking his head and smiling. He quickly went through the remainder of his Cavaliers business. The arrangements he'd requested were in place and ready to go. The last thing was to clear out his personal messages. Jim was surprised to find one from Splunk.

Jim,

I have to make a trip home to do some research. I'm sorry there wasn't time to come in person; you were already flying to Brazil. I should be back in a month or two. Please be careful. We'll have lots of organization to do on the Raknar driver recruitment program we talked about. See you as soon as I can get back.

Vok'tor *J'asa*

Splunk

It was the first time he'd gotten an email from her. Jim hadn't known she even knew how to send an email. It seemed only yesterday he'd thought she was a friendly little alien creature who'd helped him survive on an ice planet. It only made sense, since she was really a member of the ancient Dusman race, that she'd know how to send an email. They probably thought it was a quaint way to send messages.

He checked the stargate log and, sure enough, a Dusman cruiser had been logged as it departed the system two hours ago. He silently wished her luck, wondering if she could sense his thoughts light years distant. The truth was, he didn't know the extent of the Dusman's psychic abilities.

The Dusman far-talkers could communicate complicated messages halfway across the galaxy, instantaneously. Splunk and he shared a link, but only on a sort of empathic level. The other paired Raknar drivers had a link with their Dusman, as well. Maybe he should ask Splunk for more details.

The last item was a message from Chiss. As with all communications from the Aku, it was a physical package delivered via in-system courier. Jim's main concern was keeping the details of the alien's presence in the Sol system secret as long as possible. Thus, any correspondence was sent via a secure diplomatic style message case back and forth. Slow, yes, but harder to accidentally stumble across than a radio communication to a supposedly abandoned asteroid installation.

He used the DNA verification system built into the case and opened it. Inside, he found a datachip and a small case, not much bigger than a satphone. Popping it open revealed a nestled rack of what resembled metallic pipe nibs.

"Bingo," he said, setting the case aside and slipping the datachip into his personal slate. The Tri-V activated, and the tortoise-like visage of Chiss appeared.

"Great Jim Cartwright," the alien said, bowing his head.

Jim moaned and rolled his eyes. He'd tried to dissuade them from calling him that, and failed. Chiss continued.

"These are the upgraded pinplant isolators you have requested— the pinlocks. As previously discussed at our last meeting, we still believe it would be better to modify your pinplants to stop unwanted external communications. However, since you are unwilling to simply fix every pinplant, these are designed to perform the isolation function you requested."

Jim had to smile. Chiss didn't understand why you couldn't just ask every being with pinplants in the galaxy to replace them with a new model because it turned out they were an easy way for a malevolent SI—synthetic intelligence—to take over your brain.

What worried Jim more than the fact their pinplants were an easy way to turn them into automatons was the fact that *all* pinplants had that vulnerability. He guessed, since the Science Guild was ultimately responsible for the design of pinplants, including modifying them for use with new species, it only stood to reason Minerva would like such a vulnerability.

Minerva was the name assigned to the SI behind the Science Guild, a 20,000-year-old ultra-powerful intelligence that had spent the millennia carefully controlling all technological development. *Suppressing* all technological development might be a better way of saying it. Based on some of the encounters with Minerva, and the less powerful version called Ghost that worked for the Winged Hussars, Jim thought the machine considered all Humans a threat. Its attack on humanity's computer databases and attempt to lure the Four Horsemen into an ambush had been the result of that sentiment.

The Horsemen, with Dusman help, had foiled the trap. Then the Aku's technical acumen had further foiled the attempt to destroy humanity's computers. In fact, the Aku's computer specialists had called the attempt "ham fisted." More and more, the Aku were becoming Jim and humanity's secret weapon. He had to keep them secret, or they, too, might become the target of Minerva's wrath.

Jim's rapidly growing intelligence network, with help from Sansar Enkh's already impressive intelligence gathering capabilities, scoured the galaxy for any hint of another move by Minerva against the children of Earth. He lost a lot of sleep waiting for the SI's counterstrike. Sooner or later, it was only a matter of time.

"I have to make sure I don't spend too long off planet," he mumbled as he examined the gifts from Chiss. The instructions were

simple. Click the pinlock in place on your pinlink, the external connection usually located above your ear. They would interface with the
user's pinplants and provide a simple switch. Activating it would
filter all external communications. Only outgoing and simple finan-
cial transactions weren't. You could either turn it back on with the
same mental switch, or remove the pinlock manually. However, you
could activate a feature in the pinlock that made it impossible to remove without the user's acknowledgement.

"A forceful attempt to remove the pinlock is likely fatal to the
user, as you requested."

Jim nodded, took a set, and clicked them into place on his own
pinlink with a *snap*. Instantly, a simple menu option appeared on his
pinplants' communications interface menu, just as Chiss had said it
would. Under "Security" was the option "Unremovable." He selected it without thinking about it. He was *not* going to be turned into a
fucking robot for Minerva.

He put three more pairs into a case from his desk, then into a
pocket. The rest he left on his desk and sent a message to the tech
department. Chiss had included all the schematics and 3D printing
files. He wanted these in mass production and the details sent to the
other Horsemen immediately.

As he stood and stretched, a wry smile crossed his face. Unless
he was mistaken, Sansar would have these on every single member of
the Golden Horde by this time tomorrow. Good. Ultimately, he
wanted them available to every Human and alien ally, after all the
Four Horsemen had them.

"Use these well, Great Jim Cartwright, and we wish you luck on
the mission for us."

Jim nodded in the empty office and sighed. Trying to retrieve the other Aku, still enslaved in the galaxy, was the price of working with them. Oh, Chiss had never made it a condition. Jim doubted the kind-hearted alien had in it him to do such a thing. But he knew they would be greatly disappointed in him if he didn't. The problem with being the Great Jim Cartwright was you had to live up to a larger-than-life reputation.

The truth, though, was that his father, Thaddeus, would have rescued them from slavery as well, and wouldn't have rested until all of them were free. Jim could live with someone not thinking he'd done his best, but he couldn't deal with the thought of his father thinking he'd done less than physically possible, if not a little bit more.

Feeling a little morose after São Paulo and Ziva's departure, Jim decided that what he needed was a real drink. As he never kept anything harder than Coke in his control-tower apartment, this called for a trip into town. He used his pinplants to summon an aerocab, logged out of his workstations, and left the office for the night.

Not an aficionado of bars, Jim let his fingers do the walking, and used the GalNet. There were 244 distinct bars in the Houston Starport Startown, and another 109 that were also restaurants. He wasn't into eating by himself, and he wasn't hungry anyway. Then a name jumped out at him. He grinned as the robotic aerocab landed.

He used his Yack to unlock the machine and climbed in. Crime had plummeted after the formation of the Federation, but the starport and the adjacent town under its jurisdiction was still a Wild West sort of place, not subject to any of the rules outside its perimeter. He keyed in the destination, and the cab lifted into the air with a scream of ducted fans.

It set him down in the street a scant five minutes later. He'd had to scan his Yack again as he passed into starport property, of course. While coming and going from the starport was easier since the Federation took over, it was still watched and controlled. Not to keep drugs and weapons— mostly—out, but to keep dangerous aliens out. Veetanho were not welcome in the Federation, except on strict diplomatic missions.

The aerocab beeped at him as the fans slowed to an idle. "Press release to exit cab."

Jim blinked at the display. You only got that warning if the area was...less than safe. His trusty GP-90 was in a shoulder holster under the light-duty jacket he was wearing, so he hit the release. He wondered if the address was wrong when he had to put a hand up to shield his eyes from the swirling garbage as the aerocab took to the air.

It looked like an old, abandoned strip mall, not at all the place his dad had talked about. Certainly not as storied as the scuttlebutt from mercs he'd talked to over the years. He queried his pinplants again, then looked at the old, rusty street signs. Everything matched up.

He glanced up at the retreating aerocab clearance lights, shrugged, and walked off the road to the long, abandoned-appearing mall. Jim thought for a second, trying to remember the deal. Something about a blue door?

He walked until he saw a glass door with blue paper on the inside. Inside the door was the faint outline of a golden lion. "Bingo," he said. But there was no sign or button to call. He frowned and reached for the door. It seemed locked. *Maybe closed?* Examining the door and its perimeter, he spotted at least three scanners. Probably meant there were twice that many he couldn't see.

Out of curiosity, he removed the pinlock after clicking the release in his pinplants. Instantly, he had access to wireless pinlink-style menus. There was a hidden network, which also seemed to argue he was in the right place, because the block looked abandoned. The last thing an abandoned block would have is an expensive, secure network. He replaced the pinlock and thought back to when he'd heard stories about the bar.

"You go there, just stand in front of the door, and if they want, they'll let you in," was what Buddha had said once. *Or something like that*, Jim thought. The conversation had been a couple years ago, and on another planet.

So he stood there, waiting. Nothing happened. Shaking his head, he started to turn and leave, then stopped. Out of curiosity, he took out a challenge coin. Mercs *always* carried one. It was a fast way to have to buy a room full of drinks for other mercs if you didn't and headed for a bar. He held it up to one of the cameras.

"Colonel Jim Cartwright, Cartwright's Cavaliers," he said clearly. "Look, if I'm missing some ritual, I'm sorry. I didn't want to hunt up one of my mercs, and I don't know the rules."

Bzzzzz! went the door. He grabbed it and pulled. It opened easily.

"Okay, that worked," he said and entered.

Inside, a hallway led downward, then turned slightly. A couple steps in, the door closed behind him with a substantial *clunk*, locking immediately. He continued down and around the corner. When the door was well behind him, he saw a pair of hulking Lumar waiting by another door. "Hey, guys, you been juicing?"

"Amusing," one of them said, making Jim lift an eyebrow. "Welcome to the Lyon's Den. Do you know the rules?"

"I'm told the Lyon makes the rules and don't start any shit."

"Close enough," the Lumar replied. His English was remarkable. "The Lyon offers his regards and welcomes Thaddeus Cartwright's son."

"Thanks," Jim said. The door opened, and music washed over him.

As he passed inside, the place didn't feel much different than most merc pits he'd visited, minus the contract trading part. There was room for at least 50 at the massive, hexagonal bar dominating the center of the room, and at least four times that in all the tables and booths. The current patronage looked like mercs, too, though with many of the booths around the edge being in dim lighting, he could be wrong.

He half expected the Lyon himself to be washing glasses behind the bar. Of course, that was stupid. Robots appeared to be running the bar, as well as serving food and drinks. He went to the bar and took a stool away from anyone else.

"Welcome, Colonel Cartwright," a robot said, rolling over on silent treads.

"AVA?" he asked the robot, referring to an autonomous virtual assistant. They weren't as smart as AIs, but had the advantage of not being illegal in the galaxy. The thought of illegal AIs made him shake his head. The more he got behind the curtain, the more he found out the deep dark laws were more like deep dark *lies*.

"That is correct. What can I get you?"

"Rum and Coke?"

"There is a surcharge for the Coke," the robot told him.

"Of course. A good spiced rum, please."

The robot rolled away and returned in a moment. "Your father always wanted the bottle left for him." One of the robot's arms placed a plastic ½ liter bottle of Coke on the counter. It was the same type, made with real sugar in old Mexico, his father had left stashed in bars everywhere he went. It made him smile and nod. He tapped his Yack on the robot's outstretched hand, and 20 credits disappeared from his account.

The drink was perfectly mixed. Jim wasn't a big fan of alcohol, but rum and Coke had a place in the list of things he enjoyed. When the first one was gone, the robot brought another tumbler with two fingers of rum, and even poured the Coke to add the correct amount of sugary soda.

"Ahhh," he said. His appreciation of the drink was growing. With two drinks in him, he looked around the room. A surprising number of aliens were there. At one table, a trio of elSha were sharing a bowl of worms, while drinking and having a good time. Another table held a single Besquith. It wasn't covered in scars or heavily-armed, making Jim suspect the alien was a trader. Then, back in one corner, he heard, over the music, the unmistakable roar of Oogar, and they were looking at him.

He returned their stare for a moment, then all five Oogar got up and walked over to him. A lot of aliens on Earth didn't think much of him, and this could be a group of them. He was wondering whether his pistol would do more than annoy an Oogar when he suddenly recognized them.

"You are Cartwright, yes?"

"That's me," Jim said and stood from the stool. All five towered over Jim. The Oogar looked a little like terrestrial bears, except they were bipedal, had arms almost long enough to touch the floor when standing, and were purple. Not just any purple, *raging* purple. They were also loud, as in, no indoor voice. A deadly merc race, they'd earned the title "Giant Purple Don't-Care Bears" for many reasons.

"And you guys are Purple Rage, right?"

"Yes, we are!" the Oogar who'd spoken said. "We wish thank Cartwright; our music career is going good! We have many concerts and are selling songs on net. We want thank you for help with music."

"You're welcome," Jim said, beaming. When it had become clear many of the aliens on Earth couldn't get home, some had wanted to stay. The hardcore monolithic mercs were mostly deported to the nearest neutral system with merc pits: Karma. The rest, many of them non-combatants, were allowed to stay. Not all did, but a surprising number stayed.

Among them was a group of five Oogar brothers, all security specialists, not front-line mercs. They'd had a bellyful of fighting, but they'd all liked music while growing up. They'd discovered a type of music popular in the late 20th and early 21st Centuries called "Metal" and formed a band, naming it Purple Rage. When he'd heard about it, Jim had booked a concert in Houston. It had been wildly successful. He was genuinely glad they'd succeeded, and that success gave many of the resident aliens on Earth hope for a peaceful life.

He chatted with Purple Rage for a few minutes until they went back to their table. Apparently they were planning a concert tour of South America, now that Brazil was part of the Federation. Jim figured the novelty of seeing a giant purple don't-care bear playing music would take some time to wear off.

Jim put away a third rum and Coke and an order of chicken wings. The food was exceptional, something he wasn't expecting. Nobody who'd talked about the Lyon's Den had said the food was good. He didn't eat things like wings much anymore, and the rich taste brought back memories. Seemingly a lifetime ago, he'd played video games and snacked on hot wings. The memory seemed almost like someone else's.

"Hello, Jim Cartwright."

He turned toward the voice, then down to see an opSha standing there. The alien looked like a fully bipedal howler monkey, but with two tails, massive bat ears, and nearly vestigial eyes. They used a form of echolocation to move around, and their language was extremely high pitched. His translator barely caught it.

His first thought was, *What is an opSha doing on Earth?* His second thought was, *How the fuck does the little bastard know my name?* Then he realized there were at least a dozen of them.

"What do you want?" he demanded, remembering all the stories from the battle of Morgoth where the opSha were everywhere, and some strange recollection of a...hand-to-hand fight with an opSha? *When did that happen?*

"Minerva says it's time," the alien said. The translation took a fraction of a second, by which time it was already moving. Jim had a fractured image of something in the alien's hand, moving with blinding speed, touching it to his left pinlink. The opSha's expression could only be interpreted as jubilant. Nothing happened.

"Tell Minerva to go to hell," Jim said and winked.

The opSha, its expression turning to shock, focused on his pinlink. The external points for his pinplants were basically direct interfaces to his pinplants. Only they *weren't* direct interfaces anymore; a little cap-like device was fitted over them, packed with nanolayered electronics to protect the interface from any sort of attack. The Aku's pinlocks.

Jim planted a hand, open palmed, on the opSha's chest and launched it away from him. "Don't ever touch me again," he said, while making a mental note to talk to the minister of immigration. She needed to be made aware that the opSha were on the *persona non grata* list.

The opSha sent an ultrasonic screech to its fellows. It was beyond the reception of Jim's translator, and clearly meant so he couldn't understand it. After their experience with the little bastards, he pretty much knew what it meant; his quiet trip to the bar was about to turn into a shitshow.

Jim wasn't interested in just letting them get the upper hand, regardless of whether they were going to fight like monkeys in a zoo, or come at him like assassins. He triggered the speed enhancing augment now built into his pinplants. His perception of speed changed, and everything began to move much slower, including all the opSha drawing tiny, wicked-looking blades. *Game on*, he thought.

* * * * *

Chapter Three

The Lyon's Den, Houston Texas, Earth

If Jim hadn't considered the risk in advance, he probably would have been dead before he knew it. With his vastly faster reflexes, he smacked the first swing away almost casually, and the second the same way. Then the other opSha were joining the fray, and he wondered if he should have gone for the gun immediately. That ship had sailed. "You fight with what you have," Murdock, the top Cavaliers' sergeant back when he took over, had said.

The speed boost only gave him a few precious seconds of advantage, so he needed to end this, fast. As the third opSha came at him, aiming a blade at his jugular, Jim moved aside just enough that the blade missed its target, and used all his strength to slam a fist into the alien's face. He felt bone give, and ignoring the pain from his fist, he grabbed the stunned alien by its outstretched knife hand, stripped the weapon, and swung the being like a sledgehammer, completely creaming one of its cohorts.

Three other opSha went flying like tenpins in the backspin as he let it fly. He slid off the barstool and flashed out a sidekick, catching still another in the midriff. The alien folded like a bad poker hand. *Yesss!* the voice in the back of his mind exulted. *Kill them all!*

Oh, shut up, he thought as he used his left to backhand another opSha. He didn't have his hand angled perfectly, and he felt a bone pop in it as the impact shuddered up his arm. Two more jumped at him, one from each side. Because they were shorter than him, he jumped. Not as effective as it might be with a skinnier, taller man, it was still enough for him to rise above their dive, though not enough to let them pass under and crash into each other, which was what he'd been going for.

Instead, they both kinda collided with the underside of his thighs, so he let his own weight finish the move, and landed on top of them. It took two more out of the fight, but it left him on his ass, on the floor, and the speed boost was fading. Another reached for him, and he buried the blade in its throat, ripping it out sideways in a spray of blood.

Six of them leaped at the same time, and he tried to roll away from the two he'd squashed, hoping to gain range. Without the extra speed, it wasn't going to work. They were flying right toward his face—only to be intercepted by five massive sets of purple arms. His Oogar friends had joined the fray.

Jim had never seen an opSha torn in half, and he hoped to never see it again. At least the opSha weren't trying to kill him anymore. He'd just rolled to his feet, considering what to do, when the two Lumar door guards hit the scene with all eight arms, pulling opSha and Oogar apart, and holding them at bay with equal ease.

The surviving opSha didn't take the interference well; they drew compact laser pistols. This turned out to be the final bad move in a series of bad moves. Judging by the number of bullets, lasers, and sharp, pointy things that flew, Jim figured everyone in the bar had opened fire at the same time.

"That's a lot of dead monkeys," a man said as he came out a hidden door behind the bar. He held an HP-90 almost identical to Jim's casually, unfired. "Thanks, guys," he said to the two Lumar, who nodded. "Please take out the trash." They set about cleaning up the mess. "I almost didn't let them in; should have gone with that instinct."

"Lyon, I take it?" Jim asked.

"In the flesh." The man looked like he was in his 50s, with maybe an extra 10 kilos around the waist, partly balding; he radiated a certain strange atmosphere of indifference. Not a merc, then? "Your dad specialized in getting himself into trouble, too. Like father, like son."

"You knew my father?"

"Yes. He met his wife here."

Jim had to pick his jaw up off the floor. "I...didn't know that."

"Hmm," Lyon said and shrugged. "So those assholes had something to do with the trouble you guys caused at Morgoth?"

"They were operatives of the Science Guild."

"Is that so?" Lyon glanced over at the cleanup operation. Nobody else in the bar seemed to care in the least, except the Oogar, who were mildly interested. "Thaddeus did a lot of things in my bar, but he never started a fight."

"I'd argue they started it," Jim said, hooking a thumb at a dismembered opSha being loaded into a wheelbarrow by a Lumar and bots. "How often have they been in here?"

"My clientele enjoys anonymity," Lyon replied immediately.

"That anonymity is a useful tool to cause mayhem, spread viruses, and help our enemies invade the planet."

"Are you suggesting I helped the aliens invade Earth?"

"I'm suggesting you support their anonymity." Lyon's face clouded. "Do your own research, Mr. Lyon."

"Maybe you better head home, Colonel Cartwright."

"Gladly," Jim growled, and headed for the door. He tossed a 100-credit chit to the nearest Lumar as he passed. "Sorry about the mess."

"I got that reference," the Lumar said as Jim headed out the door.

It was after midnight when he got back to his control tower apartment. Jim tended to his split knuckles and a cracked metatarsal bone by using a light dosage of nanites applied topically. The pain helped clear him mind some, too.

He got in a workout, which helped him get rid of the residual anger, then had something to eat. He wasn't really surprised Lyon had acted the way he had, just disappointed. Jim doubted any of the invasion planning or help had been provided by the Lyon's Den. Was it possible? Absolutely. He also knew there were a dozen such places all over the planet where it could have been. "Don't ask, don't tell." He filed it away for later consideration.

He was putting the dishes in the washer when he realized why he felt strange; Ziva wasn't there. It would have been nice if she'd been with him at the bar. Feeling somewhat morose, he went to bed, thinking about when she would return.

Captain Su contacted Jim in the wee hours of the morning to say they'd gotten an early schedule for stargate transit, so he cut the night short and expedited his plans. By the time he was climbing out of the shower, the first *Phoenix*-class dropship was roaring into the predawn sky, filled with Cavaliers and supplies.

He set his apartment's automated assistant to take care of things, finished packing his duffle bag, and headed for the door. As he was passing through the sunken living room, he paused in confusion. His now worn and weary Rainbow Dash sat in the center of the coffee table with a note under it. It hadn't been there when we went to bed, and the security system hadn't been tripped. He picked up the note and read it.

Jim,

Don't forget who you are. See you in a few months.

Ziva

Of course, who else could have had this delivered without triggering his state-of-the-art security system, except a Depik. Fssik's name wasn't on the note, but it didn't have to be. He pocketed the note and picked up Dash, intending to put it back in the display case in his bedroom. Then he stopped and put it back where he'd found it. *Don't forget who you are.*

With a grunt, he headed for the elevator. Outside, another dropship was just roaring into the slowly brightening sky. His XO, Buddha, came jogging over as soon as he was visible.

"Ready to go, Boss?" the big man asked, his tawny skin glistening with a thin sheen of sweat. Having grown up in the tropics, Houston's climate had never bothered him. Jim had moved to Indiana as a child, so he'd never completely acclimatized.

"You bet, Lieutenant Colonel."

Buddha's expression darkened, and Jim grinned. He'd insisted Buddha try the silver oakleaf on for a contract term, and it had fit far better than the other man had expected it would. The transition from senior noncom to officer wasn't always as successful. Buddha's love of the Cavaliers and friendship with Jim helped. He was also the last original member remaining from when Jim took over.

"A and B Companies are already on board, and the last of the supplies are being loaded. Captain Su reports *Bucephalus* is ready to go, and your staff from the Ministry is en route. Major Schellenbach was briefed an hour ago."

"What's Craig's assessment of C Company?"

"They're green as the spring grass," Buddha said and winked.

C Company was the newest company, stood up just before Morgoth. He'd accepted a small contract a week ago with the full intention of sending Buddha and C Company to get them blooded. Now he needed his XO with him, especially since they were potentially entering an unknown situation. Going in light was not an option.

"Is he confident in his ability to handle the contract?"

"It's retaking a research facility," Buddha said. "Since they're only expecting a light Jivool garrison, he'll have a heavy numerical superiority."

Jim nodded in agreement. The Jivool preferred to fight up close; as long as Schellenbach didn't concede initiative to the ursines…"He's an experienced commander," Jim said.

"Plus he has a solid group of experienced NCOs, as well as his junior officers."

Jim knew the latter only too well. He'd sent Lieutenant Orpington to Schellenbach. Orpington was his most experienced junior officer. As his replacement for A Company, 2nd Platoon, he'd signed on Lieutenant Aaron Mayer.

Mayer was a bit of a special case. At 37, he was taking his first lieutenant billet. Ten years ago, he'd been a senior NCO with Burt's Bees. Colonel Earl had sent the man to officer training in the asteroid belt. All the Bees were Marines, so they trained in space. A lot.

During a training cycle, a junior pilot had screwed the Zuul, detaching from a boarding position too soon. An emergency airlock had slammed closed on Mayer's ankles, blowing the lower leg seals. Luckily for him, the Mk 8 CASPer he'd been using had progressive emergency seals. The knees both closed off, keeping the suit from decompressing. However, it had taken an hour to get the airlock mechanism to disengage. By the time they got Mayer to the infirmary, both legs below the knee were destroyed.

He damned near died anyway, but he was too damned tough. Most men would have taken the disability payout from their policy and gone home to spend more time with their remaining limbs. Mayer instead spent nine years building himself back up until he could drive a CASPer again. He had basic cybernetic replacements; he hadn't been able to afford the best. Because of that, he'd bounced around small units until the Omega War. He'd fought in a resistance group in Texas, and Sansar Enkh had dropped his name immediately when Jim mentioned he needed junior officers. That was enough for him.

So, at 37 years old, Mayer wore butter bars for the first time in his life. Most new lieutenants averaged around 24 years old in merc companies. Those junior lieutenants usually caught a lot of shit from the older NCOs. Not Mayer—he'd been one of them and had refused to call it quits. Jim liked the man for a number of reasons.

Mayer stood by the *Phoenix*, talking with the other officers. The titanium of his legs was visible in the shipboard shoes they all wore when deploying. He was laughing and joking with the other officers as if he'd deployed with them a dozen times. It was only the lack of hashes under his Cavaliers' logo that dispelled the illusion and the way he snapped to attention when he saw Jim.

"At ease, Lieutenant," Jim said, patting the man on his powerful shoulder. "Ready for this?"

"Been ready for 10 years, Colonel Cartwright." The man's eyes held a glimmer of unshed tears, and Jim patted him again. "I won't let you down, sir."

Double T, Jim's top sergeant, nodded behind the officers. Jim had run it by him before hiring Mayer. "It's a bit of a risk, sir," Double T had said. "He's got the heart, excellent record as an NCO, and seems a good fit. He's just a bit down the road for a first time LT. I say give him a run."

Of course, when they hired him, they weren't planning to send A Company out anytime soon. Jim had planned to put him in C Company, but now he couldn't leave Schellenbach with a green LT on top of mostly green troopers. You played the cards you were dealt.

"I know you won't," he said, then looked around at his officers. "Ready to go?" They all nodded. "Then pack 'em in, men." Together, they boarded the last *Phoenix*.

* * *

EMS *Bucephalus*, Secure Transit Space

Achilles drifted into the newly finished bay and looked around. The *Akl'o* had done a reasonable job in the short time they'd been given. "Any sign we were spotted coming aboard?" he asked his second.

"None," Athena responded. She cast her eyes around as the rest of the *Osk* came aboard, likewise looking around and sneering. "Someone would have to be looking out a window to notice." She examined the sleeping harnesses and snarled. "All of us in here, for weeks?"

"It's what we have," Achilles said. "At least their software has been modified to make our shuttle invisible. So much easier than begging the ship's *ske'ii* for permission to travel while guarding our charge." J'asa hadn't wanted to mess with the Humans' ships, but had ultimately relented to make guarding them easier. They did so love getting into trouble. He understood the process with Sansar Enkh had proven much more complicated.

"They should be servitors," J'op said.

She was the youngest of the team, and relatively new from Eesius. Achilles guessed she was also one of the opposition faction. J'asa had tried to be sure all of Cartwright's team were from her faction, but it had proven almost impossible.

Hector glanced around and shrugged. Nothing seemed to bother him. Ajax, the largest of the team, looked unhappy as well. He didn't appreciate tight spaces, not even their Konar. Hera smacked J'op on the back of the head as she floated by.

"Quit your crying or go back to the creche," she said. J'op's ears quivered in anger, but he stayed quiet.

"Are all the Konar secured?" Achilles asked Athena.

"All set," she said. "Good thing, too; the Humans are ready to get under way."

"Cartwright is in a hurry," Achilles said. "Maybe he's as bored with his race's politics as we are?" None of his commando team had anything to say, so they settled into the newly built space. He tried not to think about how Su, the ship's *ske'ii*, would react if she found out about their secure transport area. More than likely, if they were needed, Su wouldn't care. At least, he told himself that.

* * *

Dusman Cruiser *P'Ka*, Hyperspace

P'*ka* transited through the Sol system stargate, and instantly J'asa felt the connection with Jim Cartwright *stretch*. It was normal when either of them was in hyperspace without the other. Even so, she always felt a pang of guilt or just separation when it hit. Her sister Seldia insisted it was a normal byproduct of the bonding process. J'asa was less convinced. She missed her Human.

"Five minutes to plunge," the *ske'ii* announced over the intercom.

J'asa noted the information without looking up from her slate. She had detailed lists of her research, plans, notes, and a thousand other things. As the minutes counted down, she found it increasingly more difficult to concentrate. How long had it been since she'd gone home? She'd been on Kash-kah two years before Jim came along, and that was seven years ago.

This was more than a homecoming; it was a trip of redemption. She hadn't gone to normal space and the sentry world of Kash-kah because she wanted to; it had been a banishment for the trouble she'd caused. Kash-kah had been one of the Dusman's many factory worlds 20,000 years ago. Now it was locked in an ice age, its subsurface full of rusting equipment, and only staffed by 100 of her kind. A little like a peephole Humans put through their doors in dangerous neighborhoods. Their leaders had probably hoped she'd die there.

"Plunge in three...two...one..."

Transitioning from normal space to hyperspace was an instant of feeling as if you were unmade, then remade. Some liked it, some didn't. A few races could barely tolerate it for one reason or another. The ones who didn't often had difficulty in the transition and also struggled to deal with the 170-hour trip through hyperspace. Leaving hyperspace for normal space was a much less traumatic experience. A moment's strange falling sensation, even if you were already in zero G, and you were out.

Leaving hyperspace for 2nd level hyperspace, a process the Dusman called "The Plunge," was far worse than either entering or leaving hyperspace. The first time J'asa had experienced it, she'd thought it was like being torn apart one cell at a time, when you could feel every single instant of it, though everything happened in a split second. Despite eons of research, the process had never been improved to make it less traumatic.

"Plunge complete," the *ske'ii* said over the intercom. *"Are you well, Vok'tor?"*

"Yes," she whispered. *Entropy, that sucked!* She'd forgotten just how horrible it was. "It never gets easier, does it?"

"No," the ship's master replied, *"but you do become more inured, eventually."*

She hoped she never would.

The only good thing about the aftermath of a plunge was that it didn't leave any lasting effects. Within moments, you only had the memory. Sure, the memory sucked, but at least you didn't hurt all over like you'd been beaten up. She guessed the *ske'ii* was right—enough trips would make it tolerable. She hoped she never took enough trips.

She released the harness that had held her in place in her cabin and moved to push off before remembering the physics of 2nd level hyperspace. She plucked a stylus off her desk, where a magnet had held it in place, and tossed it. Had they still been in normal space, or even hyperspace, the stylus would have flown across the room and rebounded off the wall. Instead, the instant she released it from her hand, it quickly slowed to a stop in only centimeters.

The physics of 2nd level hyperspace were markedly different than regular space, or what the Humans sometimes called Newtonian Space, after one of their ancient scientists. You didn't drift like in zero G; you came a quick stop as if you were underwater. Only there were no sensations of gravity from the stop. In fact, you could go from a million kilometers per second to a dead stop in only meters, and not feel any sensation at all.

Starship operations in 2nd level hyperspace were challenging in many ways; maneuvering within the ship were the least of those. However, it could be embarrassing to get marooned in the middle of a compartment with no way to reach the bulkhead. Dusman who routinely operated here had a sort of lasso added to their equipment belt. She made a mental note to get one.

"*Docking in five minutes,*" the intercom announced.

J'asa nodded to herself as she reached the corridor and used the well-placed handholds to make her way amidship. She passed several crewmen en route, going about their duties. There was none of the distracting saluting and such the Humans found so important. The Dusman uniforms were also simple, unadorned affairs. They could tell rank by virtue of their race's inherent psychic sense.

The same abilities so powerful in the *k'apo* were shared with all Dusman to a minor degree. It wasn't as controlled or detailed, of course, but it was enough to tell what position another Dusman occupied, both in rank and affiliation. Not only did it make life easier in their society, because nobody carried ID, it also made it impossible to infiltrate their organizations.

She reached the ventral airlock quickly enough to get a view through the reinforced glass viewing port set just adjacent. It was her first view of home in many years. "I wasn't sure I'd ever see Eesius again," she said quietly.

"How long have you been gone, *Vok'tor?*"

She turned her head and saw a group of P'Ka's crew floating a respectful distance behind her, none a higher rank than *ske'i*; most were *ske'o*, just technicians or experts.

"I was only considering that a short time ago," she said. "Nine or ten years, I think."

"It is good to be back," the highest ranking of them said.

"None of you were planetside in normal space?" They all shook their heads. "There's a lot to be said about a planet that isn't trying to kill you." She could tell by the looks on their faces that the statement didn't quite register. She hoped if the coming conflict went well, they could eventually abandon this world. World might be a bit of an overstatement.

There were no planets in 2nd level hyperspace. As they needed a place to live, dozens of asteroids had been brought in. Once gathered, they were compacted together using powerful mass drivers at nearly point-blank range to create a worldlet. Dubbed Eesius, after the engineer who'd conceived of it, the surface was covered in thousands of atmospheric domes, factories, storehouses, and everything a race needed to survive. It was home.

The view was becoming occluded by a massive shape. Roughly pyramidal and slowly rotating, Arsenal 3-B-E came into focus, or at least part of it. The structure was four kilometers on a side, and the only reason they'd been able to construct Eesius in the first place. The arsenals were the biggest manufactories ever made. There had once been hundreds of them. Scouts were still searching normal space for more. No more had been found.

It took a minute longer for *P'Ka* to finish its docking maneuver, since the Arsenal was rotating. The pilot was skilled, and it went without issue, securing them to one of the Arsenal's myriad docks. After the computer verified a secure hard-dock, the airlock opened. The smell consisted of sweat, oil, and ozone. So familiar, if years distant in her memory, the stench was still welcoming.

As the Arsenal's rotation created pseudo gravity, the lock was now "up." She grabbed the handhold and pulled herself inside, then moved aside to let the other crewmembers through, so they could move past and on to whatever their tasks might be. She took a few hesitant steps, recalling how artificial gravity interacted with the strange physics of this dimension.

In normal space, under any sort of gravity, walking was partly stepping forward, and partly falling. Bipedal beings learned a delicate dance of timing and gravity to move about on two limbs. Here you had to move yourself forward, you couldn't lean forward and let that momentum propel you. If you were to try to run, you would freeze in space above where you started the step, and the wall would then move toward you like a flyswatter. Walking was more like a shuffle, done with care to ensure constant contact with the floor.

She'd been born and grew up on Eesius, where there was no spin. Arsenal had to constantly spend energy maintaining its spin, otherwise it would stop, like anything else in 2nd level hyperspace.

She had been just out of her creche when she took her first trip to Arsenal and broke two bones in her arm. Good times.

"*Vok'tor* J'asa," a voice said.

She turned as a young Dusman shuffle-stepped up to her and bowed his head.

"I am *Tor'o* Keenta."

"I greet you," J'asa said, confused that a low-ranking leader would greet her on Arsenal. "Do you have business?"

"I do. *Tor* Saleen requires you meet with her on Eesius at your earliest convenience."

J'asa's mouth became a line, and her ears went straight up. *Tor* was the rank of the leadership council, shared by all five members. She'd been gone too long to know any of them by name. It didn't matter, though; if a *Tor* summoned you, you responded.

"I don't have transport assigned," she explained.

"I have a skimmer." Keenta bowed her head and indicated down the corridor. "If you will follow me?"

She briefly considered denying. She was within her rights; being a *Vok'tor*, she didn't answer to the council. It wouldn't play out well, though, for it to get out that the *j'apo* who'd just won over the *kroof* Sly to her position and redirected the history of all Dusman didn't listen to the counsel of a *Tor*. "Very well, proceed," she said and followed the *tor'o*.

* * * * *

Chapter Four

EMS *Bucephalus*, Hyperspace

I

t felt good to be back on his own merc cruiser, the ship filled with Cavaliers on their way to another planet. Only they weren't heading off to kill aliens and get paid; it was a purely diplomatic mission to the colonies. Jim hadn't bothered telling his fellow ministers until he was on board *Bucephalus* and transiting through the stargate.

"Sorry, forgot to tell you. Back in a few months. I'll email reports and keep up my work remotely."

Yeah, they'll be pissed, he thought as he looked out his commander's porthole into the featureless white nothing of hyperspace. "I'm fresh out of fucks to give," he said to the empty room. What was the worst they could do, fire him? The Dusman wouldn't appreciate that. The thought prompted a little grin.

As the CO, he rated his own cabin, one of only a handful on the converted *Akaga*-class cruiser. Sure, he could have bunked with Buddha, but RHIP, right? The compartment was self-contained, too, with an airtight door, small life support backup, and a wet-head just big enough to get a shower. In truth, it was tiny, and he usually used the officers' head down the hall.

If the *Akaga* had a serious flaw, it was the lack of a gravity deck. The Izlians who'd built her, and much of the galaxy's starships, had evolved in the extreme heat, radiation, and pressure of a gas giant. They had no use for a gravity deck, so they were rare on their ships.

Since the *Akaga* was shaped more or less like a flattened spear with protruding hangars and weapons mounts, it was impossible to retrofit, too. So, they flew in zero gravity when not under thrust. Nobody wasted reaction mass in hyperspace to make gravity.

Jim watched the Tri-V on his little desk, displaying the Human sphere of influence. As he did, he remembered his father, Thaddeus Cartwright, had once strapped into the same chair, planned missions, and made the Cavaliers even greater than they'd been when he'd inherited them from Jim's grandfather. He wondered what his father would think of the way his son had run the Cavaliers. Considering what Jim had when he started, he'd like to think he'd done okay. Maybe he was wrong, and Thaddeus would shake his head and frown. Jim himself frowned thinking about it.

He pulled his attention back to the map. It held a tiny section of the galaxy's Tolo arm, which Humans had called the Sagittarius arm of the Milky Way. As Jim understood it, the names of the galaxy arms were *very* old, and thus the reason they were classified by only four arms, when in fact there were five arms and numerous spurs. Over the million or so years since the stargates were invented, it had been easier to stick everything in 'four arms' and simply change a planet's address if an arm changed shape. Whatever.

The Tolo arm, like all arms, was broken into three regions; the Coro or outer region, Gresht or inner region, and Cresht or middle region, where Earth was. The vast majority of Humans lived in the Cresht region of the Tolo arm. Jim was aware of small populations on a hundred worlds all over the galaxy. There was no way the Terran Federation could concern itself with anything outside the range of a single hyperspace jump, which basically meant the Cresht region.

When you thought of galactic geography, you also had to consider the Core region. This was the center of the galaxy, often broken into zones named after each arm, and oriented at their bases. There weren't as many populated worlds there as you'd expect, mainly because those stars tended to be old, hot, or played out.

For a second, he stared at the final arm, called simply the Fourth Arm. It was there, 20,000 years ago, that the enemy of the Dusman, known as the Kahraman, had fled. Nothing went in or out, thanks to a complicated network of hyperspace disrupting stargates. Only the Kahraman *were* trying to get out. He had to think it wasn't to make friends. He also found little coincidence with the Dusman returning at almost exactly the same time the Kahraman were doing this.

A concern for later, he thought, and he once again stared at the Human sphere, a small cluster of green, yellow, and red star systems. Green for active colonies, yellow for unknown, and red for ones that no longer existed.

There had been a total of 29 colonization efforts in the Cresht region over the 110 years since First Contact. Of those, 18 had failed and were lost for one reason or another, most from either mismanagement or aliens not appreciating new neighbors.

By the time the Omega War rolled around, there were 11 colonies remaining that each held more than 10,000 Humans. Five had been destroyed in the war, including New Persia, Victoria Bravo, and Danube, which left six remaining.

The largest, and consequently the oldest Human colony, was Taluu 211c, or Talus. Settled only 11 years after first contact, it had grown massively from various disaffected populations immigrating from Earth. Sadly, 60 years into its history, a series of civil conflicts had led to its being taken over by an authoritarian leadership not too dissimilar from the old Soviet Union. It was also the site of the biggest colony battle of the Omega War, where Jim had used his Raknar to bring the resistance to a close.

A million or more people lived on Talus, which was the main reason it was his first stop. The other reason was that the Dusman had, unbeknownst to him, put a Raknar base down there as well. When they'd liberated Talus during their counteroffensive in the Omega War, Jim had done what he could to unseat the totalitarian "Council" that had controlled the planet and welcomed aliens in. Two years later, he wondered what it looked like. He guessed he'd find out in another day.

A gentle knock on his door brought him out of his reverie. "Come."

The door cracked open to reveal the almond eyes and golden complexion of *Bucephalus'* master, Captain Su. "Colonel, you have a minute?"

"Sure," he said, and gestured to the fold-down guest chair in his cabin. It was funny that even people who spent a lot of time in space still preferred to sit and talk, even if they really weren't sitting. Just Human nature, he guessed.

Su floated in, pulling the door closed behind her, before clicking the visiting seat down and slipping into it, with the strap going over her legs. "I know your plan on this mission," she said, looking him in the eye, "but I don't know your action plan based on possible situations."

"What do you mean?"

"There could be ambiguities we're not prepared to deal with." He looked at her, confused. "Colonel, Jim, you remember what it was like during the Omega War, that Talus was under multiple influences.

Have you considered how these factors might have evolved, changed, *complicated?*"

"It's only been two years," Jim reminded her, "and the Dusman have been there for a while. At least long enough to assemble a Raknar fist."

"I've been to Talus, many times, before I joined the Cavaliers under your father. Officially, it became a totalitarian state 60 or so years ago, but it was always a mess. That's what happens when you have a quickly growing colony and no real plan. It didn't help that Earth maintained a hands-off attitude toward the colonies."

"I thought that was a better policy than trying to micromanage," Jim interjected.

"It is, if you aren't arresting people in the dead of night and creating gulags."

"Good point," Jim said. "Okay, what's your suggestion?"

"It really depends on your goals. If you're here to show the flag, maybe practice some gunboat diplomacy, you probably should have brought some Dusman firepower. They aren't likely to be impressed by an *Akaga*, especially one that's been largely disarmed."

"Not the plan," Jim said. "The minister of war doesn't participate in diplomatic negotiations. There's a minister of Colonial Affairs for that."

"I know; she's never been off the planet."

Jim made a face and avoided commenting.

"So, you're here to assess their ability to defend themselves?"

"More or less, yes. That and to see what the Dusman are doing here." She nodded in understanding. "I also want to make sure they aren't going to welcome another invader, such as maybe Minerva."

"Another good reason to visit the place," she agreed. "I just wanted you to realize Talus is a mess, and probably always will be. Being prepared for the unexpected is a good strategy."

"Since the Dusman are likely there, I don't think we have to worry about some kind of attack," Jim said.

"No, the Talusians have always preferred to come at things sideways anyway."

"Thanks for the information," he said.

"No problem. See you in the morning."

She left him in his stateroom to consider what would happen when he finally returned to Talus.

* * *

EMS *Bucephalus*, Taluu Star System

*B*ucephalus arrived at the Talus system's emergence point right on schedule. Had it been otherwise, Jim would have been really concerned. He was strapped into his customary couch in the ship's CIC, the combat information center. As a former warship, its bridge was tiny, and only used for maneuvering in port or emergencies. You didn't put your command center on the outside of the hull where it was vulnerable. The CIC was deep in the center of the ship, surrounded by reaction mass tankage and reinforced plating.

Though Captain Su was the ship's master, Jim owned the vessel and was the company commander. As such, he was entitled to a seat at the table as Su would call it. Many merc commanders preferred to be strapped in a CASPer and out of view as the shit hit the fan. Jim, growing up watching old TV shows and modern Tri-V movies, loved being in the CIC, where he could watch and listen to the ship's operations.

"Shield's up," Captain Su said sternly. "Sensor sweeps, stand by on ECM and drones." Jim cast a curious eye at her. "Remember our talk?" she asked, *sotto voce*.

He nodded in understanding, not that he'd have said anything if he disagreed. He was, after all, a guest in her home, and a guest doesn't tell you how to put out the dog.

"Confirmed the Taluu system," navigation spoke up in only a moment.

"We have radar returns on six warships picketing the emergence point." Su stiffened, leaning slightly forward in her curved gravity couch. One hand hovered over a tiny Tri-V to her side, from which she could issue rudimentary input controls to many of the ship's vital systems. "Approximately two minutes for a return from anything at the stargate to confirm if they have a high-guard."

Jim knew why they would be concerned about the stargate, though it was at the opposite LaGrange point from the emergence point. They could possibly avoid a small squadron where they were, and thus run for the stargate and escape. However, if any ships were guarding the stargate, a tactical position called high-guard, escape would be much more difficult. An emergence point was usually a few light seconds to a light minute across. Lots of room to try to interdict. A stargate was no more than a kilometer across. Forcing your way through would be running a gauntlet.

"Status on the ships here?" she asked.

"Running the data," the TacCom, or tactical command officer, replied.

Warships used a variety of special positions evolved for use on a spaceship. TacCom coordinated the ship's offense/defense using sensor data to analyze threats to choose the correct defensive action. SitCon was a sort of liaison between the ship's commanding officer, all the various department heads, and any mercs on board. In the case of a larger squadron, they handled orders from other ships as well and were often the ship's XO. DCC was the damage control coordinator. The rest, like helm, sensor ops, engineering, etc., were more easily recognizable.

"They're Dusman," sensor ops said. A second later, TacCom filled in the details.

"One *Seesius*-class light frigate, four *Feesius*-class frigates, and two *Pleesius*-class cruisers. All based on the data Colonel Cartwright provided from the Dusman."

Jim nodded; this was in line with what he was expecting if Talus was being used as a Raknar base. They were incredible war machines, yes. However, they were still vulnerable to orbital assault if caught off guard or unmanned. Sol's defensive squadron was considerably bigger, at least partly to ensure the Peacemakers didn't come nosing around. Splunk didn't think much of the galaxy's law enforcement agents.

"We're being hailed by *K'Pok-44*," the comms officer said. "One of the *Pleesius*." Su gestured at the nearest speaker, and a Dusman voice came over the air.

"*Unidentified ship, respond. This star system is under the protection of the Dusman.*"

"Rather gruff, aren't they?" Su asked Jim.

"They're not much on diplomacy," he admitted. He'd heard secondhand that the mission to acquire the Raknar from the KzSha had nearly turned into an armed conflict with the Peacemakers.

"Hmmm," she grunted. "Put me on." The comms officer activated the channel, and she spoke. "This is Captain Su of EMS *Bucephalus,* merc cruiser for Cartwright's Cavaliers, here on official business."

"*What official business is that?*"

"May I?" Jim asked. She nodded in assent. "This is *Vok'ka* Jim Cartwright, also minister of war for the Terran Federation. As my ship's captain said, I'm here on official business."

The radio was quiet for more than a minute. Jim smiled wryly as he imagined a confused *ske'ii* on the cruiser conferring with the other ship *ske'ii* on how to respond. Jim had learned a lot about the various Dusman ranks from Splunk after the last battle. His rank within the Dusman hierarchy, largely a requirement because of his Raknar command, was the equivalent of a naval squadron commander. In other words, he outranked a mere *ske'ii.*

"Is there a problem, *Ske'ii?*"

"*No,* Vok'ka," the Dusman replied instantly. "*We just didn't know to expect you.*"

"Because I sent no word I was coming." He looked at Captain Su. "Please proceed to Talus at your convenience."

"*We'll send an escort,*" the *ske'ii* said.

"That's not necessary," Captain Su replied immediately.

"*It is my pleasure,* Ske'ii *Su.*"

She looked at Jim, who shrugged in reply. Su gestured to mute the audio, then spoke to Jim. "Are they worried about us?"

"More than likely curious, more than suspicious. The Dusman are big on ritual and propriety. It's probably going to take them a while to get used to our position as allies and not servitors." The CIC main Tri-V now showed the Dusman formation a few million kilometers away, waiting patiently. He gestured to it. "Consider it an honor guard."

Su snorted and shot him a wry grin. "Okay, Colonel, you know these aliens better than anyone else."

Jim gave a single laugh. "God, I hope I'm not the preeminent authority." *They tell more lies than truth.* He didn't say the last part out loud, of course. She was nervous enough as it was.

The mute was removed. "Very well, thank you." The channel was cut, and *Bucephalus* thrust toward the distant blue dot of Talus.

As the Dusman said, a ship fell out of formation and accelerated to intercept *Bucephalus'* flight path. Jim could tell by the size it was the light frigate, a *Seesius*-class. If the Dusman had been concerned, they would have sent one of the cruisers. This was the senior *ske'ii's* attempt to fit an unexpected visit into some form of proper protocol.

Thanks to the fusion drive technology, they moved from the emergence point to Talus orbit in hours instead of weeks, as they would have in the early days of Human spaceflight. Before first contact, Humans hadn't ventured outside the Earth-Moon orbit, with the first trip to Mars only taking place in 2023.

Bucephalus executed a smooth trans-orbit injection burn, placing herself in a 400km semi-circular orbit. They hadn't exceeded 2.5 Gs the entire trip. Jim was always impressed with how tight a ship Captain Su ran.

"We're being hailed by the planet," comms reported.

"On speaker," Su ordered.

"This is Talus Orbital Control. Welcome, Bucephalus, and Minister Cartwright. While your arrival was unexpected, we are looking forward to welcoming you back."

"Can I speak to whoever is in charge of the government now?" Jim asked.

"I'm just orbital control, Minister, and not in charge of diplomatic communications. Please come down as soon as possible." The radio transmission ended.

"Well, that's not vague or troubling," Captain Su said.

Jim made a face and stared at the planet orbiting below, shown on the CIC's massive Tri-V. The world was mostly water and had a slightly higher than normal PH level, which made it unsuitable for most galactic aquatic races. That was the reason Earth was able to negotiate a lease so easily. They were passing over the eastern hemisphere, which was almost unpopulated, except for a few islands with fishing and some deep-core platinum mines. In a few minutes, the main continental mass would come into view.

The main continental mass was about seven million square kilometers, slightly larger than the old United States. Not a lot of land for a planet larger than Earth. However, it wasn't well utilized. Only around 200,000 square kilometers were inhabited, primarily around the capital city of Johnstown, just north of the equator and situated on a large body of water known as the Great Shallow Sea.

A pair of large rivers near the center of the populated area provided a less alkaline region of water, and terrestrial sea life flourished there. Johnstown was near one river to the north, and Smoker was near another to the south. The 150 kilometers of coast between the two cities held a series of fishing and tourist towns. This region accounted for two thirds of the planet's population of a million or so Humans.

"Go ahead and prep a shuttle, please," he asked Captain Su.

"You sure about that?"

"I have more faith in the Dusman than the government of Talus," Jim replied. Since they'd entered orbit, TacCom had been using the ship's sensors to catalog anything else sharing near-Talus space with them. They'd noted 122 satellites of a design never seen before.

"They have to be Dusman," TacCom said, showing an image on the Tri-V. The satellite looked like a slowly spinning diamond shape, nearly black, with antenna-like projections on all its faceted sides.

"That's a good guess," Jim agreed.

"There are also three other Dusman ships in orbit; two are cruisers, one is just big."

The Tri-V moved to show a massive, globular-looking starship with three clusters of bays along its length, and a lot of weapons as well. Jim had seen them before.

"That's a *Sleesius*-class assault carrier; it delivers Raknar and support to a planet. They used one to deliver the Raknar to Earth."

"So it's true," Su said. "There are Raknar on Talus?"

"Yes," Jim admitted. "We didn't advertise that a Talus contingent relieved our assault on the Morgoth Canavar facility."

"Are the Dusman trying to play Talus off against Earth?"

"That's part of what I'm here to find out," Jim said. "I'd rather you stayed on board, just in case."

"You don't have to ask me twice," she said.

Jim thanked her and headed aft as she ordered the shuttle prepared. On the way to his quarters, he sent a message for his XO to meet him. Buddha floated up just as he arrived.

"What's up, Boss?"

"I'm going down to Talus. I want you to stay here with B Company on ready alert."

"You think they'd do something to you?"

"No, but I'm not betting my life against it. If I call for help or don't communicate every 12 hours, coordinate with the Dusman to get my fat ass out of the frying pan."

"Your ass ain't all that fat anymore," Buddha said, "but will do." Jim was about to leave when Buddha had an idea. "What if the Dusman are the ones who've grabbed you?"

Jim snorted, then gave a deadpan reply. "Run."

A few minutes later, he and a hastily-loaded duffle bag were soaring down one of the *Akaga*-class cruiser's long bow-to-stern tunnels. They were wonderful for moving quickly throughout the ship, but when under acceleration, doors closed off every level. A 10-story fall in 3G would be instantly fatal. Since they were just drifting in orbit, the passageways were open and buzzing with crew, whisking about on whatever jobs they performed.

Bucephalus' main hangar was located in her aft section. The Cavaliers' dropships weren't moored in the bay; they docked directly on the side of the ship and rode there. From this location, it allowed quick access to troopers, easy loading and offloading of men and equipment, and each mooring point had fuel and power umbilicals.

In the modest-sized hangar, protected from the vacuum of space by large, clamshell-style doors, two shuttles were clamped to the deck, oriented so ship's thrust pushed them down. The bay doors were closed, and one of the two shuttles' clearance markers were flashing. The boarding ramp was down, and a crewman floated just inside.

"Colonel Cartwright," the man called and gestured. "We're just about ready to go."

"Good," Jim said. He carefully slung his duffle bag across his body and checked the jump. He'd spent thousands of hours in free-fall, but it wasn't as much as many of the lifetime spacers. He constantly had to relearn zero-G instincts, which were ingrained in those who lived in it all the time. He was ready to jump when a man's voice called out from behind him.

"Be right there, Colonel."

He glanced back to see Double T—Tom Tasker, his top sergeant—floating toward him, and the rest of the squad close behind. "Looking forward to seeing Talus again, but not through my cockpit view."

"Sergeant, why are you here?"

"Captain Su called us and said you must have forgotten to let us know you were going down. Maybe you were in a hurry?"

"Yeah, that must have been it," Jim said, his expression darkening.

"Oh, don't be cross, Colonel. Maybe we can check out some of those Talusian nightspots I've heard so much about."

Jim didn't comment, just made his jump across to the shuttle. The pilot noted that his one passenger had increased to nine and retreated inside. Jim waited to help make sure all his unrequested bodyguards made it across to the shuttle. Some were young, without a lot of zero-G experience.

"You know," he said to Double T, "maybe I was trying to keep a low profile."

"We left the CASPers behind," Private Zane Voss said with his typical ear-to-ear grin.

"Yeah, Colonel, we're low profile!" Private Doug Henry had a heavy machinegun in its portable carrying case, hugging it like a lover. Double T gave him a pained look.

"Swell," Jim said, pulling himself inside the shuttle.

In the rear cargo/passenger area, the pilot and his copilot were busily opening up seats from the deck and locking them into place. Jim grunted; at least *everyone* hadn't been in on it.

They buckled in, and bay depressurized in a few minutes, and finally Jim was heading for the planet's surface.

* * *

EMS *Bucephalus*, Secure Transit Space

Achilles watched the Human shuttle pull away from *Bucephalus* and head for the planet's surface. In his briefing was a full detail readout on the planet, Talus. It had belonged to a servitor race before the Betrayal, and had changed hands a hundred times in the intervening years. Apparently a sub-culture group of the Humans, of which they had a dizzying number, had settled the world just after contact with the Galactics. Being a relatively nice world close to Earth, the Humans proceeded to fight themselves over control of it.

"Their history is rather straightforward, isn't it?" Athena was leaning over him and reading the slate at the same time. "Find something they all want, proceed to kill each other over it."

"It does seem that way, doesn't it?" Achilles replied. The planet was mostly water, which explained why the Dusman hadn't been overly interested in it. Their race had evolved from arboreal hunter/gatherers. Forests were more to their liking.

"Odds of trouble while we're here?" Hector asked from across the compartment.

"Minimal," Achilles said. "The *vok'sa* F'ada reports the planet is well in hand. A number of dissidents had been trying to organize after Cartwright pacified the planet in the last war. The ones the Human *Tor* couldn't round up, F'ada took care of quietly. There are a lot of predator fish species; she said it was easy to dispose of the evidence."

Athena grinned, her ears curling upward. She approved of such methods. Some blood, a little work, no more problem.

"All the same," Achilles said, "I'd rather be prepared than destroyed. Have the Konar checked and on orbital drop stand by. Time on target from here would be less than five minutes. Cartwright has proven resilient; he'll be sure to live that long."

"If things go badly, you better hope so," Athena said to him quietly. "He's bonded to *Vok'tor* J'asa. If we were to lose him…"

"I know my job," he snarled at Athena. "Do yours, *Osk'i.*"

She nodded, her eyes narrowed, and she went to oversee the Konar's readiness. Because of how they'd travelled, in a hidden space on *Bucephalus*, the Konar were stored on the outside of the hull. They'd look like nothing more than instrumentation or vents to someone else. The Human ships were ugly messes anyway, with projections, turrets, antennae, and anything else you could imagine poking out at odd angles. Honestly, if they didn't want the Dusman coming along, all they had to do was make ships that were hard to hide on.

Achilles turned his attention back to the monitor and tapped into the shuttle's flight and monitoring circuits. He had access to every channel and control on the ship, and all its sub craft. If push came to shove, he could operate the entire ship from their secure transit space. The *Nee'Akee* said this had always been one of his race's fundamental abilities, stealth and deception. The Dusman didn't have to rely on other races to do their spying; they were masters at it.

The shuttle was entering the atmosphere, and despite *Vok'sa* F'ada's confidence, Achilles would still watch the following events with some nervousness.

* * * * *

Chapter Five

Leadership Dome, Eesius, 2nd Level Hyperspace

The skimmer was similar to the orbital work pods the Humans used in space docks. Room for two to four people, a clear cockpit dome, rear chassis containing life support, avionics, and other controls, and maneuvering thrusters. They were perfect for 2nd level hyperspace, where they just skimmed around, hence their name. J'asa would rather have been in a Raknar dropping into the midst of a thousand Canavar.

For a few minutes after they detached from *P'Ka*, she considered grilling Keenta on what the leader wanted with her. It would be a waste of time, though. A *tor'o* was a young assistant—a trainee, really. Maybe in a few years she could answer her questions, or maybe not.

The skimmer flew from where *P'Ka* was docked to the Arsenal, which itself was only 15 kilometers above Eesius, at a proximity impossible in normal space. The only gravity found in 2nd level hyperspace was whatever you made yourself. The inside of the Arsenal, with its spin, and some of the domes had rotating gravity decks, but the multi-trillion-ton bulk of Eesius would be the same distance from the Arsenal, forever.

She examined the settlement as they flew across the intervening nothingness. While 2nd level hyperspace looked like regular space, in that it was black and without air, visible light didn't travel infinite distances; the space there consumed light in mere kilometers. It varied from place to place, but the Dusman had measured it at no more than 100 kilometers. In many places, it was far less. Power flowed differently as well, and travel was adversely affected by the strange braking action. Day to day life was always a challenge, even without considering their neighbors.

Several of the domes on Eesius were dark now, unused. They'd moved forward with recolonization. She nodded in approval. The question was, how much and where.

Keenta parked the skimmer, and they passed through into one of the Eesius domes. J'asa thought it might be 21-K'oon. It had been too long; she wasn't certain. The leadership dome didn't have its own dock. As they passed inside, dozens of Dusman were passing by, and her senses were assailed by rank and purpose. It felt good to be home.

Her guide took her through several intra-dome passages utilizing the glideways, similar to those found in the Union. That only made sense, since the Dusman had perfected the pneumatic transports. She didn't need to be told when she entered the leadership dome; it was large with only a single towering structure in it, a spire that rose almost to the dome's transparent top. The floor was crisscrossed with tiny ropes on guys, used to move about in the unusual nature of 2nd level hyperspace, something unnecessary in the original building on Capital.

"I understand it looks just like the one on Capital," Keenta said.

"It does," J'asa replied. For the first time, Keenta looked taken aback. "I've seen it," she explained.

"It must be difficult to be amidst all the traitorous races who stood by and allowed us to come to this."

J'asa didn't reply, instead gesturing for her to finish discharging her task. The younger Dusman stared at her for a moment, then continued leading her into the duplicate of the capital spire. For herself, J'asa had always thought the structure morbid. The First Republic was 20,000 years dead.

Inside were many offices and places for meetings, but the grand hall where the *Tor* presided on major events was the same chamber where the Mercenary Council in the Union held court. She'd never missed the irony of choosing that place, of all the other locations available in the Capital Spire, to put the Mercenary Guild council chambers. *More like a poke in the eye socket*, she thought as they reached the chamber.

J'asa expected to be led further; instead, Keenta stopped and waited by the door. J'asa was about to ask where she was to go when a voice spoke from up on the plinth.

"Welcome home, *J'apo.*"

She looked up to see a single Dusman sitting in one of the leaders' chairs. "*Tor* Saleen?" she asked. The figure nodded. Looking up so far hurt her neck. It had to be intentional. "You summoned me?"

"I did," Saleen replied and disappeared from sight. A moment later, she heard a door open at the base of the plinth, and the other emerged, pulling herself on a line. The *Tor* was older than J'asa; she'd expected that. What she hadn't expected was the high-ranking leader wasn't *much* older. They were close enough in age, J'asa couldn't guess how much older Saleen might be.

Has there been a major change? she wondered. At the same time, she glanced around. They were alone. Strange.

"May I ask why? Am I being detained?"

The *Tor* smiled, but her ears didn't curl to echo the facial expression. Instantly, J'asa was on full alert. This was a dangerous situation.

"No, *J'apo*, you're not being detained."

Yet, she thought at the continued use of her title. She crossed her arms over her chest and cocked her head, ears going straight out, curling down at the tips.

"Now, now, *J'apo,* why the distrust?"

"I come back to do some research, maybe visit my babies in the creche, and I'm summoned to the leadership dome, where I find just one *Tor.* I've been in normal space for years, with no idea of what's gone on here in my absence, except what the *kroof* has relayed to me."

"Yes, this is true; you have no idea what's gone on here since you were relocated to normal space."

"You mean *banished.*"

The same fake smile. "Let's not resort to hyperbole."

"I'm the first *j'apo* since the Betrayal," she said, her tone cold, "yet my visions were nearly my demise." Saleen rolled her eyes. "Your faction hoped sending me to normal space would either silence or kill me." She was now certain Saleen was part of the faction that'd had her banished. The *Tor's* expression instantly darkened, and J'asa knew she'd struck home.

"I didn't send you to normal space," she complained.

"You personally? No, of course not. You weren't a *Tor,* more likely a *tor'u,* or *tor'o,* like young Keenta back there." She gestured to the doorway, where Keenta was doing a poor job of feigning disinterest. "Yet you agreed with it, supported it, pushed for it." Saleen's mouth was a tight line of anger. "You lost. It's over."

"Maybe it's less over than you think, *J'apo.*" Saleen almost snarled the title, more curse than rank. "You've put us on a path to destruction."

"I've done nothing except what my visions have led me to."

"Visions," Saleen spat. "Dreams, you mean? What good are the *dreams* of a young Dusman?"

"The last *j'apo* born foresaw the Betrayal," she shot back, her own anger growing. "What happened to that *j'apo*?" Saleen glared at her. "She was *banished* as well, only remembered after we were thrown low, all but destroyed. A hundred billion Dusman, with barely a thousand survivors."

"My job is to protect our future, not dwell on the stories of the past. Abandon this insanity. We've been safe here; we can remain so."

"Thousands of our young fighters die every year to hold this place. The numbers have slowly increased as the enemy learns our means. This isn't our future. The past is our window *into the future*, you fool!" She did it, she lost per patience and screamed at the *Tor*.

Everything about their race's caste structure, their natural ability to fit within those structures and to recognize where each of them sat, backed up her ability to do what she just did. A *j'apo* held the same status in Dusman society as a *Tor*, or even a *kroof*. They were leaders, in their own way, to be listened to, understood, and heeded. In the aftermath of her own rage, J'asa wondered, *Is this how the last* J'apo *ended her life?* Nobody remained to tell the tale, of course, or maybe their path would be clearer. Wouldn't it?

"Get out," Saleen snarled. J'asa didn't move; though she was breathing hard, she forced a tiny smile on her face, and her ears quivered in anticipation. "Leave, *J'apo*." This time the rank *was* a curse, but propriety had been observed.

She bowed her head slightly. "As you wish, *Tor* Saleen." She turned smartly, remembering to keep a hand on one of the ropes, and pulled herself back to the door, where the young *tor'o* stared in stunned disbelief. Keenta moved to follow her.

"I think I can find my way," J'asa said dismissively. "You might want to see if *Tor* Saleen needs medical attention; I've delivered quite a shock to her system by not rolling over and playing dead on command."

* * *

EMS *Bucephalus* Shuttle, Talus

The shuttle certainly wasn't a dropship; it was far more comfortable. The pilot treated him like a VIP instead of a company commander, taking a slow, easy reentry interface through Talus' atmosphere. The last time he'd been there, Jim had come in on a HALD drop, laser and MAC fire lighting up the sky as the alien defenders tried their level best to kill him.

He poked Double T in the ribs. "All things being equal, this is better than the last time we were here." The confused look on his face forced him to remember that the last time he'd come to Talus, Hargrave was still alive and his XO. "Sorry, I forgot."

"No problem, Colonel. I was with Roaring Saints on Canopy."

"The Horde ran that assault," Jim noted. Double T nodded.

"Not many Cavaliers made it through the war, did they?"

"No," Jim said. "Lieutenant Colonel Buddha, then top sergeant, made it with about a platoon. They were securing the perimeter when Peepo blew up the government building. Most of the Cavaliers were inside, trying to secure the rat bitch. She was 1,000 kilometers away, safe and sound. I was landing with the Raknar, didn't know what happened till days later. Peepo played us well."

"She played everyone," Double T said. The two nodded as super-heated plasma roared against the shuttle's hull. "Did anyone ever figure out who killed her?"

"It was a Depik," Jim said. Double T's mouth made an O. "Yeah, apparently the biggest piece left of her was her head. Nigel confirmed it through the Peacemakers."

"Couldn't happen to a nicer rat," Double T said.

"That's for sure." *I still wish she'd told us what was happening,* he thought. *There's no guarantee humanity would have helped keep the Kahraman out, but at least a lot of people wouldn't have died.* He considered for a moment and wondered if that was really true.

The shuttle banked, and the pilot came on. *"We're under approach control; no sign of an armed response."*

"Good to hear," Jim replied then turned to his security detail. "Maintain decorum, you're only authorized to fire if fired upon. The Talusians are very impressed with themselves and are likely to try to order you around. Don't fall for it. You're Cavaliers and representatives of the Federation government. Understood?" They all nodded. "Good, oh, and Henry? Leave the heavy machine gun in the shuttle."

"Aw, but Colonel—"

"Shut up and stow it," said Corporal Pam Walder, known as Paragon. The private mumbled but secured the cased weapon in one of the many gun harnesses built into the cargo area. Double T shot Jim a wink, and Jim struggled not to laugh. The kid was gung-ho, and that was good. Except when you were trying to be one big, happy family, of course.

A few minutes later, the shuttle's landing gear came down, and the pilot performed a short runway landing. Looking out one of the small armored windows, Jim tried to place the location and failed.

Johnstown's starport was just north of the Rapid River, but he couldn't see a river to the south.

The shuttle finished taxiing and stopped with a terminal in the near distance. A pair of flyers flew over the shuttle, spun around, and landed on their ducted fans. Neither looked like any design he'd ever seen before. Jim felt his men tense around him.

"At ease," Jim said under his breath as he saw the lead car was full of Dusman, and the second one of Humans. "I think we're fine." While he didn't recognize the Dusman, he recognized a woman who was walking toward the shuttle—Former Colonel Jennings, whom he'd last seen on Morgoth.

"Let's open her up," Jim said to the pilot over the intercom.

"*Roger that, Colonel.*" The forward loading ramp slid down under the cockpit, and the hatch hissed as pressure equalized. The smell of asphalt and sea spray made itself known as the portal slid open. In the moments between spotting the cars and opening the door, the occupants of both cars had rushed forward to create a line on either side. As soon as he set a foot out, someone yelled.

"Atennnn, SHUN!" All the Humans came to attention; the Dusman stood where they were.

"*Vok'ka* Cartwright, welcome to Raknar Station Talus."

As soon as he walked out from under the cockpit, he knew why he hadn't recognized the location. They were closer to the mountains, and everything was new, including the line of 15 Raknar standing next to a smaller version of the base now being built on Cavaliers' land back in Houston.

"Holy crap!" He gawked. The Dusman opposite Colonel Jennings grinned, her ears curling upward the same way Splunk's did when she was amused. Jim came to attention and saluted the assemblage. Jennings and the other Humans returned it in kind, and the Dusman with fist to heart in their own way.

"Welcome, Colonel," Jennings said, coming to shake his hand. "Or is it Minister Cartwright?"

She had a firm hand and a genuine smile. "It's Minister for this trip," he said. "You've been busy."

"We have less red tape to deal with here than on Earth. Plus, you guys did such a good job of levelling the area for our use."

"Yeah, this was one of the enemy merc missile bases, if I remember right?" He glanced around at the surrounding territory, accessing his pinplants. They were north and east of Johnstown, maybe 40 kilometers. He hadn't fought there personally. The entire campaign had been a nonstop rollercoaster of carnage and despair. Earth was still recovering.

"Yes, it was flattened in the early part of the invasion," Jennings said.

"We decided it was the perfect location for the Raknar facilities," said *Vok'sa* F'ada, Jennings' Raknar partner. Like Splunk, F'ada had a Human nickname, Glimmer. "It was close enough to the city to take advantage of available labor, as well as the existing, though inferior, starport. Yet the location was far enough from the city to allow maximum defensive measures to be installed."

Jim nodded, then considered what that meant. He'd never really inquired into what sorts of defensive systems were being installed at the Raknar base near his home. F'ada took note of the squad waiting behind Jim, and her grin turned wry.

"Were you concerned about our intent, *Vok'ka?*"

"Your intent? Not really. The locals?" He glanced at Jennings and winked. "Absolutely."

"I think you'll find a lot has changed," Jennings said. "For now, would the minister of war care to conduct a personal inspection?"

"I would." He gestured. "Lead on, Colonel."

While they were going through introductions, a third flyer had arrived. Jennings and Glimmer joined Jim and his squad, and all piled into the newly arrived vehicle as ground support crews attached a tug and moved the shuttle toward a hangar where more crews waited. *Very efficient operation*, Jim thought. The flyer he'd boarded screamed to life and leaped into the air. In moments, they were flying toward the Raknar building.

Like everything around Raknar, it was big. *Really* big. Since Raknar themselves were over 30 meters tall, you need taller buildings to house them. Maintenance on the towering war machines required cranes taller than the Raknar. To move them around, even taller buildings. The result was a structure pretty easy to recognize. There weren't many industrial structures commonly 50 meters tall, made of massive, reinforced materials—Raknar are heavy too—and without windows. Earth-made industrial structures tended to take advantage of natural light, which was more aesthetically pleasing.

Dusman didn't care about aesthetics. Everything about their construction lent itself toward utilitarianism. Jim suspected the Spartans would have appreciated Dusman architecture. Raknar facilities never had windows. In fact, they would make decent forts, if overly tall. The building was identical in most aspects to the ones on Earth. Jim realized they were probably manufactured on some Dusman planet and delivered ready to assemble. Where were these factories?

His eye was drawn to a difference from the facility on Earth. He pointed. "Is that a laser turret?"

Jennings followed his gesture and smiled. "Yes. When it went up, our Dusman allies didn't have the defensive satellite array in orbit. As you know, it takes more than a few minutes to get Raknar up and running. Even more to get them ready to fly to orbit." Jim nodded in agreement. "The base's defenses include shields and starship-class lasers. It might not stop a heavy assault, but it would slow it down, or give the enemy pause. We also have the old missile base at Redoubt back in operation. That would help, or at least draw fire from the Raknar base."

"We anticipate some time before most potential enemies understand exactly what the Raknar facilities are for," Glimmer said. "Initially, they'll mistake them for industrial targets."

"And thus of secondary concern to defenses," Jim added. The Dusman gave him a nod of acknowledgment.

"J'asa's assessment of your ability as a commander was not in error."

"You know her personally?" They'd switched to a series of small electric vehicles to tour the inside of the Raknar complex. Like the outside, it was nearly identical to the facility on Earth. Smaller, but with room to expand.

"We are from the same creche."

"How long are Dusman in a creche?" Double T asked.

Glimmer glanced curiously at the senior NCO before answering. "It depends somewhat on their future caste, but generally three years."

"That's not very long," Jim said. "Are you adults at that point?"

"Certainly not. After leaving the creche, young Dusman enter a period known as the *J'Zha*. I think Humans would think of it as college, or maybe an internship."

"So they can decide what they want to do?" Double T asked.

"More or less," she replied, "but it's deeper. Young Dusman already have a direction for their lives, the *J'Zha* merely solidifies that direction into a specific caste, as well as deciding what sex they will be."

"I wondered when that happened," Corporal Paragon said. She caught the eye of Private Erica Glendale, the only other female member of the squad, and winked. The women had a strange fascination with the Dusman, who started out as neither male nor female, but eventually changed into one or the other.

"Not always at that point," one of the other Dusman with them said. "Some never pick. They are the *coo*, the ones who run the creche."

The rest of the tour completed, they were brought to the main barracks, where he got to see the rest of the Raknar star, which was two fists, for a total of 14 Raknar.

"We took what we learned in setting up Earth's base and applied it here," an older, grisled-looking Dusman who reminded Jim of Dante, explained. "There wasn't much demolition to do, after all."

It was only after the inspection that Jim realized almost all the Human Raknar drivers were women! They had lunch in the base cafeteria, and Jim asked Jennings about it.

"All except two are from the Hellcats," she explained. The Hellcats had been her unit, partly lost on Earth at the beginning of the invasion. They'd been the only Human merc unit that was all women, at least to Jim's knowledge. "We were all compatible."

Not one to discard the possibilities, Jim wondered if they could tweak recruitment on Earth more toward women. Mercs in general, especially CASPer drivers, tended to be upwards of 80–85% men.

"All the women?"

"Yeah," Jennings said. "The two men in our star also came from the Hellcats. One was a mechanic." She gestured, and a young man nodded. "The other a pilot." Another older man, bald with a grin, waved.

Lunch had been a variety of seabass and local greens. It was delicious. He felt better than he'd expected when he'd decided to come to Talus. Deep down, he hoped the Dusman had brought some sense of control to the chaotic planet. But with such a history as the world had experienced, he found it difficult to believe it could be so quiet. So peaceful.

"Everything looks great," he said, finishing a cold Coke. Someone must have told them. "But what about the government here? Can you give me a breakdown of the current political situation?"

Jennings popped a brownie bite into her mouth and gave a wry smile. She glanced at her Dusman, Glimmer, then shrugged.

"It is best if you meet them in person," the Dusman said. "You have a meeting with the governor in an hour."

"Governor?" Jim asked. His detail didn't react, beyond glancing around curiously. Most of them had never been to Talus, only having heard about it from basic education or Tri-V news stories. "Okay, let's go."

* * * * *

Chapter Six

Talus Government Complex, Johnstown, Talus

They departed the Raknar complex with only a single large flyer holding Jim, his squad, Jennings, and her partner Glimmer. As they lifted off, the hustle and bustle of the base fell away behind them. Jim nodded in appreciation. To see the efforts of Houston so readily duplicated here, even slightly further along, spoke volumes of the Dusman's abilities and intent.

The last time he'd seen Johnstown, it had been war ravaged and dysfunctional. He'd left a group in charge as a provisional government; there simply hadn't been time to thoroughly root out and neutralize the former leadership, which had sold the colony out to Peepo. Sadly, that was a common scenario, though nowhere worse than on Talus.

The Rapid River had been dammed just above Clover Bay, the water used for both a reservoir and entertainment. Hydroelectric power had been some of the first energy generated on Talus, largely supplanted later by a planetary fusion powerplant installed several kilometers north of the dam on the coast. Water discharging from the hydro plant and spillway split into two tributaries for the final kilometers to the ocean, the northern route passing cheap workers' housing and industrial concerns, the southern branch a sprawling business district and entertainment center. The island created by these two waterways held the old government building (largely destroyed in the fighting), luxury housing with views of the Johnstown Reservoir, and the city's main docks.

As the flyers took them along the river and over the reservoir, Jim instantly saw the city had grown. Quite a bit, actually. The old city government buildings were gone, while the luxury district that had been adjacent it had grown. He began to frown until he realized they were headed for that district. There were no grandiose signs on the buildings, or advertisements for luxury housing, affordable to only the richest or well placed. Instead, a Tri-V displayed the words "Johnstown, Talus" rotating steadily.

"The new government complex?" Jim asked the Dusman piloting his flyer.

"Yes, *Vok'sa*. We provided bots to aid in the redesign."

Jim nodded. That was a good sign. It was early afternoon, the Talus star slowly heading toward the horizon. It was bigger and brighter than Sol, but the planet had a thicker atmosphere to shield the surface. The weather was mild and nice, a hallmark of life on Talus that made its political problems that much more profound.

The city was alive with flyers, of standard Union design and clearly Dusman manufactured. The roads below were likewise teeming with all manner of vehicles and foot traffic. Jim could see no signs of roadblocks or any attempt to control the traffic, beyond that required by expediency to keep it moving. Slowly he smiled.

They flew past the southern perimeter of the starport, and he was further pleased to see several free traders—smallish merchant starships of varying designs found in the galaxy. They were usually owned by individuals or small corporations and plied their way between smaller planets, buying and selling for profit. They were often sparsely armed, so finding them on Talus was yet another good sign.

The flyer left the starport behind and flew over the old hydro dam. Water gushed in hundred-meter-long arcs from the power-house, throwing up spray that reached well into the sky. The pilot angled their approach, and they descended to a large landing pad on top of a building. It looked like it might have once been a rooftop party area, or a restaurant. For the first time, Jim saw signs of securi-ty. A small, armed detachment waited for them to land before form-ing a line. An honor guard. There was also a small group—unmistakably journalists—a respectful distance to the side, being held in check by a functionary.

He came to a stop in confusion and surprise. It took Jim a sec-ond to collect himself and proceed down the ramp.

Standing at the end of the assembled guards was a man Jim thought was familiar, though he couldn't place the face. Jim walked down the assembled honor guard, Jennings and Glimmer flanking him on either side, and his own squad behind them. Double T looked decidedly uncomfortable in light combat armor with all the soldiers in ceremonial garb.

The man at the end of the procession smiled and held out his hand. "Minister Cartwright, I'm Governor Edgar G. Allen. I would like to officially welcome you to the Commonwealth of Talus."

Jim took the hand and shook it. "I thank you, and as an official representative of the Terran Federation, I'd like to inquire if the Commonwealth of Talus is to be considered *part* of the Terran Fed-eration, the defunct Earth Republic, or something else?"

Allen's eyes took on a twinkle, and he gave a slight smile. "While there's a good amount of discussion remaining to hammer out the details, including verification of a treaty with the Board of Mayors, I'm pleased to tell you, we proudly consider ourselves part of the

Terran Federation." He gestured, and the reporters came forward. He again took Jim's hand, and the two smiled and shook again. Jim also quietly breathed a sigh of relief. Dusman presence notwithstanding, he hadn't been confident in how this would go.

"If you and your men would accompany me," Governor Allen said, "we've prepared a small reception to welcome the first official visit from a Terran Federation official."

Jim began to understand that the meeting with the Dusman had been a delaying tactic to allow Allen to prepare the reception, including summoning a large number of town mayors from around the planet. As he was ushered into the reception hall, which was nicely appointed without being ostentatious, the mayors were just arriving. More than a few looked windswept or out of breath.

The hall held hundreds more guests, maybe as many as a thousand. Jim groaned inwardly. That hadn't been his intention for this visit; the minister of affairs or even the prime minister should have been there for this sort of dog and pony show. The guests were a mixture of nicely dressed and more common apparel.

His security detail was directed to a waiting area just behind the hall. As Jim and the governor entered, all eyes turned to examine the arrivals. He saw them immediately spot him, and conversation rose noticeably. A few pointed to their friends or those seated next to him. His apprehension immediately rose.

"Ladies, gentlemen, and community leaders," a voice boomed over the public address system. "Please rise and welcome Jim Cartwright, commander of Cartwright's Cavaliers, and minister of war for the Terran Republic!"

For the second time, he came to a surprised stop as the room came to their feet, and thunderous applause rolled over him. "Holy shit," he said out loud, and was instantly grateful that nobody could hear him.

Of course there were speeches, for which he was completely unprepared. Luckily for Jim, he'd gotten somewhat used to giving speeches during his tenure as minister of war on Earth. It wasn't until the third person used a handheld microphone to thank Jim for rescuing them from the alien invasion that it came to him.

He turned to Allen, who just happened to be looking at him. "I remember you," he said. Allen smiled even wider. "You were about to be executed in a quick and dirty trial just after we took the city."

Allen nodded somberly. "More later, Minister."

"Call me Jim."

He smiled again. "And please, call me Ed."

An hour later, they were in the governor's office, which Jim was pleased to see wasn't nearly as ostentatious as you'd expect from a planetary governor. Another ice-cold Coke had been provided for him, and the two were alone.

"Your memory serves you well, Jim," Ed said. "I was one of about 100 men and women Avery Bates, along with his toadies, rounded up after the invasion."

"Your wife was nearby, trying to deal with the fact that you were about to die," Jim said, taking a sip of the sweet beverage. Strangely, it didn't taste as good as it used to. "I think it was your son, about five?"

"He's seven now."

"Right, he asked me if I was going to kill his daddy. I was pretty wasted after the fighting, but I listened. Your wife said they'd been hostages, forcing you to work."

"I ran the fusion plant," Ed said. "When Peepo invaded, the Council helped and provided names of people like me, who were necessary to keep the lights on. Our houses were hit by Goka and Aposa mercs, who rounded up our families. I was one of the lucky ones; the Aposa got my family. The Goka killed more than a few they were supposed to bring in."

"Sounds like Goka."

"Anyway, we did what they said. Avery and his crew played both sides, said if we cooperated, eventually they would get a chance to strike back, if we bided our time. 'After all, the Council has our best interests at heart.'"

"He was with the fucking Council?" Jim snarled, cursing himself. The Council was part Politburo, part Nazi Gestapo. They'd ruled Talus for decades, somehow managing to hold onto power during multiple coup attempts. There had been a round of executions by the aliens just before Jim's forces neutralized the last of the resistance. He'd assumed it was the Council being liquidated by the aliens. There'd been some testimony to that point.

He should have stayed a while longer to make sure of the situation. Instead, the cursed Council had been behind it all along. Which only made sense; Peepo had probably discussed it with them. The entire invasion of Talus had been more similar to that of Earth than he'd suspected at the time.

"What happened after we left?"

"Avery Bates was rewarded by the Council and made chief administrator. They figured with Earth subjugated, this was their big chance. Yeah, Earth never got involved much in Talus politics, but there was always the threat. The Council was like a bunch of bullies, always worried the teachers would figure them out."

"They were overconfident enough to not worry about me and the ones they'd helped hold hostage. Only I and others gathered all the records of what they did. Bates thought everyone was happy the occupation was over, and because you'd endorsed his trials, they figured he was on the good guys' side. Until we released our research on the AetherNet."

"Bates didn't have you rounded up?"

"He would have, if he hadn't been shot dead in front of his house the next morning."

"Woah, one of your allies?"

"Nope, never found out who. In fact, as far as we can tell, the entire Council was killed over the next week. Maybe even a few who weren't part of it. When you guys left, you turned over all the alien weapons to my friends, remember? We kept them, too. That night, everyone used them."

Jim considered his words carefully. In the end, he hadn't suggested more might have died who weren't actually on the Council or working with them. Things were seldom that cut and dried. Only problem was, what good would it do to say as much? From the brief time he'd spent talking with the mayors and seeing people and the way things appeared to be going, life was better. Wasn't it?

"Talus looks safe and peaceful now," Jim ultimately said. "How's the crime rate?"

"Going up, unfortunately. Talus before used secret police to enforce laws. You didn't commit crimes if you didn't have the right connections or weren't desperate. Now that we have courts working, and police or peace officers, some of the worst elements are beginning to show themselves."

"Have you considered relaxing weapons laws?"

For the first time, Ed looked uncomfortable. "We've never been that sort of colony."

"That's not entirely true," Jim said and took out his slate. He instructed it to project a Tri-V display of the planet's original constitution, filed back on Earth with the Republic at the time Talus became an official colony. "It's a simple version of the United States' old Constitution, right down to the Bill of Rights. Notably absent is the so called 'Green Bill of Rights' and the 'Right of Reparations,' added just before First Contact. Smart move, there."

Ed looked caught, which was exactly what Jim had been after. "You were able to resist being subjugated because I *armed* you, Ed. That was my goal. You used those tools to throw off tyranny, and Talus is free again. Mostly."

"The majority of our citizens aren't familiar with weapons."

"So teach them." Ed nodded slowly. "It's your planet..."

"No, it's the people's planet," Ed corrected.

"Good, you're right. But it's your decision and theirs; I won't pressure you. There are no requirements for Federation colonies, outside the basic Human rights of life, liberty, and all that. Drug laws, abortion, guns?" Jim shrugged. "We don't have any of those laws on Earth in the Federation territories. Well, most of them. A few European areas and the Middle East are still coming to grips on freedom of marriage and abortion, but we're making progress. Anyway, it's up to Talusians, but I hope you make the right decision."

"They could turn those guns on us," Ed pointed out.

"Don't give them a reason to." The other man looked annoyed, then shook his head and laughed.

"Jim, you sure don't sound like a man only in his 20s."

"I've done a lot more than most people my age." He activated a new file. "So, let's talk about Federation security, shall we?" A large spreadsheet with force projections, budgets, and proposals appeared between them. Ed narrowed his eyes and slowly nodded as Jim talked.

* * *

Eesius, 2nd Level Hyperspace

J'asa pretended to throw the ball with all her might, then flipped it around and handed it to another child. The momentary confusion caught most of the 2-year-old Dusman completely by surprise, but not a handful. It was the second time she'd pulled the maneuver in the simplified version of L'oopo. She was particularly pleased to see two of the ones who hadn't bit on the feint were her own children.

"Nice try, Mother!" one of them screamed as the young one tackled the kid she'd given the ball to. In a second, there was a screaming, laughing, snarling pile of adolescent Dusman fighting for the ball.

She'd played L'oopo on Eesius growing up, and on Kash-kah during her long banishment. The Dusman community in the old industrial complex, now a listening post, had several teams to pass the time. It was a very different game when played in gravity, and the ball could be bounced and passed. Here in the strange physics of 2nd level, even the strongest Dusman could only throw the ball maybe two meters. To compensate, there were extra players called drones who ran with the ball in whatever direction they felt like. You had to chase them down and take the ball without physically injuring or even deflecting them. Of course, the young didn't follow that rule very well.

"Both have been exceptional studies," the *coo'i*, a well-schooled teacher in charge of this creche, was gray and slow to move. Unlike many *coo*, he was a sexed male. He was missing an ear, and part of his skull was shining metal. A victim of the war to maintain their home, he'd likely become *coo* to remain useful.

J'asa guessed he could no longer father young, either. As most of their war veterans injured so were young, it was a possibility. So, this would be the closest he got to having his own children. Most Dusman harbored fond memories of their *coo*. J'asa, not so much.

"Any sign of the gift in either?" she asked of him.

"Of *j'apo*, or *k'apo*?"

"Either?"

The old Dusman shook his head. "No, *J'apo*. From what we understand, being like you would be unprecedented."

"Everything feels unprecedented these days."

They watched the young play, as it devolved into a general fracas. Right on time, a young pair of *coo'u* with a *coo'o* in charge of them waded into the battle to break it up before anyone needed medical attention.

"More than a few warriors in that batch," the *coo'u* noted.

"We're going to need them in the coming years," J'asa said.

She'd spent the last three days splitting her time between visiting her children at the creche and research. Most of the latter was remote only; she hadn't yet been granted the access she needed, and she was getting annoyed. Of course, her children weren't allowed to come back to the temporary quarters she'd acquired. Dusman young didn't leave the creche until they'd completed primary conditioning. Then it was to begin the *J'Zha* teaching for their future lives.

"Your two should be leaving in a few months."

"The first in their creche?"

A creche was kept together until they were conditioned, if the population was large enough to allow it. The population of Eesius was more than large enough. As young came in after being weaned, they were paired with others within a week or so of the same birthday. Once enough were present, conditioning could begin. They stayed from as little as two years, to as long as three. J'asa and Seldia had been first to leave their creche.

"Probably. You aren't surprised?"

"No, my sister and I were the first as well."

The *coo'u* nodded and made a note in his slate. "Not that it hasn't been pleasant to have the *J'apo* visit…"

She smiled and nodded, hint taken. "I'm hoping I can get the access I need soon," J'asa said. "When I do, I'll be far too busy to spend time at the creche." She longed to ask the *coo'u* what the children's decisions would be. Soon they would pick names, and their options for *J'Zha* would be presented to them. However, it wasn't a parent's place to know these decisions before they were made, lest the inquiries influence the child's future.

It was normally considered forbidden to even visit them once enrolled in a creche. J'asa admitted to herself, she'd pulled rank to get access. It didn't hurt that the *coo'a* was clearly on her faction. The more she interacted with her kind on Eesius, the more she was seeing, despite the *kroof*'s arbitration, many were unhappy with the outcome. Only time would tell if matters became worse.

She was about to say something when the little comm unit on her belt buzzed. "Excuse me, *Coo'u* she said, and moved to the edge of the room. "*Vok'tor* J'asa," she said into it.

"Vok'tor, *you are granted access to the Nee'Akee.*" The transmission cut off automatically. She grunted and put the device back. It was a computerized message, not a live person. Interesting.

She nodded to the *coo'u* and glanced at the creche group one last time. They were at the far end of the chamber, with the young being settled into comfortable little alcoves, each equipped with a miniature Tri-V and audio system. Rapid iterations, from physical challenges, to learning, or even rest was a common later stage of the conditioning. Some were taking it better than others. Her children were already concentrating on the displays. Without a word, she left.

After several days back in Eesius, her old instincts were returning. She'd only been marooned in an open space twice. Both times, a passerby had rescued her without comment. More than a few had returned from long stays in normal space, so situations like hers weren't unheard of. They were all respectful, and she often found others moving aside to make room for her on a glideway or a lift as soon as they sensed her caste and title.

With those familiarities came a general lay of the land, as Humans would call it. Of course, Eesius had changed in those years, but there were limits to what could change. A restaurant or service might relocate, but the leadership building and the science dome wouldn't move. The *Nee'Akee* was one such thing. It hadn't moved in 20,000 years.

J'asa made her way through three habitation domes and an entertainment dome en route to her destination. Her memory was years old and colored by time among the Humans, but Eesius seemed less crowded, and in places almost empty. As she waited for space on a well-used glideway, she used her slate to see if anything special had been scheduled: a concert, L'oopo game, or anything else. There was nothing on the network. Her space came, and she boarded the glideway.

When she exited the glideway, another Dusman caught her eye— a female who'd been watching her for some time. She tried to sense the other's caste, and got nothing. That made J'asa pause in confusion. She shook her head and moved toward the female, but she was gone. "What?" she said aloud. A few others using the glideway looked at her curiously.

She spun around and used her full concentration, searching for the strange, casteless female. There was no sign of her. J'asa spent several minutes searching the corridor without luck. It had already been half an hour since she'd gotten the message, and she didn't want to risk angering the *Nee*.

Eventually, she reached the airlock separating the rest of Eesius from the *Nee'Akee*. Two Dusman in Konar stood guard, both saluting with the whine of high powered electromuscular actuators as she approached.

"Welcome, *Vok'tor*," the *osk'i* of the pair said.

"Thank you," she replied and returned their salute.

"Your purpose for this visit to the *Nee'Akee*?"

"I seek knowledge, *Vok'i*, and have been invited by the *nee'a* to proceed."

"Very well." The two braced their suits in specially installed leg holds and pulled.

The ancient door groaned, and the vibration was translated through the pressure-tight walls to reach her hand where it gripped a protrusion. She'd grown up and spent half her life on Eesius, but despite having learned about the *Nee'Akee* way back in her creche, she'd never visited it. Strange, to grow up Dusman, but never to come here. It seemed the door could only open about a quarter of the way, because the two armored Dusman stopped when the hinges screeched in protest. The *osk'i* gestured, and J'asa found handholds and pulled herself through the lock.

Inside, an old Dusman waited, floating within reach of a doorway, a male with almost pure white fur, and only a few tufts of hair left on his tail. Like all the *nee*, he wore a fold of black fabric wrapped around his eyes. Eyes that had been blind from the day he'd left the creche.

"*Vok'tor,*" he said and inclined his head slightly. The shine of brightly-polished interfaces just above his ears was jarring, despite her expecting it.

"*Nee'o,*" she replied.

"Are you prepared to walk the shores of *Nee'Akee?*"

"I am."

"Then come with me," the old Dusman replied, grabbed the nearest handhold, and headed down the old, dusty corridor.

How long do you have to move about the same space before you can find your way without sight? she wondered.

"A lifetime, *Vok'tor.*"

J'asa gave a shudder. She'd also forgotten the *nee* were supposed to be particularly powerful telepaths, perhaps even more accomplished than the *k'apo*, who could only talk to other *k'apo* effectively.

She followed the *nee* without thinking anything that might require a response. The corridors and doors were so deteriorated, it was difficult to believe they were inside a starship. She guessed it wasn't actually a starship anymore, and hadn't been for a long time. About 20,000 years, to be precise.

After a short time, they reached their goal—the *Nee'Akee*. She'd seen pictures of the *Nee'Akee*; all young Dusman did. The pictures didn't give you the scale of what she was seeing. The ship had been a *Behemoth*-class, like many that still plied the stargates, providing food and other goods to the far corners of the galaxy. This particular *Behemoth* had been one of the few ships to arrive in 2nd level hyperspace after the Betrayal, bringing the ragged survivors who'd managed to evacuate.

The *Behemoths* were of several designs. The *Nee'Akee* was inside one of the biggest, with a massive central main cargo bay, and a thousand small, honeycomb-style sub-bays all around its periphery. The main area was dimly lit by tiny spotlights shining out from many of the honeycomb-shaped bays. In the center, floating unsupported, was an icosahedron-shaped construct built entirely of smaller computers networked together. The *Nee'Akee*, or living memory.

Like much of the Dusman language, words could have multiple meanings, depending on who said them, the context the word was used in, and even the subtle telepathic emphasis added to the word. It had taken J'asa months to learn how to communicate with Jim in the Humans' overly simple, almost two-dimensional language. It was somewhat amusing that their race was more emotional, yet less able to express it. *Nee'Akee* had a many layered meaning to Dusman, beyond the simple translation. It could also be interpreted as heart of life.

"First time seeing it in person?"

"Yes," J'asa whispered. "How many recordings?"

"We're still indexing them."

20,000 years later, she thought, *and they're still sorting it out.* "Where do I start?"

"What are you interested in?"

"Raknar, of course."

The *nee'o* grunted in an unsurprised manner. "Only makes sense." He paused for a moment, and the *Nee'Akee* came alive, all 20 sides flashing in a hypnotic pattern. "There isn't much," the old Dusman said. "Only a couple *Vok* made it back. The Betrayal cost them everything."

"I am aware, *Nee'o.*"

The other nodded, his head turning as if he heard something imperceptible. "Is your mesh talking to you?" she asked.

"It is," he said. "Do not covet what you dare not have."

"Billions in the galaxy have the simpler versions. We hoped they might be immune. They weren't."

"As we warned the *Tor.*" He was silent for a moment. "I have summoned a guide for you. One you might find familiar."

J'asa wondered who it might be. She had only maintained contact with one from her creche, her sister Seldia. "Who is it?"

"Wait here; it will not be long."

She stared at the *Nee* flashing its strange, hypnotic patterns, then noticed a couple of the small honeycomb chambers were glowing in order with the pulses. She knew the *Nee* had told her to wait, but she didn't care. She moved up the side of the honeycombs, using ropes attached next to each one. Each was dark as she passed. In a moment, she came abreast of one and looked in.

The interior was three meters on a side, with a single slate mounted on the wall furthest from the entrance. Unlike the others, this one was alive, casting its dim light across the huge open expanse toward the *Nee'Akee*, floating out in the center of the bay. The slate's light reflected perfectly on that facet.

Drawn by the light like a moth to a candle, J'asa pulled herself into the cell and up to the slate. When she was mere centimeters away, it came to life. The Tri-V projector must have been ancient; it flickered and shimmered as it displayed a young, incredibly weary-looking Dusman, who stared back at her, then spoke across the gulf of time.

"*Vok'or* T'eep, 210th Vanguard, 13th Star. Our assault on K-449 was in the latter stage. Attempts to pacify the locals failed, so they were neutralized. The enemy had maybe three stars of Canavar, no more than five. Half our strength. As *vok'or*, it was my call, and I made it. We began the assault at 1434 local time. By 1600, we were pushing toward the enemy LZ. All our mesh were destroyed at 1605. Everything stopped working. Everything. The transports, the field control support units, the fighters...and the Raknar."

The *vok'sa* shook his head. "Our interfaces were worse off than we were. Without our mesh, we'd lost a lot. Without theirs, they lost everything. The selective breeding left them no more capable than children fresh in the creche."

The look on the *vok'sa's* face was full of confusion and despair. "We expected to die. It was a trick of the Kahraman. They'd played a fool's decoy, like in *L'oopo*. This thing, this Betrayal, was complete. The Canavar would roll in, and we were helpless. Only from the roof of our dead Raknar, we could see the monsters laying there, moving listlessly. The enemy was just as dead as we were. Nobody understood. I still didn't, even as we managed to board an old ship we'd salvaged from the locals and flew into space."

The *Vok'sa*'s image faded out and another replaced it. But before this one could speak, another voice spoke behind her. "Greetings, *Vok'tor.*"

J'asa looked back and blinked in surprise. Recognition took a second. She sighed. "Hello, Mother."

* * * * *

Chapter Seven

Talus Government Complex, Johnstown, Talus

Considering his expectations for his visit to Talus, Jim was agog at the results. After the initial meetings, receptions, luncheons, etc., he authorized the remaining forces on *Bucephalus* to come down for shore leave. The real reason was simple—verification. He wouldn't say out loud that he was suspicious about the turnaround on Talus. He didn't have to.

"We'll check things out," Buddha said and winked. He'd been on Talus more than once, and the expression on his face said it all. He was skeptical as well.

They put him and his officers up in suites within the government complex—which, after a busy day, was appreciated. He'd suggested they could stay at the Raknar base, which the governor waved off.

In the morning there was, of all things, a parade in his honor. His security detail went into apoplectic fits at the idea of him parading down the street like JFK in Dallas, Texas. However, it ended up being a short one, and only through the main downtown area. The Dusman were on hand, both on foot and in their tiny versions of CASPers known as Konar.

At the end of the parade, he was taken to the site of the trials that had taken place after he'd finished the conquest, where they showed him the worst part—a 5-meter-tall statue of him, standing triumphant, next to a CASPer with its cockpit open.

"Oh, for fuck's sake," he hissed when he saw it.

"Nice," Buddha said, nodding in appreciation. Jim glared at his XO, who laughed and clapped a huge hand on his shoulder. "There are several statues of your dad on Earth, Jimbo. He hated every one of them."

"You're taller than the CASPer," Double T pointed out.

"You aren't helping," Jim snarled. The senior NCO grinned, and Jim rolled his eyes.

"What do you think?" Ed asked. The governor was smiling from ear to ear.

"I think I'm not some hero who needs a statue," Jim said, speaking his mind. "I'm not Julius Caesar."

Governor Allen's expression turned somber. "Read the plaque, Jim." He did.

"Dedicated to Colonel Jim Cartwright, Cartwright's Cavaliers, and all the mercenaries who spilled their blood rescuing the citizens of Talus from ourselves. Thanks to your bravery and Colonel Cartwright's belief in us, we finally stood up and became the people our heritage meant us to be. Free." Under the dedication was a list of everyone who'd died fighting for Talus.

"Wow," Jim said. It wasn't about him; he was just a symbol. "I'm honored, and I'm sure the mercs who fought with me will be as well."

The rest of the day was meetings with the planet's nominal military leadership, which had to change.

"Here's the thing," Jim said. "We got rolled by the aliens for one reason; we didn't take our defense seriously."

"How do other races avoid that?" the commander of the Talus 'navy' asked.

"They hire mercs, or if they're a merc race, they use their own people. Keep in mind, monolithic merc races are more common than races like ours—non-monolithic. The Aposo are mostly fighters or workers. Attacking their colonies is like rolling in an ant nest.

"The other non-monolithic merc races are much older than we are. They've won massive fortunes and used them to build deep defenses. I don't have the time or the money. We have to go back to Human basics; we need an army and a navy."

"Everyone who wants to fight becomes a merc," said the military commander, Colonel Matthew Parker.

"Not necessarily," Buddha interjected. Now that Jim was sure it wasn't all an elaborate trap, he'd brought in his other senior officers. "Merc service is, if anything, *more* dangerous than military service was. If you look at the numbers from the 21st Century, the last data we have before First Contact, even if you factor in areas with excessive warfare, only 1 in 1,000 people in military service died. After the Omega War, we're sitting closer to 1 in 20. Sure, there's more money in being a merc, but a lot of it is paid out in death benefits."

Ed nodded. "I didn't know that."

"No," Jim said, "you wouldn't. The MST, or mercenary service track, taught in schools talked up merc service because it brought millions of credits in taxes. It also stripped the planet of militaries and left us a soft target. Your most recent census showed Talus with a population of 1.2 million?"

"That's close," Ed said. "Might be closer to 1.3, factoring in small settlements."

"Okay, we'd like to see you raise a standing army of 25,000." The Talusians gasped and started to complain. Jim raised his hands for silence. "First, realize that only about a third of those are actual trigger-pullers. The rest are everything from pilots to cooks. We're only talking about 2% of your population."

"And how do we pay for that?" the Talus finance secretary asked.

"Merc taxes," Jim said. "The same place you'll draw the core of your soldiers from." He explained his idea of deferring merc taxes through service to the planetary military.

"You're going to implement this on Earth?" Ed asked.

"Already are; it started months ago. Sure, there's some squabbling, but the young mercs love it. We give them the option of working their whole career for free in exchange for a promise of two years of service up front, or five years after they've served as a merc for ten years. The ones who serve at the end of their career are used as training, if injured, or to infuse the command structure with experienced officers and NCOs if they're still fit. We had hundreds of retired mercs turn up to serve. None of them liked seeing Earth under Peepo's thumb."

"I'm sure you'll find a lot here who feel the same," Lieutenant Mayer said.

Colonel Parker agreed. "We already have a few, but we didn't offer that tax incentive."

"Money and mercs, hand in hand forever," Jim said. All his officers and NCOs grinned; a couple gave thumbs up.

"We'll consider that," the governor said.

"I need you to do more than consider it, Ed," Jim said.

"What do you mean?"

"I mean this is a Federation thing. If you expect aid from Earth, especially naval aid, we expect you to have forces ready to deploy."

"That sounds a little like extortion, Jim."

"No, it's called a treaty. Ships are expensive. I'm dumping millions into getting the first Human navy up, Winged Hussars notwithstanding. Asking them to protect us as well as their own interests isn't exactly reasonable. Extending that to all the colonies is completely unrealistic. All the Human colonies are within a single jump of each other. When you add it up, that's a lot of throw weight, ready to go.

"When Peepo hit us, we all stood alone, and fell. The Peacemakers have a saying, "Stand or fall." That's us, because the next time someone comes, it probably won't be for conquest. These galactics don't play for points." He stopped short of talking about the Kahraman. *Get their military stood up first, then the real potentially bad news later.*

"Okay, say we go with his plan, what about weapons and gear?"

"We'll arrange that on Earth, with an eye toward getting a small arms and armor operation going here on Talus. It could be a lucrative business. I know for a fact Binnig is interested in putting a facility down."

"It'll cost millions to equip all those soldiers with CASPers," the finance secretary said, looking up from her slate where she'd been making notes.

"We don't expect that," Jim said. "Oh, sure, a couple companies, even a battalion of CASPers will be important. But after the Omega War, we don't have enough trained mercs to form a training cadre on the scale you'd need for complete CASPer forces. We're struggling on Earth to put together just two brigades. Five battalions per brigade, two companies per battalion, two platoons per company, each platoon with two squads of ten. That's 10 battalions, 40 platoons, and 800 trained CASPer pilots. Figure another 10% for officers, and double that for techs and medics."

"Woah, woah, woah!" Ed laughed and held up his hands. "Okay, 5,000 or so trained infantry sounds a lot easier."

Jim smiled and nodded. He held out a datachip. "It's all on here, including expected costs and times of development. We'd expect you to be at 80% readiness in a year." Colonel Parker was shaking his head. "You can do it," Jim assured him. "The numbers I gave you are *very* conservative. You might find you can do better. We'd like you to try."

"What do you think?" Jennings asked, catching up to Jim as he left the final meeting.

"Of Governor Allen, or the chances he'll come through with their military commitment?"

"Yes."

Jim laughed and shook his head. He sometimes forgot she was a seasoned merc commander, complete with a double scoop of pessimism and jaded nuts on top. "I think he's the kind of ruler Talus should have had for decades. I think if he'd been running things when the Omega War happened, Talus wouldn't have been rolled in the first place." Jennings nodded, a tiny smile on her face.

"However," Jim continued, "there are still forces here that don't want him to succeed. Every public event I attended was carefully guarded. The Dusman had my back, with probably 10 times more than I could see. He's at least conscious of his precarious position, which is why I've promised to get as much manufacturing moved here as possible. This will help him in his position, and help us decentralize Federation manufacturing. With all this in mind, I think he likes the idea of being able to protect Talus, and he's going to at least try to meet their obligations. That about cover it?"

"You don't miss much, do you, Minister?"

"Call me Jim."

"Marge," she said as the elevator reached the ground floor.

"Keep an eye on things here, Marge."

"That's my job." He was about to turn when she put a hand on his arm. "There's going to be a war, isn't there?"

"There have already been a couple at least," Jim said.

"No, I mean a *big* war, like the great one 20,000 years ago."

He considered his answer for a second before speaking. "Yes, Marge, I think we're going to have another war. But I don't think it will be as big as that one; there just aren't enough armies this time."

"Safe travels, Jim," she said. They shook hands, and he left for his shuttle back to *Bucephalus*.

* * *

Nee'Akee, Eesius, 2nd Level Hyperspace

"I didn't know you'd joined the *nee*," J'asa said. It was hard to look at her, knowing she couldn't look back.

"I'm here to assist you, *Vok'tor*. What specifically are you looking for?"

J'asa paused, fighting her emotions. Though Dusman didn't hold familial attachments to the degree Humans did, she was still hurt. The last time she'd spoken to her mother had been just before she was banished to Kash-kah in normal space. Her mother had always said she was honored to have the first *j'apo* since the Betrayal, and a *k'apo* far talker as well. The people who took the *Nee* were always motivated by something in their lives, usually bad.

"I'm researching Raknar," she said.

"I have been informed. Please provide additional details."

J'asa considered for a second. "I'm looking for more information on *cood*, and interfaces."

Her mother lowered her head for a moment. Outside, the *Nee'Akee* flashed a new pattern, and J'asa could see some of the cells light up, and others go dark.

"Which subject first?"

"Both together."

Another head down moment, much fewer. "As you have already perceived, the learning is kept in the cells. Each contains many *Akee*. If there are multiple in one cell, the slate will show you. If you need more, touch the *Nee'Akee*, and I will return." She turned and pulled herself out of the cell without another word.

J'asa watched her go, catching a glint of her mesh implant over her ear as she turned. It didn't make any sense. She couldn't ask her father; he'd died in a battle while J'asa was still in her creche. If she wanted to take the time, she could check Eesius records and find out when her mother had taken the *Nee*. Just now, her time was better used in her research.

Out of 1,000 or so cells, it looked like 50 were lit, a depressingly small number. When Jim Cartwright got the two Raknars shortly after she'd befriended him, J'asa had begun studying them. Since she was in normal space and had left Kash-kah, she hadn't had access to the Dusman's records. The GalNet had had to suffice, and it was pathetic.

Now looking at the sum of their living memory—*Nee'Akee*—on Raknar, she wondered if the galactics knew more than the Raknar inventors now knew. Ever since she'd begun her efforts to move the Dusman to return to normal space, she'd felt more and more how much they'd lost in the Betrayal.

But much of the data she needed wasn't there, either. She'd pieced together enough to bring the current Raknar project back online, even with Sla'etou aiming most of the efforts at space forces. She'd done all this without returning to Eesius for more research. Mostly because she knew there wasn't an overwhelming amount of information there, and partly because she'd been too proud to come back with the specter of the banishment hanging over her head.

Now she had no choice, because a problem was rearing its head. So, she spent every waking moment in the *Nee'Akee*, going through memories one at a time. Some recordings were hours or even days long, and none of it had been indexed…

The end of the third day, J'asa found a rope and pulled herself over to the *Nee'Akee*. Uncertain what to expect, she hesitantly touched the metallic surface and felt a strange hum run up her arm—

only for a second, then it was gone. A moment later, she saw one of the *nee* coming across the space toward her. As it got closer, she could see it was her mother again. *Great.*

"Yes, *Vok'tor?*"

"Can you tell me why the information around Raknar wasn't indexed?"

"Some of it has been, as you see."

"Yes, but most of it is not. When I had my vision, it was decided to move the Raknar memories up in importance, which they were. Then it stopped."

Her mother floated in place for a moment before responding, "The priorities were changed seven years ago."

"Seven years ago," she repeated, the idea processing in her mind through a growing fog of anger. "How long ago did you take the *Nee?*"

"Seven years ago."

J'asa was so enraged, she forgot where she was and tried to jump for the nearest door, making it a little more than a meter. Luckily she'd picked up a grapple belt the previous day, after getting stuck in a corridor center one too many times.

The harness held a pair of small rope launchers, which used rechargeable electric fan drivers and tiny grappling arms. Aim them at a handhold and activate them, and they would fly where indicated, latch on, then reel in the rope, bringing you along with it. Largely used by Dusman going to large open spaces for work, it was considered comical for an adult to use one. She didn't care.

She used the grapple to pull herself to the exit, retrieved it, and raced along the corridor, using hands and feet to move as fast as she could. If it weren't 2nd level hyperspace, it would have been a dangerous move. Miss a handhold, and you could collide head-on with a bulkhead. In fact, she was so focused on moving as fast as she could, that she didn't notice the group that fell in behind her, see them catch up, or see the fist until it connected with her head.

The impact caused an explosion behind her eyes and imparted a partial spin, causing her to lose her grip on the rope she'd been using to move along. She spun about 90 degrees from the impact before 2nd level hyperspace physics caused her to stop. As her vision cleared, she saw four Dusman, not wearing any clothing, and giving off no feelings of caste.

Po'Froo, J'asa realized. *Here, in the central domes?*

Two of them brandished crude knives, and the other two snarled with overly long teeth and claws allowed to grow like an animal's. She cast about for the sense of anyone nearby. She'd chosen as direct a path to her destination as possible. It was a little-used side corridor, so nobody was in sight.

"You're making a mistake," she warned them. "You do not want to do this."

"Oh, but we do," one of them said, a male with two visible scars in his fur.

Things had gone downhill since she left. Years ago, the *Po'Froo* would never have dared come into the main habitation area to cause trouble.

All four of them still had contact with the walls or a guild line, but J'asa had the grapple harness. In a flash she drew and fired the grappler aimed at the scarred *Po'Froo*, who tried to dodge aside, as you'd expect. Except the grappler was guided, meant to track a target, if necessary, not really caring what the target was. The other Dusman grunted as the powered grappler arms smacked into his abdomen and latched on. J'asa jerked with all her might, racing forward, feet first, into the *Po'Froo*'s face.

The surprise move was enough to shift the advantage in her favor. J'asa grabbed the nearest handhold with her tail and swung blindly behind her. Her claws contacted lightly-furred flesh and felt wet. The swipe was followed by a scream. The two remaining *Po'Froo* came at her as one. She locked a leg around a rope, grabbed the still stunned one she'd hit first, and flung him into the other two, nearly losing her grip on the wall in the process.

She was about to make her escape when the one she'd clawed grabbed her around the neck from behind and put her in a choke hold. J'asa tried to pry the fingers loose, without success. *Am I about to die?* she thought desperately.

Her vision swam, and she felt more hands grasp her. She fought any way she could, but it was no use. The hands around her throat loosened their grip, and hope flooded her, only to be replaced by terror as the coldness of steel replaced them. Her eyes went wide, and she thought she heard an insectoid chittering. Then something hit her, and she fell into darkness.

* * * * *

Chapter Eight

EMS *Bucephalus*, Talus Stargate

"Is there a chance it's sabotage?"

Captain Su glanced at Jim and shook her head as she examined the Tri-V dominating her ready room, just off the CIC.

Jim had been in a similar space aboard *Pegasus*, the Winged Hussars' flagship. Unlike *Bucephalus*, *Pegasus* was a dedicated warship, and its commanding officer, Alexis Cromwell, had a ready room that would have made Jean Luc Picard smile. Captain Su's ready room, by comparison, wasn't much larger than Jim's quarters aboard.

"My crew is above suspicion, and nobody else has been aboard since we left Sol," she explained. "No, it's just a matter of wear and tear. *Bucephalus* has logged a *lot* of hours in hyperspace, and that was after her conversion from an *Akaga*-class by the gas bags." Su didn't think much of the Izlians who'd designed and later refit her ship.

The problem they were both looking at was a redundant hyperspacial relay. If Jim understood it correctly, the hyperspace generator created a wave effect that was channeled out to the ship's hyperspace nodes via these relays. The devices looked almost identical to regular superconducting power relays, and even functioned similarly. The only difference was, at their core, they were made with Astatine-222.

A222, as it was often called, had the singular distinction of being the only element in the galaxy rarer than F11. It was *so* rare Jim had never even heard of it until a year ago, when he heard second-hand about a dispute between the Engineering Guild and a Zuul merc unit. This dispute apparently involved ownership of the only known reserves of A222, and now nobody knew who owned or controlled it.

"Everyone's putting off routine maintenance," Su continued. "These components are only good for so many hours. The hyperspatial wave effect deteriorates it. Whatever process they use to make A222, eventually wears out. These components need retreatment intermittently in a ship's life. It's just our rotten luck that this one chooses now to go out."

"So it's toast?" Jim asked.

"No, it's just flagged itself in a routine diagnostic check. That means it has less than a 75% chance of working if called upon."

"We still have the main one, right?"

"It flagged before we left Sol," she said dourly. "The chief engineer has been saying we needed them fixed since Morgoth. With the backup showing okay, we were fine. However, it's been tapped more than a few times recently, so it's now beginning to fail, too."

"Why haven't we fixed it? Are they expensive?"

"Moderately. Less pricey than an F11 flush, actually. The problem is nobody has any A222."

"Nobody?" She shook her head. "That's bad, right?"

"Yes. I've heard rumors of ships gathering at repair depots waiting for A222 to repair components. I've also heard lost ships are on the rise. Likely from a failed hyperdrive during jump. As your Dusman friends explained to me, an uncontrolled failure in hyperspace often results in a destroyed ship. The ones that survive to 2nd level hyperspace..."

"Have no way home," Jim finished for her. Apparently it took powerful computers to manage it, as well as specialized computations. "There are also forces there that are quite dangerous."

"So I've heard."

"What do we do, go back to Earth now? I'd hate to stop at just Talus, but the alternative is to keep rolling the dice."

"There might be an alternative." Jim looked at her expectantly.

"The Yovaz system."

"I've heard of it, a backwater mining planet with poor agriculture, mostly due to polluting their own planet from mining." He thought for a second. "Colony of the Reyq? Electric eels?"

"Yes, but it's now their principal world. Their home world was cooked by a gamma ray burster 11 years ago. Only a few thousand got out alive."

"What? The Science Guild should have…" Jim stopped and sighed. "Fuck me. What's special about them?"

"Not a clue," she admitted. "Never seen one in person, just what you see in the GalNet, which is precious little."

"Do they mine A222 there?"

"No. However, they have a side business—starship breaking."

"Oh, ho!" Jim said. "Let me guess, there's an old *Akaga* there?"

"Right in one," she said and winked. "Two, actually. We've bought parts off them in the past, so they've left them in a deep orbit. I guess spaceship junkyard is a sometimes profitable income source."

"Hold on," Jim said. "Why didn't we just buy the parts before we left Earth?"

"There's the rub," Su said. "They haven't responded to inquiries." She changed the Tri-V to a map showing Yovaz in relation to Talus and Earth.

Jim could see all the Human colonies as well as Karma off to one side, more toward the coreward side of their region. "One jump," he said.

"Easily."

"Well," Jim said and shrugged, "let's pay the Reyq a visit, shall we?"

"Already have the course set, just waiting for your approval."

Jim grinned. He really did like Captain Su.

* * *

EMS *Bucephalus*, Yovaz System Emergence Point

Of course, Jim warned the Cavaliers of the risks of another hyperspace jump. However, it was the same risk whether they went home or on to Yovaz. It was unlikely anyone would wander by with a cargo hold full of Astatine-222 and volunteer to sell some, so they went. Captain Su put the odds of a catastrophic failure at under 5 percent, and sure enough, they arrived without incident.

"Anyone at the emergence point?" she asked once they'd fallen back to normal space.

"Sensors only show some debris."

Jim was suddenly alert. Debris in an emergence area was something most races wouldn't tolerate. Ships often came through with significant velocity. The best way to find your system off the visiting list was to allow ships to get hulled by junk when they arrived.

"Scan it," Su ordered. A minute later, responses came in from sensor ops.

"Remains of several ships, so exploded ordnance and a few life pods. Looks like a battle, Captain."

"Any signals from the pods?"

"Negative, and there are no indications of power from them, either. I'd say whatever happened, we missed it by weeks, maybe months."

"Not a good sign," Su said, mostly for Jim's benefit. Her CIC crew already knew full well they might have fallen into the shit. "Sit-Con, drones out, extend our view. Sensor ops, bring the high gain around at the planet; see if *anyone* is talking, even encrypted. TacCom, shields at full. Helm, give me 2Gs toward the stargate."

"Getting out of here?" Jim asked.

"Just moving that way, in case," she said. "If everything is okay, we can always redirect to the planet without too much wasted delta-V."

Jim nodded, understanding. He did what a ground commander always did when hostilities in space were a possibility; wait impatiently. His memory was pulled back to his early career. They'd had a simple relief of assault mission, and ended up jumping into the midst of a pitched space battle. Their merc cruiser at the time, *Traveler*, had been destroyed by enemy fire. All the CASPers got off in dropships, but there were still casualties. That mission had been the first time he'd faced off against Canavar.

Minor shudders through the hull spoke of drones being launched and weapon systems readied. *Bucephalus* carried both missiles and lasers for offense and defense. She was far more capable at defense, which was ubiquitous among merc cruisers. They'd traded offensive punch for speed, defense, and troop capacity. In his father's day, the Cavaliers would sometimes hire space navy elements when more firepower was needed on specific contracts. The only Human mercs with sizeable space assets were his fellow Horsemen, with the Winged Hussars.

"There are at least two dozen ships in orbit," TacCom reported once their drones were broadening the ship's sensor capacity. "Many have battle damage."

"What kind of warships?" Su asked.

"None appear to be warships. At least, they weren't originally."

"TacCom, can you explain that?"

"I'm putting up radar and thermal compositions on the main Tri-V."

The display at the center of Bucephalus' CIC came alive with the images of many ships. From Jim's limited ship experience, he thought they looked like freighters or ore haulers. One might be a troop transport, but he doubted it. All of them had chunks missing and glowing spots, and a few looked to be actively burning—a bad thing for any spaceship.

"What are we seeing?" Jim wondered aloud.

"That is a really good question," Captain Su replied. "Comms, anything on the planet?"

"There's chatter," the comms officer replied, his eyes closed as he used pinplants to go over data. "It's mostly low power UHF. Calls for help, coordinates, situational reports. It's hard to put together a coherent picture because it's all on a data carrier so I can't tell who's who. What I *can* tell you is an invasion is underway."

"There's no way that's a merc operation," Su said, pointing at the ragtag fleet.

Jim had begun running contracts through his pinplants. Like any starship, every time *Bucephalus* transited a stargate, it got an update to the GalNet, various personal emails archived for forwarding to the next stargate. In addition, because she was a merc cruiser, she also got updated files from the Mercenary Guild, including contracts underway, requests, and completions. Because of the small number of contracts, it only took him a few seconds to confirm there was nothing active in the Yovaz system. He gave her the results.

"Unsanctioned?" she asked him.

"According to Guild law, that's a risky proposition. Sure, it happens, but why bring that junk? Even a Pushtal would be embarrassed to fly around in that. Looks more like whatever junk still flew was pushed into service." He pointed at the ships. "Entropy, could this be *territorial?*"

"You mean a planet putting together their own military and launching an attack?"

Jim nodded. The CIC was silent, except for the quiet chatter between department team members and the constant hum of life support. "I wonder if Nigel knows about this, and if it's a trend," Jim mumbled under his breath.

"Helm, set course for the stargate, 2G nominal acceleration."

"Roger that, Captain."

"We getting out of here?" Jim asked.

"No way to pay, nobody answering, better to just leave."

"We've bought from these people before, right? For *Bucephalus?*"

"Yes, they're a nearby source of parts for more than a few ships in use by Human mercs, all old and out of date, of course. What are you getting at, Colonel?"

"Follow me here," Jim said. "If we've paid them before, we have their account information." He gestured at the planet. "Where are the ships?"

"In a geosynchronous orbit with all the other junk ships." She used her pinplants to change the view to a large cluster of ships high above the planet. None were recognizable as *Akaga*-class.

"Well, if the parts are there, and we have their Banking Guild codes, can't we just transfer them the funds we would have paid? Add like 25% and get them ourselves. They used to call it Pick-n-Pull back in the 20th Century on Earth."

Captain Su looked at the Tri-V display and rubbed her chin, considering. "There's some risk attached," she told him.

"I'm willing to take it, but it's your ship and your call."

"If you're willing, so am I, Colonel." Jim nodded. "Very well. Helm, belay the previous orders and make for the junkyard, 1G nominal."

Jim glanced at her questioningly.

"Better to take it slow and save reaction mass. That way, things go south, it won't happen quite so quickly. If we're breaking in at higher G, we have fewer options."

"Understood," he said.

It would take just over six hours to reach their destination, so Jim used the time to catch a few hours' sleep in his quarters, then brief his senior officers and NCOs. As his quarters were only the size of a small car, most of them had to stand in the corridor and peek around the corner.

"It's a simple grab and go on the surface," Jim explained. "We're going to wire the locals credits for the parts, park next to the wrecks, and *Bucephalus'* engineering team will retrieve what we need for repairs. While that's going on, Cavaliers will suit up, go EVA, and cover them, in case trouble comes a callin'."

"Sounds straightforward," Buddha said, grinning. "You know what that means?"

"Shit sandwich," Sergeant Mayer said.

"Extra cheese," Double T agreed.

"We don't know that," Jim said, trying to sound like a commander around the grin on his face, "but I'm setting the RoE as fire only if fired upon or with command staff approval."

The NCOs groaned; none of them liked having strict Rules of Engagement. Jim didn't like the idea of a group of undetected locals who worked in the junkyard popping up suddenly and his men shooting the shit out of them, either.

"Regardless, that's how it needs to be. Buddha, assemble two squads of the most experienced zero-G troopers we have. Get the armorers to prep their CASPers for space with two squads for backup. We'll have *Bucephalus* watching our six, so that should be all we need. However, I want the whole contingent on alert."

Buddha nodded, making notes with his pinplants. "Who's commanding the EVA op?"

"Me," Jim replied. "I'm one of the most experienced Cavaliers in space, anyway." None of his officers had anything to add, so they went to work.

Captain Su managed their approach to the parking orbit—high in geosynchronous—closely, using a minimum of fuel, while observing a maximum defensive posture. Far too often in the galaxy, small, less-well-armed adversaries would take advantage of an enemy's complacency to turn it into opportunity. Jim imagined even a lightly armed cruiser would give its master a certain feeling of invulnerability.

His family's personal yacht, *Pale Rider*, which he'd taken out several times, had once been a scout frigate, bought cheaply by his grandfather, and converted into a personal craft. It was still a pretty good-sized ship. However, its shields were minimal, and it only had one laser and missile apiece. Most alien systems prohibited nuclear weapons aboard non-merc ships (which was impossible to enforce anyway), which meant her offensive punch was all but nonexistent. Enough to keep lightly armed opportunists at bay; that was about it.

"Debris," sensor ops called out.

"Avoid?" Captain Su asked.

"Unlikely, Captain."

"Very well. TacCom, shields to full power, maximum forward deflection."

"Shields full power, aye. Maximum forward deflection, aye."

A few moments later, a series of tiny shudders ran through the ship, kinetic energy of the impacts translated through the field effect generated by the shields. *More tech we don't fully understand,* Jim thought. The GalNet articles on shields predated the First Republic, the government run by the Dusman 20,000 years ago. All he knew was it had something to do with the nuclear strong force and electromagnetic fields, which weren't even related. Maybe if he was bored when he got back and needed to get to sleep, he would ask an Aku to explain them.

"Wait…" the sensor ops tech said a split second before a hammer blow hit the ship.

They'd been coasting nose on toward the junkyard. Enough of *Bucephalus'* forward momentum had already been canceled by her main engines, allowing her to flip over and use bow thrusters to finish her approach. Like most warships, her best shields and weapons pointed forward. Getting caught in an engagement while trying to lose velocity was suboptimal, for a lot of reasons. A fusion torch required a hole in your aft shields.

"Low order nuclear detonation!" TacCom said. "Shields damaged."

"What the hell was that?" Captain Su demanded.

"I'm picking up low level neutron readings in the debris field. I only detected them when we were under a kilometer away. Lost it in the star's neutron flux."

"Mines?" Jim asked.

"More likely repurposed missiles," Su replied. "Almost nobody uses mines—too messy—but when they do, they're usually megaton range, not the little kiloton firecracker. If we'd hit one of those big boys, we'd be having this conversation in hell. Helm, all stop!"

Everyone in the bridge grabbed something as the ship's forward thruster burned hard. *Boom!* They hit another nuclear weapon as the last of the ship's speed was canceled. The Tri-V showed the junkyard, 20 kilometers distant. *Bucephalus* was still at a higher orbit, which meant the junkyard was slowly slipping behind them.

"Detailed scan underway," sensor ops said. The Tri-V changed so *Bucephalus* was a tiny miniature in the center of the field. In the distance ahead was the mishmash of the junkyard, and all around them were little red dots, a small sea of them.

"Tell me those aren't all nuclear weapons," Su spat.

"Uncertain," sensor ops said. "They all have neutron emissions higher than the background. Let me redirect the main sensor dish and perform detailed scans." Minutes ticked by as a cluster of 10 targets were scanned. After five minutes, seven had been eliminated; three now pulsed red. Sensor ops and TacCom conferred for a second.

"These three are definitely armed weapons," TacCom said.

"But the other seven could simply be unarmed," sensor ops said.

"How are they holding the higher orbit adjacent to the junkyard?" Su asked.

"The orbital distance is only a couple kilometers," SitCon said. "They could have station-keeping ability, and simply went dark when they detected a target."

"There are more behind us," sensor ops said.

"I'd have to say, the minefield didn't activate until we were deep in the danger zone," SitCon said.

"Well, *that* was a twist I wasn't expecting," Captain Su said.

* * *

EMS *Bucephalus*, Secure Transit Space

"We can help them, you know?" Ajax suggested.

"I'm aware of that, *Osk'i*," Achilles snapped. Ajax shrugged and went back to the game he'd been playing with Hector. The problem was, Ajax was right. The Humans had blundered into a minefield, which he could probably deal with easily enough, but not without letting the *ske'ii* know they were there. *Vok'tor* J'asa had given him strict instructions to only break silence if absolutely necessary. Currently, he didn't believe it was *absolutely* necessary.

Of course, the problem was, if he waited until it *was* absolutely necessary, they might all be dead. The Humans had come here for parts, and ended up in the middle of a battle. *They're their own worst enemies*, he mused. "No, we'll continue to monitor, but keep the Konar active."

"Again?" J'op complained.

"Yes, *again*." He increasingly wished she'd stayed in 2nd level hyperspace and off his team.

* * * * *

Chapter Nine

Eesius, 2nd Level Hyperspace

She floated alone in the void. No sound—not even of her
own breathing—penetrated the nothingness. She was
neither alive nor dead. Time, like space, had no meaning.
Slowly, like emerging from a fog, images began to surface.

I'm having another dream, she realized in excitement and terror.

She saw a brain's neurons, but they were scattered across the galaxy, each one a star. Hundreds of them were infected, a growing malignancy. One arm of the galaxy/brain had been clean; now the disease spread there as well.

A thousand Raknar stood like trees in an old-growth forest, covered in improbable amounts of dust, mildew, and vines. As one, their lights came on, and they shuddered to life, breaking free of the decay that had enclosed them. Renewed and shiny, they fell into formation, and marched toward a fogbank. Behind the mist, monstrous shapes writhed in anticipation.

A man and woman, naked and holding hands, stood amidst a huge crowd of aliens, also paired by whatever sexual group was common to them. Slowly, the myriad of races moved and formed groups. First a couple, then many, until two sides formed. The Humans were joined by SalSha and two aquatic races she'd never seen. Then there was a fifth race; it reminded her of a little of her own race, and a little of the Humans.

The groupings continued. There were all the mercenary races she knew, together. Then suddenly they were no more, moving off to join groups. The Dusman appeared, and the KzSha went to join them, as did several of the former merc races. Others joined the Humans, the Zuul, the Sumatozou, and surprisingly, the MinSha. But there was a new group.

This group appeared, just like the Dusman. They were shadowed and indistinct. There might have been two of them, or one larger one? She couldn't tell. Instantly, other races moved to join them, and J'asa knew they were the Kahraman, still shrouded in mystery and confusion. Two sides had been created, with only a few bunched between them.

One or two changed sides, then a few from the middle picked a side. One of the aquatics with the Humans left and joined the other side, and the rest watched them go, while the other aquatic race wept. The indistinct image of the Kahraman slithered forward, as did the Dusman, Humans by their side. The scene flashed and was gone.

Stars. A million stars, the populated worlds of the galaxy, shone with an indescribable light. They began to wink out, starting from the tip of one galactic arm and moving inward. Then an actual star flashed and died. Another, then another, then a flurry. J'asa watched in horror as trillions died, just like before, but in weeks, not centuries. The galaxy screamed her name. And then...

J'asa opened her eyes and looked around. She was in a medical bed in one of Eesius' combat trauma centers. She'd seen them during training, shortly before her exile into normal space, but never as a patient. She struggled to remember how she'd ended up there.

"You are conscious," a chittering voice said.

"The dream," J'asa said. "Another dream. Fates and entropy, what have I seen?"

"You've seen death," the speaker said.

J'asa forced her eyes to focus on the speaker. She saw a heart-shaped head with pale, milky-red compound eyes, pinkish in color. A pair of antennae waved in her direction. The creature's body was covered in chiton that was dark green, yet faded, and it looked somehow fragile.

"Hello, Cheka," J'asa said. "I didn't know you were back."

"I come and go as I wish. It is a courtesy afforded me, as you know."

"I do," she replied. The memory of the attack suddenly forced the dream aside. "*No*," she cursed and fought to hold the memory fresh, even with its symbolism and horrors. So different from her first, and so much more terrifying.

"There are not many of us left," Cheka said. "We've slowly decreased in number over 20,000 years. No more than a few hundred Minchantaa'Sha remain."

"Have you had this dream as well?"

"The destruction of all?" J'asa nodded. "In one form or another. It is one of the dreams I am haunted by."

J'asa grunted and unhooked the strap holding her in the medical bed. "Do I have you to thank for rescuing me from the *Po'Froo*?"

"Yes," Cheka said. "Why were they attacking you?"

"I don't know," J'asa admitted. "Have the *Po'Froo* been causing more trouble?"

"Not that I am aware of, but I have only just returned."

"Were any of them detained?"

"No. I summoned protectors, of course. They arrived long after your attackers had fled. They seemed confused by my presence." The Minchantaa'Sha cocked his head, antennae waving. "Maybe they have never seen one of us?"

"Possible," J'asa said. A *skaa'o*, a healer, came by to check on her. "Are you feeling well enough, *Vok'tor*?"

"Yes, thank you."

"There were no serious injuries. You may leave." The healer glanced at Cheka, then went away.

J'asa stayed there for a moment, considering. Her mind was still swirling around the dream she'd just received, trying desperately not to spin it in any way. Only, how could she not? The vision was clearly apocalyptic, any way you chose to examine it. *Why now?* she wondered. *And why always me?* She knew the answer—because she was *j'apo*.

<Are you well?>

J'asa gave a start. It was always a surprise when Seldia contacted her. Her voice arrived in her mind as if she were mere centimeters away, whispering in her ear. As a full-fledged *k'apo*, or far talker, she could reach out to any other *k'apo* anywhere, even in 2nd level hyperspace, no matter how far away. J'asa could do the same, but with great difficulty.

She closed her eyes and concentrated. *<Fine>*.

<You were never a good liar. What happened?>

She sighed and looked at Cheka. He couldn't 'look' back at her, being blind, but his head was facing her, antennae aimed her way as well, listening. No doubt he knew something was happening. Concentrating again, she sent another message. *<I was attacked by a Po'Froo on Eesius.>*

<I didn't know you were home.> There was a pause during which J'asa hoped Seldia had been distracted by a bug or something. *<Since you are alive, this does not explain your sudden sensations of terror and foreboding moments ago. What else happened?>*

"Is something wrong?" Cheka asked.

"My sister in normal space sensed my unease at the dream."

"Understandable, if your visions are similar to mine."

Probably worse, J'asa thought.

<I am not going away.>

<When do you ever?> Silence. *<I had another* j'apo *dream. It was...bad.>*

Seldia didn't reply, so J'asa dropped it. Maybe that had been enough to get her sister off her back. Somehow she doubted it, though. Seldia was a flake, but she was a persistent flake. The last time she'd gone in front of the *Tor* and tore them a new one—

She stopped in her thought process, eyes narrowing. *The* Tor*,* she thought with a mental snarl.

"Thank you for saving me, Cheka. I need to go."

"You are burdened by glorious purpose; I can sense it."

"You could think of it that way," J'asa said as she caught a cord and raced for the medical exit.

This time she stuck to the main routes through each dome, not the most direct. That meant more traffic and a longer trip. She considered it prudent at this point. J'asa wondered if this was how Seldia felt when she was on one of her 'missions' to put something right. She considered that what she was doing was probably dangerous. *More dangerous than being attacked in the open?* No, of course not.

J'asa reached the leadership dome portal and found it closed. A pair of Dusman in Konar armor barred the way. "Move aside, *Osk'i*," she snapped without bothering to sense what their rank might be.

"*Tor* is in meeting, *Vok'tor*," the one on the right said, which she now sensed was an *osk'ka*, a fist leader. "None may enter."

"I am not here as *vok'tor*, I am here as *j'apo*." She couldn't see inside their armor, of course, but she sensed their immediate trepidation. You couldn't sense a *j'apo* rank, as it wasn't a normal caste. How could it be, with one every 20,000 years or more? It did, however, often cause one's senses to tingle unusually—or so she'd been told.

"*J'apo*, I am sorry, but—"

"Do not be sorry, stand aside."

They didn't immediately respond, and J'asa began to wonder if she'd have to make it personal. Then both the Konar's sensors angled past her, and they moved uncertainly. As much as she didn't want to, she glanced over her shoulder. Cheka was floating there, his antennae swishing back and forth.

"J'asa needs to speak to the *Tor*," he said. "Open the hall."

The two *Osk* didn't know what to do. Caught between duty and propriety, they chose the latter, and opened the doors. Cheka gestured with one of his razor-sharp forelimbs, and J'asa grabbed a rope and pulled herself inside.

All in, she thought, entering as if she owned the place.

Inside was the entire leadership, all nine of the *Tor* on their plinths, talking. Talking, talking, talking, always talking. They'd talked her into exile, and had that cost them any chance of survival? The *galaxy* a chance at survival?

"What are you doing here?" Saleen demanded, cutting off another of the *Tor* mid-sentence. "You are not allowed in here during our sessions." She caught sight of Cheka and blanched.

"Are you going to say I have no right to be here?" Cheka demanded. "Or has the *Tor* forgotten the debt owed to the Minchantaa'Sha as well?"

"*Tor* Saleen might have misspoken," one of the other eight *Tor* said. Saleen scowled, her ears straight out in anger. "*J'apo*, this council will always have time for you, and the Minchantaa'Sha, as well."

J'asa would have smiled if she wasn't so angry herself. *So, there's no unified front, after all.* She'd initially been afraid she'd returned to an enraged KzSha nest.

"Fine," Saleen said through clenched teeth. "What does the *j'apo* want?" She managed to make the title sound like a curse.

"I've had another dream." The silence put the depths of space to shame.

* * *

EMS *Bucephalus*, Yovaz System, Geosynchronous Orbit, Yovaz

"Confirm stationary orbit," helm reported.

They'd managed to secure their orbit without triggering any more weapons, which was good, because *Bucephalus'* forward shield generators were damaged.

"Best I can manage is about 45% forward shields," TacCom said.

"Get damage control teams on it," Captain Su said and turned to Jim. "I'm open to suggestions, Colonel." On the CIC Tri-V, just over 200 confirmed nuclear weapons were within 100 kilometers of their orbit. None we bigger than 2-kilotons, sure, but quantity has a quality all its own. Once *Bucephalus*' shields were down, even one 2-kiloton nuke going off against her hull would be catastrophic.

"How far are we from the junkyard?" Jim asked.

She checked the navigational data. "Looks like about 29 kilometers, but because of the orbital differences, the distance is opening by two kilometers per hour."

"So we only have a few hours before we'll have to deal with even more nukes?"

"Reasonable to assume whoever did this went all in and emptied an arsenal into orbit. These improvised mines aren't sophisticated, and they don't care what they're attacking. They'd work against anyone."

"Still worried about paying these people for the parts?"

"No," she admitted. "I'm more interested in getting out of here alive."

"That goes without saying, but without those parts, we're back where we started. Can you clear a path out of the minefield?"

"Pretty sure we can. Ironically, down will be easier than up. It'll take hours to plot it out, as well. It's possible whoever launched them also has a code to deactivate them, and if that's the case, we can leave without having to play Russian Roulette."

Jim put together a quick plan, keeping it simple. "Okay, since we have a map, I'll take a squad of CASPers with EVA capability, and one of your shuttles. We'll use light weapons to neutralize enough bombs to reach the junkyard. Your people ride in the shuttle, get the parts, then we'll exit on the other side and rendezvous with you as *Bucephalus* makes its way into a lower orbit."

"Lot of risk in that plan," Su said. Jim shrugged. "You're just going to shoot the bombs with laser rifles?"

"Anti-air lasers," he said. "All the EVA CASPers have modular shoulder hardpoints. You wouldn't normally bother, since a drone could swat you before you knew it was there, but the software is simple. It'll let us engage and destroy the bombs at least a kilometer away." He was pulling the range calculation out of his ass; however, he *knew* the anti-air lasers could engage airborne missiles and fighters at more than a kilometer. They should do better in space.

"That's pretty up close and personal to be shooting nuclear weapons, don't you think?"

"I've been up close and personal with a fusion-powered tank going up. The EVA CASPers are heavily radiation shielded, and your shuttle has shields, right?"

She nodded. "Not very powerful."

"Better than nothing. We'll stay inside the shields when we fire."

"I can have TacCom give you the shield harmonics; that'll let your lasers fire through the shields."

"I'd take one of the *Phoenix*, but they're not designed for space operations like this—no airlock."

"I'd be more comfortable if one of your senior officers took this op, Colonel."

"None of them have as much time in space as I do, and that's just not the Cavalier way."

She grunted, then gave a grudging nod. "Very well, Colonel. Plan to launch in 20 minutes."

Jim gave her a salute and released the belt on his seat, heading aft and calling his armorer.

"You're going to do *what*?" Buddha asked, floating into the bay where Cavalier techs were frantically attaching and removing equipment from 10 CASPers.

"You saw the briefing," Jim said as he helped maneuver one of the last anti-air laser pods onto his own Mk 7 CASPer. It barely had enough power to run the weapon, but he couldn't get his butt into a MK 8. "Name anyone else with half the hours I have in zero G." Buddha scowled. "Look, my friend, compared to some of the shit I've done, this is a walk in the park."

"There are more factors than that," Buddha said.

"Yes, there are," Jim said. Buddha looked triumphant. "And I still rank top for all of them." He pulled himself closer. "I know I was the boss' little kid once, Akamai." Using Buddha's real first name made the other man sober. "I'm not that boy anymore; I'm the colonel. Do what I say."

"Yes, sir," Buddha said, a frown on his face.

They were ready exactly on time. Jim had assembled a squad of those most experienced in zero G based on the data in his pinplants. Privates Bob "Breaker" Beard, Joseph DeLory, James Cockle, Martin Wright, Scott "JJ" Johnson, Leo "Champ" Champion, Corporals Pam "Paragon" Walder, and Travis Solberg, and Lieutenant Aaron Mayer. Mayer, despite having recently signed on, had as many hours as Jim in zero G. Truth be told, Jim didn't trust him enough yet to lead the operation. This would be a good chance to vet him, though.

Buttoned into his CASPer, Jim double-checked the haptic suit connections as well as his pinplant connections. Unfortunately, it wasn't possible yet to interface with the suits *and* keep a pinlock on. The Aku were working on that, as well, but because of how many connections the armored combat suits had, it was a difficult task.

Once the startup sequence was complete, he linked with his onboard computer and activated the squadnet, allowing him to see what everyone else saw and act as battlefield commander.

"Squad, report in."

"Mayer online."

"Solberg online."

"Paragon online."

"Breaker online."

"DeLory online."

"Cockle online."

"Wright online."

"Champ online."

"Red Five, standing by."

"Enough of that shit, Johnson," Mayer snapped. JJ was in his platoon, so he'd be the most familiar with the private's antics.

"Okay," Jim said. "Let's keep this straight and by the numbers. Make no mistake, this is a high-risk operation, but losing the drive in hyperspace is higher risk. As you all know, we're here for essential parts, but the locals are restless. We might have wandered into the middle of a brush war; we don't know. So we go in, escort *Bucephalus'* engineers, extract the parts, then rendezvous with the ship at a lower orbit. Hopefully we'll be below the interference and can talk to the planet owners. Any questions?"

"We have backup, sir?" Paragon asked.

"Not readily, no. There's a backup shuttle and our four drop-ships locked on the hull, but it'll be difficult to extract us if things go sideways."

"We'll be shooting down nukes, Paragon," Breaker said. "What do you think will be the result if we blow it?"

"Stray atoms," Champ said.

"He ain't wrong," Lieutenant Mayer said. "Just because there's no atmosphere doesn't mean a nuke isn't dangerous. Radiation propagates faster in a vacuum. You might have to get close to a ship, but we don't have meter-thick armor or shields in these suits."

Jim nodded in his suit. Mayer had used just enough grim reality to take the amusement out of the situation, which was just as well.

"We're Cavaliers," Jim said. "We're not marines, but we do what needs to be done. No charge this time, but we'll lead the way, regardless. Extra fuel is on the shuttle for our maneuvering packs. Be careful on the jumpjets, only use them in extremis. Let's go."

He led them from the armory to *Bucephalus'* hangar deck, where her two shuttles were magnetically locked to the deck. The cigar-shaped small craft's wings were retracted and cargo doors open. Experienced in operating CASPers in zero G, the 10 mercs moved easily across the open bay and into the shuttle.

Bucephalus' hangar crew watched them go. The officer of the deck gave Jim a salute as he passed; Jim returned it as best he could. They loaded up, finding an engineering crew of six already waiting in spacesuits. The cargo/passenger area was crowded with 10 CASPers and six EVA-suited engineers. The shuttle doors closed.

"*Colonel Cartwright,*" the pilot called on internal comms, "*welcome aboard. I hope you aren't crazy.*"

Jim chuckled as he replied, "Me too." A minute later, the bay depressurized, and they moved into space.

* * *

EMS *Bucephalus,* Secure Transit Space

"Entropy!" Achilles cursed, watching the shuttle leave the bay. One, maybe two of them could have snuck aboard the shuttle, but without their Konar. They would be of little use in that situation.

"We can still use our own small craft," Athena reminded him.

"It's invisible to the Humans, not to the other aliens on the planet or in orbit," he reminded her. "If we draw fire, that'll make it pretty obvious to Su that something isn't right."

"They're preparing to get the ship underway," Hera said. She was monitoring *Bucephalus* status.

Achilles snarled in frustration, balancing risk against reward. Cartwright was definitely going into extreme danger, yet his instincts told him it was within his ability to handle. Sit still and wait was the right call. Even at a higher orbit, they'd be able to reach him in their Konar, not even needing the small craft.

"No, we wait again. But prep the small craft and load the Konar. Once *Bucephalus* is in lower orbit and Cartwright links up, we'll drop to the planet ahead of them."

"You sure he's going down himself?" Hector asked.

"Without a doubt. J'asa said he'd never let his people go into danger without him. He would make a good *osk*."

"Their CASPers are a lot like Konar," Athena said. "It only stands to reason he'd act like an *osk*."

"Primitive by comparison," Agamemnon said. He was the oldest member of the commando *osk* team, and similar to J'op, a recent arrival. Unlike J'op, though, he was clearly in J'asa's faction, and had quickly adopted the team as family, including picking a Greek origin name he liked. Achilles wasn't sure if he liked the name choice, though.

"I agree, they're primitive by comparison," Achilles said. "Then you should consider the CASPer with the Konar. Our armor is superior in every way you care to compare them. Correct?" All the *osk* nodded. "Our Konar represent many thousands of years of development, and more thousands adapting them from what we had before the Betrayal. Though they are a pale shadow compared to what our predecessors had, they're still superior to the Human version.

"The version they've developed in less than 100 years. What do you think they'll be able to come up with in 1,000 years?"

Ajax gave a grunt. "Now I wonder whether we should be afraid of the Kahraman, or of the Humans."

* * * * *

Chapter Ten

EMS *Bucephalus* Shuttle, Yovaz System, Junkyard,
Geosynchronous Orbit, Yovaz

"*First series of mines are two kilometers distant,*" the shuttle pilot said. "*You guys ready to play Asteroids?*"

Jim's team voiced their confusion; Jim just chuckled. The pilot was a man after his own heart, bringing up a 130-year-old videogame. "Let's hope there are no flying saucers," he replied, further mystifying his men. "Everyone, check your suit integrity," he ordered.

The Cavaliers ran internal checks. Their suit atmospheric cyclers shut down, as the pressure was monitored to the precise millibar. Nobody reported any leaks. Jim had checked his as well. A slow leak in a space suit was potentially worse than a fast leak if your suit didn't keep a close eye on the data. CASPers weren't designed as space suits so they weren't as finicky with such matters as a true EVA spacesuit was.

"Cargo hold ready to depressurize," he reported.

"*Roger that; depressurization beginning.*"

Jim's suit blared an alarm that the outside atmosphere was falling off precipitously as the shuttle pumped out the air for reuse. He acknowledged the alarm with his pinplants and waited. His mind traveled back to his first HALD drop years ago and how scared he'd been. He smiled for a moment, but then he didn't feel the furry warmth of his friend against his thigh.

Splunk—or J'asa now—had always ridden into battle in the thigh compartment of Jim's Mk 7 CASPer. The space was intended for tools or extra equipment. Since she'd been as good as a mobile repair system, and they were inseparable, it made more sense to leave the gear and bring her. She'd fixed his suit dozens of times in battle. Her technical prowess made more sense as a Dusman than as a Fae.

The space reached vacuum, and the doors opened. "Cavalier Actual, we're in the black," he reported to the pilot.

"*Roger that,*" the pilot replied. "*Be aware, shields are up.*"

Jim floated out of the shuttle with gentle bumps of the suit's maneuvering jets, a pack on the back used for this sort of operation. *Bucephalus* was moving sideways to their position, an occasional flash of green laser light showing its slow progress deeper into the planet's orbit.

The planet was large to one side of their embarkation angle, a dirtball with tiny seas and spots of green. There was a slightly off tint to the atmosphere's color. They had to get down there to find the way out. It was like some crazy game puzzle with a side quest.

"I hate side quests," he mumbled.

"*Sorry, Colonel?*" Mayer said.

"Nothing. Okay, lets get to this." He used his battlespace to incorporate targeting data from *Bucephalus*. The field of nuclear mines spread out all around them. *Damned natives must have got a bulk discount,* he thought. "As we discussed, left is DeLory and Wright, with Corporal Solberg. Right is Cockle, JJ, and Paragon. Breaker, Camp, and Mayer with me, in the center. Let's clear the road for the shuttle."

The progress was slower than he'd hoped. The mines were less than a meter long and much narrower, owing to their previous life as missiles. Hitting them with the anti-air lasers from more than a kilometer away proved difficult.

"We're going through ammo pretty fast," Mayer said.

"How long at this rate?"

"Another hour, tops."

Jim ran the calculations through his pinplants. There were still 29 nukes between them and the junkyard. They'd taken out 13 so far. He'd been forced to task two CASPers per mine to ensure a kill. If they just nicked a bomb and it went off anyway...They weren't going to have enough ammo, and the squad had taken every ounce of laser ammo aboard *Bucephalus*. He honestly hadn't thought they'd need more. Stupid, the stuff didn't require a large amount of space. *Last time I leave home without more*, he thought.

"Shuttle," Jim called, "do you think we can narrow our approach corridor?"

While *Bucephalus* had detonated several of the mines, they hadn't gathered enough data on the extent of the mines' triggering zones. It was somewhere between one and three kilometers. They'd been keeping it to three kilometers.

"*What about the exit corridor out the other side?*" the pilot asked.

Jim had been aware of that problem an hour ago. Their rate of ammo consumption from the beginning argued that they wouldn't be able to shoot themselves back out the other side. Going back to higher orbit didn't help; *Bucephalus* was long gone, well on her way to low orbit. *Fuck.*

"We'll cross that obstacle when we get to it, Pilot. What about that approach corridor?"

"I wouldn't feel comfortable below two kilometers, Colonel."

Jim ran the numbers with a two-kilometer safety zone, which dropped the number of mines in the danger zone to 11. They should be able to make that. "Thanks. I think you gave us the margin we need." He looked at their dispersion. Only one problem. "Cavaliers, we need to concentrate in a narrow area, which means we need to work outside the shuttle's shields. We'll do it in rotation. My group first."

They had to move outside the shields to triangulate fire more effectively. The junkyard and all the ruined ships had gone from an indistinct sparkling spot of reflected sunlight to a clearly manufactured artifact.

Solberg's group took the first three nuclear bombs. As with the others, none of them detonated. At least that was one problem they hadn't encountered. After expending half their remaining ammo, they pulled back, and Paragon's team took it up. This time one of the nukes gave a flash.

"Uh, oh," the pilot said as the shield glowed slightly.

"That wasn't a detonation, was it?" Jim asked.

"No," the pilot replied. *"It was a neutron flash, but not enough for a high order detonation."*

"Must have been a fizzle," Champ said.

"What's that?" Jim asked. Nuclear bombs not being his thing, he'd never heard the term fizzle.

"When a nuke tries to detonate but does so improperly. It's a failed nuclear explosion."

"What's the radiation readings on your team's suits, Paragon?"

"We took a few rads, not too much."

"Okay, switch out."

"We're still set for two more shots," the corporal complained.

"Yes, you are, but I'm rotating you into the shields now to keep your radiation exposure down. Move it, Corporal."

"Yes, Colonel," he replied, and they moved back under the shuttle's nominal shields. Once they were safe, Jim and the three on his team split and moved away from the shuttle in four directions. Since they were the only group of four, they could fire in even groups, and had the most ammo left. "Everyone in position?"

"All set," they reported back.

"First target up," Jim said and relayed targeting data. "Breaker, Champ, take this first one."

"Roger that," Champ said.

"Locking on," Breaker concurred. Both of their suit indicators lit when they'd set targets. *"Firing."*

The anti-aircraft lasers were a megawatt in raw yield each, designed to damage and disable a plane or a missile. The beams were angular, designed for maximum damage against fast-moving targets. A longer beam meant more surface effect. With a target two kilometers away, it was impossible to see what the lasers did to the mine. They relied upon any change in the target radar aspect. The mine they'd just fired at suddenly showed a spray of tiny returns, and the mine began to move.

"Hit," Jim said. The laser had melted off a cloud of molten debris, and the burning ejecta had imparted thrust. After a second, the biggest part of the target split in two. "Good hit. Looks like this one split it. Mayer, with me, here's the coordinates."

"Got it," Mayer replied. *"Locking in."*

Jim fed the coordinates into his targeting computer. The anti-air laser snapped up over his shoulder, coming online and analyzing the target. It overthought everything, not being designed for a stationary target. As they'd done several times, he overrode the motion tracking controls and locked the target. "I'm locked."

"*Same here*," Mayer replied.

"Fire."

They triggered their weapons. This time the mine was torn apart, creating a large halo of spreading debris. The decreased range was working in their favor.

The other pair took out another mine, and then it was Jim and Mayer's turn. Jim was feeling optimistic that they'd reach the junkyard with some ammo left, when something hit him, a shot through his mind that made him jerk uncontrollably and give a cry of surprise.

"*Colonel, you okay?*"

He realized he'd blacked out for a moment and was almost a kilometer from the shuttle. Two CASPers were closing in on him. *What the fuck was that?* Had he had a stroke or something? He stabilized his flight path and gave a short burst back toward the shuttle. "I'm fine," he transmitted. "Just had a glitch in my computer."

That was a lie, of course, and a sloppy one at that, but none of the men seemed bothered by it. They halted their momentum and fell in as he slowly returned to the shuttle. They encountered the shuttle's shield, like temporarily pushing through a wind, then they were back inside.

"How many left?" he asked, though the data was on his battlespace.

"*We're through, Colonel*," Mayer said and pointed with his CASPer. Only 100 meters away was the hulk of a starship.

"Good," he said. "Good. Have the engineers locate our specific target and get to it. I'm going aboard and buttoning up so I can check my CASPer."

A short time later, the engineers were out, being escorted by the rest of his squad. Jim had the cargo hold to himself. He used the control to close the doors and repressurize before popping his cockpit. It was good timing, because no sooner was the clamshell-style cockpit split and rotated out of the way than he leaned forward and vomited his guts out.

The ejecta spread out and splattered against the far bulkhead, floating bits and globules spinning around the bay. "For fuck's sake," he snarled. Grabbing a rag from the utility compartment inside his CASPer, he swept away the closest bits, then closed the cockpit. Resealed, he decompressed the bay once more. The evidence was boiled off into space, except for a few larger pieces. Opening the doors, he swept them into space.

Still alone in the dark bay, he floated with his eyes closed for a long time. Only the humming of his CASPer's life support intruded on his thoughts. He felt fine, the voice was quiet, only one thing made sense. *Splunk*, he thought. *Did something just happen to her?* Lightyears from Earth—and who knew where she'd gone—there was no way to answer the question. He only knew that fear lived just behind his heart and wasn't going anywhere.

* * *

Eesius, 2nd Level Hyperspace

"You cannot be serious," Saleen snapped.

"I've never been more serious," J'asa replied. "I had my first dream in the creche, before I was old enough to realize what it was. Years passed as the dream's imagery cleared and solidified in my mind. This one was much more fully formed from the beginning. Maybe because I'm an adult now, or maybe because it's simply more powerful, I don't know."

"What does the dream tell us?" another of the *Tor* asked.

"It was more abstract than the first one," she explained. "However, it confirms our path. War is coming, and it will be cataclysmic."

"Was the war before the Betrayal not cataclysmic enough?" still another *Tor* asked.

"Apparently not," J'asa replied, "because the one coming is much worse."

"How can it be worse?" Saleen demanded. "We are a pale *shadow* of our might before the Betrayal."

"Because we weren't there when the war began," J'asa threw back in her face. Cheka's head turned as he listened without comment.

"What are you saying?"

"That if my first dream had been heeded, 10 years ago, when I first understood what it meant, we would be a decade further down the road of mobilizing to reestablish ourselves in the galaxy. We Dusman have always stood for order. Under our stewardship, the galaxy enjoyed 100,000 years of peace, prosperity, and growth. Then we got complacent, we tolerated dangerous behavior, and ultimately, it cost us everything. Us, and billions who got between us and the enemy.

"So here we are, 20,000 years after our complacency and arrogance led to the Betrayal, and we're going to do it again. Only this time, it won't be complacency and arrogance, it'll be indifference." She looked directly at Saleen. "And larceny."

"What are you suggesting?" another *Tor* asked.

"Ask Saleen; she's the one who forced my mother to take the *Nee* to silence her defense of me before I was banished, and afterwards." Saleen was glaring at J'asa, her deep blue-on-blue eyes full of fury. "You didn't count on Cheka coming to my aid in the service corridor, did you?"

"I have no idea what you're talking about," Saleen said dismissively, as if what J'asa said didn't interest her at all, but her ears were up and alert.

"You also didn't count on one of the *Po'Froo* being caught and telling us who sent them to intercept me."

The room was as quiet as when J'asa had said she'd had another prophetic dream. "Explain," one of the *Tor* instructed.

"When enough of the *Tor* voted to banish me for doing what my birth demanded I do, my mother stood up for me. Eventually, she realized I'd been banished because I was right. She studied the *Nee'Akee* and found another prophesy, like mine, that happened 90 years before I was born. That one, like me, was discredited and eventually died. Nobody would say why, or how. It would have been lost to the ages, if that *j'apo* hadn't gone to the *Nee'Akee* and recorded her story.

"When my mother discovered this story, you threatened her." J'asa never took her eyes off Saleen. "You threatened to have me killed if my mother didn't take the *Nee*."

"How *dare* you!" Saleen roared.

"Only, unlike the previous *j'apo*," J'asa continued, "my prophesy wasn't many decades in the future. Mine was more akin to a final warning. And by exiling me, you didn't end my dream's prophesy, you brought it true. My return threatened to unravel your plots, so you sent *Po'Froo* to have me killed."

Saleen looked at J'asa with wild eyes. The others of the *Tor* looked between Saleen and J'asa.

"Is this true?" one asked Saleen.

"It's ridiculous," Saleen said.

"That didn't answer the question," said another, the first to speak to J'asa. He looked at Cheka. "Is what J'apo says the truth?"

"I cannot discredit what she says," Cheka replied.

J'asa would have laughed if it wasn't such a dangerous situation. Cheka hadn't answered one way or the other. "No comment," was more like it.

"Baseless innuendo," Saleen said, waving her away. "You will put together your *vision* so the *Tor* can review it for—"

Saleen was cut off as the doors once again opened, this time to admit another Dusman. The pair of Konar guarding the door floated outside, watching the new arrival make her entrance. J'asa gawked as her sister, Seldia—whom she'd spoken to via their link less than an hour ago, while she was in normal space—entered.

"How did you get here so quickly?" J'asa asked as her sister came abreast of her.

"I simply appropriated an *Ogleesius* that was nearby."

It was J'asa's turn to gawk. Simply appropriating a battlecruiser wasn't something you just did. Of course, she doubted there was anyone who could deny Seldia, once the *k'apo* had set her mind to something.

"Why are you here?" Saleen demanded, then looked down at a slate when a message arrived. "You demanded *Q'puk-Os*, an *Ogleesius-*

class battlecruiser, detach from its fleet and bring you here immediately? Under what authority?"

"My own," Seldia said, blinking, and her ears curling in amusement. "I did so when you tried to have my sister *killed*, you dung-eating scavenger."

A gasp went up around the room. J'asa closed her eyes and shook her head. Along with self-assurance many orders of magnitude above her station, Seldia also lacked the ability to hold her tongue when it came to speaking her mind.

Now J'asa saw it; four members of the *Tor* looked at Saleen with concern, the others with outrage. *So, the division is still here, and it forced them to action. I wonder if* Sla'etou *knows about this back in normal space?*" It didn't seem so in the face of such evidence. Maybe they'd hidden it from him? She didn't know, and at that moment, it didn't matter.

"You have no proof of anything," Saleen said.

J'asa was stuck. Of course they didn't have one of the *Po'Froo*, that had been a bluff to try to get Saleen to admit what she'd done. Maybe if they could—

"No, she doesn't have one of the *Po'Froo*," Seldia said.

J'asa could have killed her sister right there. Of course, that was just Seldia being Seldia. The plan to bring this conspiracy into the open was probably doomed from the moment her sister entered the chamber. She glanced at Seldia and didn't see her common airy, slightly disinterested look. Instead, there was one of keen interest and anger.

"Thank you for letting us know the *j'apo* was lying about the attack," one of the *Tor* said. "Naturally this reflects poorly on her reliability as a *j'apo*."

This might well have been their plan all along, J'asa thought. *Or rather, if the murder plot failed, this was a backup?*

"Oh, she was lying, alright," Seldia said, "but not about the attack."

"You have no more proof than she does, *K'apo,*" Saleen said. "You're merely rushing to your sister's defense."

"I am, since you tried to have her killed. Proof? Have you forgotten that because J'asa is my sister, we would both have been *k'apo?* I share her memories when she wants, or when she is under *extreme stress!*" Saleen looked like she'd been slapped. "You want the proof?" Seldia asked, looking around the semicircle of *Tor.* "Join me in *Akee* and see the proof."

"You would bring us all down!" Saleen screamed at J'asa. "You want to drag us, the last of the Dusman, from this safe place to die for these, these, *vermin* called Humans. And for what, your ridiculous dreams? Half of us have already left. We rapidly approach the point when we may have to abandon Eesius to the others, or risk being overrun. *You have no right!*"

Quick as a flash, Saleen produced a small laser pistol and leveled it at J'asa. There was no time to react. Unlike normal space, she couldn't just dive to the side and roll under cover. The nearest cover was 10 meters away, and she'd have to pull herself there. Any attempt to dive would end in less than a meter, suspending her in air as an easy target. J'asa grabbed at her sidearm in a vain attempt to stop the attack, knowing full well she was behind the draw.

Twin lasers flashed, piercing Saleen's torso. The *Tor* jerked, still trying to aim. Another shot, this one squarely center mass, and the gun fell free from her hand, suspended in air where she'd released it.

J'asa grabbed a rope to pull herself toward the plinth, then up to the top. The *Tor* circled Saleen, looking on in shock or sadness, depending on what side they'd been on.

"You have killed us," Saleen said, coughing blood that floated just past her lips in globules.

"No, I hope I've saved us all."

Saleen's eyes unfocused as she died.

The two Konar who'd fired from the door flew over the crowd of *Tor* and others, their sensors moving this way and that. "Are you safe, *J'apo*?"

"I am," she said. "Thank you."

"We merely did our duty to the Dusman."

J'asa looked at the *Tor*. "Those aligned with Saleen, did you know of this?" They shook their heads. "Yet you condoned her dissent, even after the *kroof* had rendered his decision?"

"Saleen was convincing in her arguments," one of them said.

"So not a conspirator, but complicit, then?" They wouldn't meet her eyes. J'asa spat a curse and grabbed a line, pulling herself away. She cast half a glance back at the death scene before leaving the plinth for the floor, then headed toward the door. She stopped when she reached Seldia and Cheka. The Minchantaa'Sha hadn't moved, and neither had her sister. "You're aware of what just happened?" she asked Cheka.

"I am blind, not stupid."

"Did you dream this coming?"

"I dreamt many outcomes; this was one of the better."

"But not the best?" Seldia asked.

"No."

J'asa looked at Seldia. "You never said you could see through me in times of stress. Why didn't you tell me?"

"Because I cannot."

J'asa gawked for a moment, then shook her head. "I didn't think you could lie."

"Neither did I until I tried."

"Remind me to teach you the Human game of poker; you have a fantastic poker face."

"It sounds painful," Seldia said.

Now that sounded like her sister. J'asa grunted and went to leave.

"Where are you going now?" her sister asked.

"Back to work. I didn't come here to kill anyone." She made it to the door before Cheka spoke.

"Sometimes the killing comes to you, *J'apo.*"

"Isn't that the cursed truth."

* * * * *

Chapter Eleven

J im and his squad watched from the shuttle as the engineers of *Bucephalus* found the *Akaga*-class cruiser and looked for the required parts. Like all of Captain Su's crew, they were skilled and efficient. They had the necessary parts in less than an hour.

While the engineers worked, the Cavaliers recharged life support and checked their suits. They also got a little time outside the CAS-Pers, which was always good on an extended op. The suits were excellent for emergency life support and even long-term survival— what they weren't, was comfortable.

"Grab a bite if you can," Mayer suggested to the squad. He was the only one trained as a marine. "Just not too much." He winked, and they laughed. The team was still in zero G. Though everyone had trained and spent many hours in zero G, eating food in a stressful situation could severely hamper your ability to hold it down. Jim had puked once in space recently; he wasn't about to do it again. He didn't eat.

They were all buttoned back up as the engineers returned. The lock was too small to allow them to move the parts in. It turned out the hyperspatial relays were larger than a CASPer. Funny, Jim had thought they were little. Each one weighed a ton, and after the four the engineers had salvaged were secured in the shuttle's hold, there was barely enough room left for the CASPers.

Jim knew they wouldn't be in there for long anyway. Now they needed to make a way out. He activated comms through the shuttle in his suit.

"*Bucephalus*, this is Cartwright Actual."

"*Cartwright Actual, this is* Bucephalus *Actual, go ahead.*"

"We've secured the payload and are examining extraction options."

"*Stay put at this point; we're working a problem.*"

"Nature of the problem, *Bucephalus?*"

There was a marked pause, and Jim was about to call again when Captain Su spoke.

"*The ships in orbit aren't armed themselves, but they do have drones. We're currently engaged pretty deep in the planet's gravity well. I don't like so little room to maneuver. We're below the orbit of the mines, at least.*"

Jim considered how long they could hold at the junkyard. Not long was the answer. The shuttle was likely capable of supporting a crew for weeks. The shuttle crew was two, but there were now six engineers and ten troopers breathing the air. He doubted they would last much more than 24 hours.

"We're mercs, we'll hold while we can, *Bucephalus*. Just part of the job. But…"

"*I'm aware of your primary concern of consumables, Colonel—*"

The transmission was interrupted by a squelch of static that made him turn down the receiver's volume. "Pilot, are we being jammed?"

"*Negative, Colonel,* Bucephalus' *carrier wave is being overwhelmed. Direction of signal is from the planet.*"

"*Ship in the salvage yard, can you hear me?*" Jim's pinplant translator rendered the popping, gurgling sounds into English automatically, which meant it was a known language, or close enough. Strange one, too. It sounded like there was an electrical arcing mixed in with the speech.

"Yes, we read you," Jim replied. Sure, why not talk to them? It wasn't like he had anywhere to go at present.

"*Do I understand you said you are mercenaries?*"

"That's correct. This is Colonel Jim Cartwright, Cartwright's Cavaliers."

A pause. "*Humans?*"

"Yes. We came here to purchase salvage as we have in the past."

"*I see. There is not much time; the transmitter will be targeted shortly. Colonel, we wish to hire the Cavaliers for aid.*"

"Under normal circumstances, I would be open to it, though we aren't currently deployed for a contract. However, the Mercenary Guild has put special rules in place. All contracts must be approved by the Guild Council."

A short pause. "*My name is Lureli, and I invoke Article #351, Section 5, Rule A of the Mercenary Guild Charter.*"

Jim blinked and accessed the pertinent files. He knew a lot of the charter by memory; most commanders with more than a year or so did. They were often quoted simply by article in contracts instead of detailing the clause. The typical Mercenary Guild contract was already the size of a large novel. With the inclusion of quoted articles, clauses, and rules, each contract would probably be too big to store on any known medium.

Mercenary Guild Charter Part II – Articles of Control. Article #351 pertained to how merc units handled combat against each other. Section 5 more specifically governed merc units not on a contract coming into potential combat actions in proximity to another unit. Rule A stated, "Any mercenary unit, or more specifically mercenary race, as recognized by the Mercenary Guild Governing Body (see Part I, Articles of Anointment, Article #5-44), may as it so choses request assistance from any other licensed mercenary unit at hand to render assistance against a non-mercenary aggressor force. Compensation shall be covered under Part I, Articles of Pay…"

It went on for another few thousand words. He'd already gotten the gist of it and had been completely unaware of the clause. Of course, as he reread it, Peepo's motive for blockading Earth suddenly became clear. The Mercenary Guild action against Earth *could* have been interpreted as a non-merc aggressor force, since, by the Guild Charter, the sort of action undertaken against Earth had been illegal. At least, from a certain point of view.

Jim checked the language being spoken and was unsurprised to find it was Reyq. *Explains the electric zapping sounds in their language*, he thought. "Lureli, I acknowledge your request with the understanding I'm not required to render aid without payment. However, prior to that point, since you said time is short, what are your aggressors, exactly?"

"They are Lotar, who live in a neighboring system. We purchased rights to this planet some time ago, and they want it back. Since mercs were not available, they gathered an army and invaded themselves. As for payment, I offer whatever goods you have already taken from the salvage yard."

"Lureli, I already have those goods."

"Yes, and the mines are all still there. It might be an improvised defense, but it is effective. Your merc cruiser is also engaged with the Lotar. I am not offering much, yes. However, were the Humans not similarly besieged on your own world recently?"

"Knows what buttons to push, doesn't it?" Captain Su commed to him on another channel, this one secure.

"Yes, and it has a point."

"Nobody came to our aid, Colonel."

"That doesn't mean we can't be better than the others. At least for now, I see no reason not to accommodate them, as long as certain conditions can be met."

"Colonel, the transmitter is under attack," Lureli said. *"I need your answer."*

"I agree," Jim said, "on the conditions that the minefield is disabled, and you accept a provisional second round of rate negotiations after you are relieved." There was no reply. "Lureli, do you agree?"

"Looks like the transmitter was destroyed," Captain Su said. *"We don't know if they received our demands. The enemy drones have pulled back. However, they were already pulling back when Lureli contacted you."*

"One way to find out. Pilot, we have drones on board?"

"Just two, Colonel, and they're sensor drones only."

"That's fine, please launch one to intercept the nearest mine."

"Captain?" the pilot asked for confirmation of the order.

"Follow the colonel's order, Baker."

"Launching drone, aye, aye."

Jim didn't have a shared feed, so he had to wait several minutes while the pilot operated the drone before Baker came back.

"Colonel, the nearest mine is unresponsive. I don't know if the drone is big enough to trigger it, but I flew a few laps around the mine, and even bumped it several times. In fact, the mine orbit was shifted by the impacts, and it hasn't attempted to correct its orbit."

"I think we have our answer," Jim said.

"It could be a trap," Captain Su said. *"I'm going to maneuver* Bucephalus *within range of a couple and see what happens. Don't worry, Colonel, she can take it."*

More minutes passed, Jim aware of the shuttle's limited endurance the whole time. Eventually Su's light Chinese accent returned.

"Colonel, the mines are deactivated. You can proceed to rendezvous with us at your convenience. Proceed with caution; the enemy ships in orbit could launch their drones again at any time."

"Roger that, *Bucephalus*." A moment later the shuttle's engines moved them away from the junkyard.

"Well done, Colonel," Mayer said. *"That gets us out of a tight spot."*

"Let's just hope it isn't into an even tighter one."

* * *

Eesius, 2nd Level Hyperspace

The tranquility of the *Nee'Akee* was welcome after the previous day. J'asa had returned after the horrible confrontation at the *Tor* to study more, only to give up after less than an hour and return to her quarters. Nobody disturbed her, so she slept in peace.

When she awoke, J'asa got something to eat and returned to the *Nee'Akee*, rested and ready to pick up where she'd left off.

The Tri-V in the cubicle her mother had shown her to was where it had been left, the unindexed requested knowledge available and waiting. Thousands of memories from survivors of the Betrayal.

Without any sort of indexing, what she found was completely random. The memories that were indexed mainly came from the first arrivals, and few if any of them had worked with Raknar. She was nearly desperate to find information regarding the *cood*, and there was nothing there. These survivors were mostly shellshocked, desperate refugees fleeing the early wave of the Betrayal.

Abandoning what little had been indexed, J'asa delved into the mire of random memories. They weren't even stored chronologically. While they did have date indexing, it was no help to her. She found herself flipping through random memories, only listening to a few seconds of each. The criteria was anything dealing with Raknar, and many merely mentioned them in passing. Either they'd been involved in logistics operations for deploying them, maintenance, secondary manufacturing, or some other mundane aspect.

Part way through the day, J'asa finally encountered a *vok'o*, or Raknar technician, but she was nearly incomprehensible. Something about an uprising on the world she'd been garrisoned on, and an aftermath of the Betrayal.

"We couldn't get any of them out of the Raknar," she said, crying. "We knew they were dying, could hear their pleas for help, and there was nothing we could do. None of our mesh survived, of course, so the tools wouldn't work!" She went on about her mate being one of the operators, then descended into sobs. J'asa moved on to another one.

"I am Eesius," the memory said, making J'asa gawk in surprise. "I was *nee'tor*. When it happened, I was on Ja'kuapa, overseeing the Phase 5 Raknar upgrade project. The *Behemoth* at my command served as a base for me to evacuate as much of my staff as I could. Without our mesh, many were trapped in desperate situations and completely without guidance. We depended on them for everything. They operated cities, controlled powerplants, and flew our ships."

J'asa didn't want to move or even *breathe*. She was listening to the actual voice of Eesius, the greatest Dusman mind in any recent era of their long history. She'd learned in the creche, just like all young, that Eesius was the one who'd founded the colony in 2nd level hyperspace. She'd set up the structures, planned the defenses, brought so many of them here when it was all but impossible. Then, after toiling ceaselessly to save as many lives as she could, she spent every remaining moment of her life recreating all the science and history she could.

Eesius was right; they'd depended on the mesh for everything. Interconnected super computers in their brains, a billion-billion AIs interconnected via planetary and ship SIs, the sum of all knowledge and information woven into their brains almost from birth. And then, it was all gone. All except this wondrous female she was watching speak.

"There was so much I couldn't get, so little time. I had to choose between life and technology." Eesius sighed. "I chose life. I knew if we were to ever have a chance to return and set right what was done to us, this betrayal by our most trusted partners, we had to survive as a species. I reasoned if the lives were spared, the technology could be reconstructed. I might have been in error.

"Much of our Raknar were not of our making. The combination of the mesh deep logic and the *cood.*" Eesius shook her head; she appeared so tired. She was already old when the Betrayal happened, out of retirement only to help when the war began to go badly. "Maybe we could have put the pieces back together without the mesh, if only the *cood* had survived. It didn't, though, and here in our exile, there is no way to search for more. We dare not let them know we're alive here. The Raknar are lost to us."

The reader went dark, leaving J'asa wide eyed at what she'd just learned. "Mesh helped operate the Raknar," she said, alive. Maybe the lack of it would account for Jim's unbalanced behavior, then? If, though, why him and none of the other interfaces? She really didn't understand why it took two of them. Yet she couldn't directly join *Akee* with the machine, even after they'd found the sample of *cood* and cultivated it.

"The combination of the mesh deep logic and the *cood*." Eesius had said it wasn't of their making, meaning the Dusman. Then who? She'd always thought their ancient ally-turned-enemy had produced the *cood*. It had been a well-accepted theory, after all. But theory was all they'd had until Jim had found the Raknar with *cood*, just like she'd dreamed.

The presence of the Raknar in numbers would bring many of the unruly galactics around to the proper way of thinking. A few dozen servitor races falling in line, and they'd be ready to finish the Kahraman once and for all. J'asa knew they were vulnerable. She also knew that vulnerability was ending. Her new dream—that had to be what it meant. But the rot spreading and consuming the galaxy from the end of one arm? What did that mean? Maybe this war between the guilds?

"Too many things," she mumbled. "Too many things." If what Eesius had said was true—and it must be because she was *nee'tor*—they were missing a vital piece of the Raknar, a mesh designed to help them operate. That would explain why the only Raknar she could get to come back online was the most conventional of the variants. None of the others would operate outside maintenance or transport mode.

"Without all the types of Raknar, we cannot defeat our enemies," she said. She cursed several times. Months searching the galaxy for other samples of *cood* or some vital part of the Raknar she thought was missing, and it turned out to be something likely destroyed 20,000 years ago. No working mesh remained outside the *Nee'Akee* inside Eesius, and never would. The proclamation against mesh had been the first rule Eesius made when she'd arrived.

"We can never again be vulnerable to another betrayal like the one that destroyed us," had been Eesius' words, even as she worked herself to an early death.

But clearly the very Raknar J'asa needed was driving her interface insane. *He's more than an interface to me*, she thought, despite Dante's admonition against becoming entangled with a piece of wetware, as he called the Humans.

"I'm stuck," she said.

"Do you require assistance, *Vok'tor*?"

J'asa looked at her mother, holding onto a rope and floating just outside the cell she was watching memories in. She almost said no, then reconsidered. "Have you studied any of Eesius' memories in the *Nee'Akee*?"

"Many of them, yes."

"Does she mention anything about the *cood*?"

"Not often. You just listened to one of the few instances."

"If I can't get more *cood* as samples, or some of the science behind them, I've failed and have to go back to the beginning." She'd taken the samples found in the first Raknar Jim had bought and had a team of Dusman begin breeding the material. As a genetically engineered lifeform, it seemed simple enough. Modified by the Kahraman eons ago, it facilitated the link with a Raknar's systems, and also protected and buffered the occupants against the incredible forces of combat.

But when Jim began acting erratically, J'asa had worried it was the *cood*, or 'green ooze,' as he called it. After all, the stuff completely suffused their bodies when in *Akee* with the war machines. If the sample she'd gotten had been somehow polluted, how could she tell? The *nee*, or scientists, with her initial team didn't understand the *cood* any better than she did. The more they studied it, the less they seemed to understand. It was *not* a simple organism. They told her the genetics were extremely complicated.

"Did you fully observe the last memory from Eesius?"

J'asa turned her head and looked at the Tri-V, which displayed "Memory Complete." "Yes."

"I would recommend *Vok'tor* listen to it again."

Curious what she might have missed, J'asa restarted the memory.

"I am Eesius; I was *nee'tor*. When it happened, I was on Ja'kuapa overseeing the Phase 5 Raknar upgrade project."

She stopped the playback. *Ja'kuapa? Why does that sound so familiar?* She grabbed her personal slate and typed the name in. The coordinates of the world appeared from the Dusman database, now 20,000 years out of date. J'asa entered them into the Cartography Guild locator application and was informed the system was Ja-ku-Tapa.

"Holy shit," she said in English, taking a page out of Jim's book. Her mother cocked her head curiously. "Ja'kuapa is called Ja-ku-Tapa by the galactics. I've been there, twice. We found a huge reserve of Raknar. Eesius was doing an upgrade project there, so there must be a Raknar lab hidden somewhere as well." She gave the barest of smiles.

"I am gladdened the *Vok'tor* has found what she wants."

"Thank you for helping."

"*Nee* do not help seekers; we simply allow access so you can find what you want."

J'asa nodded, her own little smile on her face. She wanted to touch her mother, to hug her, to remember what it felt like to be little, and give it back some of what she'd felt when she'd touched her own children days ago in the creche. It wasn't allowed. The *Nee* were apart of Dusman society. That was the price she'd paid for resisting Saleen. Her mother moved to leave.

"May I ask you something?" J'asa said.

"Of course."

"Why do the *nee* blind themselves?"

"That we can truly see." Then her mother left.

J'asa returned to her quarters to prepare to depart Eesius for normal space. Shortly after beginning to pack, she heard a gentle yet strange tap on the room's lone door. Curious, she opened it to find Cheka, his red eyes with the milky sheen cocked oddly as antennae sensed shapes in his blindness. "Greetings, J'asa."

"Come to bid me farewell?" she wondered, then she spotted Seldia. Her sister looked concerned. "Why are you here, too?" Seldia wasn't one for social niceties, even less so than most Dusman.

"Come with us," Cheka said, motioning her into the corridor with a mid-arm.

"What's happened?"

"Something fascinating," Seldia said, the expression on her face and ears unreadable.

J'asa left her bag contents floating where they were in mid-packing. "Very well," she said. "I hope it's important; I need to get back."

"I think you will find it worth your time," Cheka said and led the way through the corridors.

* * * * *

Chapter Twelve

EMS *Bucephalus*, Yovaz System, Low Orbit, Yovaz

"Lureli, this is *Bucephalus*, can you read us?"

"They said their transmitter was under attack," Jim said, back in the CIC after rendezvousing with the cruiser an hour earlier.

"We're mapping right now," Captain Su said, watching the slowly developing planetary map on the Tri-V. Some data was always available through the GalNet. The Cartography Guild compiled star maps and planetary reference details, which tended toward orbital calculations, rotation rates, gravity, and star types. They didn't concern themselves with the planet beyond basic statistics, though. Maybe some details on climate, land mass, or oceans. Yovaz lacked even that small amount, so they were mapping it themselves.

"Primary combat is taking place here," sensor ops said, and a section of map flashed white, "in the remains of a city with industrial facilities and a starport." The view zoomed in, and multiple targets showed weapons fire.

"Looks like old-school tanks," Jim noted. "Kinda like the old 20th Century M-1 Abrams or maybe the Challenger 2?"

"Tanks aren't my thing, Colonel," Su said with a wry smile, "but I didn't think anyone used tanks much."

"They have a niche, if a small one." He grunted as he recalled his first encounter with a tank as a mercenary. It was his first mission as the Cavaliers' commander. Even with his fumbling attempts to oper-

165

ate his CASPer, he'd managed to take it out. Truthfully, tanks had proven far too big, slow, and vulnerable against the weapons systems fielded in merc combat. Even the behemoth he'd faced, fusion powered with particle accelerator cannon and shields, hadn't been a match for a CASPer.

The one thing a tank excelled at was dealing large amounts of damage and controlling vast areas of land. Give a force of tanks enough room and an open approach without cover, and it could be a serious threat to an equal force of CASPers. CASPers gave Humans an edge in city fighting, industrial complexes, even woods and mountains. Mobility and portable firepower were their biggest advantages. They also made merc combat survivable for the delicate Humans inside—or at least *more* survivable.

"We're getting a laser from the surface," comms reported, and a crackling voice spoke.

"*Cavaliers, this is Lureli. Thank you for coming to our aid.*"

"Why are you under attack?" Jim asked. "And who are they? You said Lotar?"

"*The Lotar once possessed this system; we obtained it 11 years ago. They believed the minerals were played out, but our research suggested this was an error. After we purchased the lease, we moved most of our industrial capacity here. Our research proved correct, and massive reserve of Uranium, Gallium, Yttrium, and Terbium were located.*"

Lureli gave a single laugh and continued. "*The Lotar are effective traders. Their attempt at mining concerns were not successful. They were afraid of us. We are a merc race, you know.*"

"I do," Jim replied. "However, you haven't been active for some time."

"Correct. Our home world was destroyed in a cataclysm nearly two centuries ago. We have lived on temporary leaseholds ever since. Our merc ships still exist, but they are now old and decrepit, like our reputation. All we had was substantial stores of missiles. When the Lotar learned of our good fortune here, they tried to obtain a merc force to assault and retake the planet, but couldn't get a contract."

Jim grunted. "Yeah, that's kinda a big problem right now. Let me guess, they decided to do it themselves?"

"Apparently. We heard a lot of planets have been buying up surplus arms. Without mercs fighting, weapons and munitions are cheap and plentiful. The Lotar said we had a month to abandon the world that was rightfully theirs. We verified our lease with the Cartography Guild and told the Lotar to go to entropy. They attacked right on schedule. Nobody was more surprised than we were."

"We can lift the siege," Jim said.

"And your price, Colonel Cartwright?"

"Just the parts."

Lureli was silent for a moment. *"Nothing is cheap in this galaxy."*

"True. Your statement about nobody coming to our aid struck a nerve. You have a point. I can't do it for free; Guild law forbids it in this situation. The parts are valuable to us, though. Do you accept?"

"We do."

"Ships in our threat box," TacCom called. "Six of the improvised ships are coming up to intercept our orbit."

"They don't have a lot of guns," Su said, "but they've got excellent shields. I need to maneuver to keep them from overrunning our position."

"Lureli, we have to change orbits out of your lascom range."

"You have your parts, and now you are leaving?"

"No," Jim assured the alien, "but we need time to figure out how to get past the Lotar ships."

"*Very well, we have no choice but to trust you.*"

"Maneuvering," the helmsman reported.

Lureli began to say something, then *Bucephalus'* engines fired, and the ship accelerated. The ground-based laser lost its lock on the ship's receiver, and the alien's voice ended mid-word.

* * *

Jim grimaced as *Bucephalus* strained under 5Gs of thrust. The ship shuddered as a trio of missiles were ejected into space. On the Tri-V they accelerated away at 100 gravities of acceleration.

"We're running low on missiles," Captain Su said. "Six hours of combat, and we've only disabled one of those six ships."

"They really did a number on their shields," the SitCon said. "Probably gutted a half dozen additional ships to beef these up. Since they don't have a lot of energy weapons, and they're big, fat, old freighters, nothing else to use the power on but shields."

Captain Su grunted under the acceleration; she had no energy remaining to nod. The arm of her acceleration couch had a miniature set of ship status displays. From where Jim was, in a similar chair, he could see that one of the ship's consumables was yellow, another nearly the same.

"We're running low on reaction mass, too?"

"Yes," Su said. "*Bucephalus* has good legs, but one of those hits while you were in the junkyard caused a significant leak on reaction mass tank #2. We have about 200 G-hours of endurance remaining, and 22 missiles in the battery." The ship shuddered as lasers hit her aft shields.

"One of our missiles was intercepted; the other two hit, but with no significant effect," TacCom reported.

"Maybe if we had more than three missile tubes or a spinal mounted laser," she said and shrugged. "It's a standoff, and our reaction mass is the ticking clock. We'll run out of missiles before reaction mass, but without some of the latter remaining, we'll be stuck here. We can't even get into position to allow you to do a combat drop."

"They'd shoot the dropships down before we made atmosphere," Jim agreed. They were going to have to abandon the Reyq, it seemed, and he didn't want to be forced to do that. He thought for a second as the shields were hit twice more. It wasn't worth risking his ship, and his people, on a losing gambit.

At best, he could have *Bucephalus* do a parabolic dip into the atmosphere, releasing the Cavaliers' CASPers directly. But they hadn't come out here expecting a combat drop, and there were only 25 drop pods on board, just enough for a single platoon. Plus, with only 25 CASPers in the air, they'd make easier targets. A HALD—High Altitude, Low Deploy—drop counted on larger numbers to increase individual troopers' survival odds. Each pod deployed multiple decoys, so a company-sized drop could put hundreds of fake targets in the sky.

"Okay," he said. "Let's get out of here. You can install the parts in transit to the stargate."

Captain Su gave the order, and the ship changed direction, making for a higher orbit.

"Activity at the emergence point," sensor ops called out. "Single ship, high residual delta-V. They're under thrust, trying to correct their course for the stargate."

"Any transponder?" Su asked.

"Checking," Comms said. "Identifies as EMS *Naitoheron.*"

Jim chuckled. "Nightbirds."

"You know them?"

"I know their commander, Oda Shoji; I rescued him from Karma in the Omega War. I think they have two or three ships. They specialize in space navy escort. Can you send them a signal?"

"No reason why not." She nodded to comms then spoke. "*Naitoheron*, this is *Bucephalus* Actual, you read me?"

"Bucephalus *Actual, this* Naitoheron *Actual. Strange meeting you here.*"

"*Naitoheron*, we've kinda gotten caught in a situation here."

"*Looks that way,*" *Naitoheron* responded.

"*Naitoheron*, this is Cartwright Actual."

"*Oh, I thought the ship's name was familiar. Colonel Cartwright-sama, it's an honor to see you again.*"

"I'd trade the honor for a hand." Jim explained their situation.

"*I've never heard of the Reyq, but the GalNet does list them as a merc race. We're not big on pro bono work, though, Colonel.*"

"How about on helping out a Horseman?" There was a pause. "I assume this is Commander Oda Shoji?"

"*It is, Colonel Cartwright.*"

"I would love it if you'd give us a hand, like I did for you at Karma."

"*Certainly. You need extraction?*"

"No, I need you to clear these assholes away so I can relieve the Reyq." Another pause. "Look, Commander, if you're worried about being paid, I'll pay myself. Out of my own pocket."

Shoji laughed. *"That is not required, Colonel. I owe you a debt for rescuing my people and me; it would be my honor to repay you in kind. Captain Su, orbit around, and we'll come at your aggressors from behind."*

With the addition of another merc cruiser, the improvised warships were seriously out of their league. *Naitoheron* dropped into orbit tail first, burning her fusion torch to scrub off velocity. She flipped end over end at the last minute and took the trailing ship under fire with her twin forward-mounted lasers. Su flipped *Bucephalus* and added her heavy lasers as well. The combined fire breached the enemy ship's shields and sliced into its hull.

Secondary explosions bloomed across the huge freighter's superstructure. It quickly yawed out of control and fell toward the planet's atmosphere. Now there were four enemy, and they quickly showed their lack of tactical experience by trying to engage both merc cruisers at the same time. *Bucephalus* and *Naitoheron* concentrated on a single target again. When its shields went down, all four survivors ran for higher orbit.

"Pursuit?" Shoji asked from *Naitoheron*.

"No," Jim said. "Let them run. They'll think twice before trying us together again."

"What's your plan now?"

"We're going down to relieve the Reyq."

"And then?"

"I'll figure that out afterward."

* * *

Eesius, 2nd Level Hyperspace

J'asa's second visit to the leadership dome was quite different than the first. The Konar guarding the door saluted, fist to armored chest. She returned the salute and pushed the doors open. Inside there were nine plinths the *Tor* would sit upon. There was no sign of the killing that had taken place the last time she was there, and of course the body of the dead *Tor* Saleen was gone.

Five of the nine plinths were occupied by the *Tor*, watching her pull herself into the chamber with one of the guide ropes. She glanced back and saw both Seldia and Cheka waiting just inside the door, which remained open.

"You requested my presence?"

"We did, *Vok'tor*," one of the *Tor* said.

"It looks like your numbers are reduced."

"They are. All the *Tor* who opposed you have been removed. We confirmed *Tor* Saleen tried to have you killed, and they were duplicitous in her plot. She and her coconspirators acted out of fear for the Dusman as a whole. As more and more leave for normal space, our forces here dwindle dangerously. Saleen was convinced our opposition here would mount an offensive we would be unable to resist."

"Then we leave this place."

"After 20,000 years, it would not be an easy thing, *Vok'tor*."

"Yes, it would!" J'asa yelled. "It was *hard* to move here; it will be *easy* to leave. We abandoned the galaxy ages ago, abandoned them to our ancient adversary, and the newer one as well. We cannot do this yet again. My dream shows the stakes have grown immensely." She shuddered as the imagery played in her mind's eye. Trillions dying in fire, screaming her name. "Everything is on the line. *Everything.*"

"We do not begin to understand your ability, *J'apo*. Likewise, we cannot deny its existence. To do so risks bringing ruin down on our heads."

"Yes," J'asa agreed. "Worse ruin than the last time a *j'apo* was ignored." The *Tor* looked down or away from her. "All the Dusman must be united in this, or we surely fail, and take every living being with us to our doom."

"Since the early days, the *Tor* have led the Dusman. We've always tried to heed the *J'pa*."

The sprits of the fallen? J'asa wondered. *I didn't know many still followed the old faith.* "You're some of the few who do, then."

"Sadly, you are correct."

"As honored as I am to speak with the *Tor*, especially while they're not shooting at me, I need to get back to normal space to continue my work."

"Our work is your work, *J'apo*."

"There are only five of you now," she said. "The *Tor* cannot function without the nine. It's always been this way."

"It has," the same speaker said, then sighed. "Until now." She and the other four rose from their plinths and pulled themselves down to the floor where J'asa floated. As a group, they moved toward the doors.

"Where are you going?"

The female *Tor* who'd spoken came abreast of her and stopped. "We are leaving," she said.

"What about the *Tor*?"

"The *Tor* is no more, *J'apo*. We've done what should have been done when the *J'pa* chose the *j'apo* before the Betrayal."

"The Dusman need leadership."

"They have it, in you. *J'apo*, you are now the leader of the Dusman. *You* are the *Tor.*"

They departed the leadership dome, leaving J'asa, Cheka, and Seldia alone.

"Didn't I tell you it was fascinating?" Seldia said in her normal dreamy tone.

Cheka chuckled in his clicking way. "Sometimes the best events are the ones you do not dream about. Wouldn't you agree, *Tor?*"

J'asa sighed. "I hate you both."

* * * * *

Chapter Thirteen

Phoenix-Class Dropship, Yovaz System, Yovaz

*T*his is more like it, Jim thought as the planet's atmosphere clawed at the dropship. The superheated plasma made a screaming sound as it rebounded off the bow shock of their hypersonic trajectory.

"*Well, here we are again,*" Double T said over the squadnet, and the rest of the men chuckled or grunted. "*Always wondered what it would be like if one of these buckets was shot out from underneath me.*"

"You don't want to know," Jim said.

"*Holy shit!*" Private Erica Glendale exclaimed. "*You've been shot down, Colonel?*"

"Once," Jim said. "*Traveler,* the first merc cruiser I took out shortly after taking command, was toast. We jumped into the middle of a space battle. We didn't stand a chance, so the ship's commander, Captain Winslow, decided to eject all the dropships so we could make a run for the objective planet. He stayed in the fight long enough to buy us the time we needed. Then my dropship got hit, nearly cut in half. Last thing I remember was being thrown clear as the ship tore apart."

"*I heard about that,*" Double T said. "*That's where Murdock bought it?*"

"He's alive, actually."

"*You gotta be shittin me,*" Double T said then laughed. "*You know what? That old fucker is too tough to die so I don't doubt it one bit.*"

"Yeah, he ended up helping in the rescue op that got me and the other Raknar drivers away from Peepo at the end of the war."

"*Any idea where he is now?*" Double T asked.

"Not a clue."

They rode in silence as the pilot pulled up their trajectory. Jim kept waiting for the multiple *thud* indicating the small craft was ejecting flares and ECM decoys, but it never came.

"*We were scanned a couple times by air defenses, but never engaged,*" the pilot told them. "*All dropships are on final to the edge of the city.*"

"Roger that," Jim said. "Okay, Cavaliers, time to go to work."

Less than a minute later, the *Phoenix* flared hard, its variable-angle engines rotating down to allow a short landing. Heavy landing gear slammed against the ground, the rear loading door, which was as wide as the fuselage, dropped automatically, and the electromagnetic grapples that had been holding them in place released.

"*Out, out, out!*" Double T yelled.

Jim was first out, as had been the Cavaliers' way since his great grandfather's time. First in, last out. It didn't matter if it was a hot LZ or just arriving for a simple garrison contract. Cavalier Actual was *always* the first out the door and last to board a dropship home.

His CASPer told him Yovaz' atmosphere was not quite Earth normal, though close enough. A little too much CO_2, a bit too little O_2, and elevated levels of a dozen heavy metals made it far from safe to breathe. They'd be wearing face masks the whole time they were there, which Jim hoped wouldn't be too long. Gravity was a little less, at least.

As the last trooper of his squad stepped onto the rubble-strewn roadway they'd chosen for a landing zone, the *Phoenix's* engines screamed back to full power, and it jumped back into the cloudless sky, the ramp retracting, and the pilot banking away to make himself a harder target.

The second *Phoenix* assigned to his platoon was just finished unloading to their east, while 50 meters away another pair of *Phoenix* were delivering 2nd Platoon of A Company.

"Mayer, Sitrep," Jim called on the squadnet, set for platoon level comms.

"*All clear and 100%,*" the former marine said.

"It'll take about 20 minutes for the *Phoenix* to return to *Bucephalus*, refuel, and load B Company. About 15 minutes to drop."

"*If everything goes by the numbers,*" Mayer replied.

"Exactly. We have orbital scans of the enemy's basic disposition and direction of assault. If we're lucky, they have no idea what's landed at their flank. If we're unlucky—well, we'll deal with that later."

"*Roger that, Colonel. Order of battle?*"

"I don't want to hit them head on; tanks can still be dangerous, and this city isn't very tall. Without many buildings over two stories, we're short on cover. If we get locked up with the enemy, we'll be stuck waiting on Buddha to pull our asses out of the fire instead of him landing to the east and linking up with us. Send out your second squad as scout/skirmishers. I don't want to waste the few drones we have with us."

"*Roger that, sir,*" Mayer said and issued orders.

Jim used his pinplants to build as detailed a battlespace as he could manage. Between the scans *Bucephalus* had generated from orbit, and what they'd gotten on descent, it wasn't a terrible map. He'd had worse. The majority of the enemy was 2.1 kilometers roughly north, assembled mostly around their landing craft. A lot of them were assaulting various targets in the city, but Jim guessed if he could secure their landing craft, they'd fold.

His CASPer CNC, command and control, computer beeped that he had orbital comms. "Cartwright Actual."

"*How's the beachhead, Colonel?*" Buddha asked in his familiar Polynesian accent.

"We're down, zero casualties. Didn't even take fire on approach. Pretty clear these aren't mercs; any of them would have done their best to light us up."

"*Good to hear, but that means we might have a hotter job of it.*"

Data came in from Lieutenant Mayer's scouts as they probed around the enemy's flank. There were no units to their rear. None. *Holy shit,* Jim thought. *Jackpot.*

"You might not need to worry about that."

"*What's that supposed to mean?*"

"That means the dropships are en route back to *Bucephalus.* Comm me when you begin loading."

"*Colonel,* Jim, *don't do anything stupid.*"

"Not going to happen," Jim assured him and cut the comm. "Mayer," he called over the squadnet on the commander's channel, "you see what I see?"

"*A barn door, wide open and welcoming?*"

"Yup!"

"*Could be a trap.*"

"I doubt they're that sophisticated," Jim said. "Have your scouts hold and provide uplink." He switched to company-wide. "All other squads outside the scouts form up on my position. All up?"

"*Lead the charge!*" the company called out.

* * *

Achilles and his commando team of Konar touched down in almost perfect synchronization. They'd dropped from *Bucephalus* mere minutes after Cartwright in his dropships. The Dusman had their own versions of dropships. Of course, theirs were much more advanced and versatile, not to mention they had shields, and weren't easy targets, unlike the Humans'.

Achilles had made the call to let Cartwright drop in his primitive ship, and for his team of Konar to go down separately. That was, again, a risk. Bringing his team down as a separate element from the Humans was a major tactical advantage and increased the chances they'd never be spotted.

"Have you thought of how we're getting back up afterward?" Athena asked.

"No," he said. "One problem at a time."

Since they'd dropped as a joined unit, all 10 of the Konar automatically gathered petabytes of data on the ground below them. By the time they released from each other, flared their aerobrakes, and prepared for a landing burn, Achilles had an incredibly detailed map of the terrain and every enemy unit deployed. He also knew where all the so-called friendlies were, though he didn't have a lot of trust for the Reyq. His records indicated they'd fought for the Kahraman.

"How do we want to do this?" Athena asked. "Right up the middle, trash them completely, leave a couple for Cartwright so he feels useful?"

Achilles rolled his eyes, which wasn't visible to her inside his Konar. "Don't you think the Humans would be a little bit suspicious?"

"Probably."

"Okay, so let's be more specific." He sent coordinates to the rest of the Konar in his team.

"I like the way you think," Ajax said. They leaped as one.

* * *

The 30 CASPers crossed the intervening kilometer in a little over two minutes. Jim ordered running only, no jumpjets. The low-lying buildings gave them cover as they advanced. If they jumped, though, they'd be easily spotted.

"*Didn't they even* look *in our direction?*" Paragon asked the rest of the squad. "*I mean, a fucking* Phoenix-*class dropship isn't exactly a dainty target.*"

Jim nodded in his suit. The biggest downside of the *Phoenix*-class was its massive radar cross section. She was as stealthy as a cinderblock dropped from orbit. All the newer, alien-made classes were far harder to notice or hit. The venerable *Phoenix* didn't even have adaptive cooling on her reentry surfaces. She threw a plasma contrail visible from another continent. He guessed coming in on a daylight assault had worked in their favor this time.

"Scouts, report!" Jim called.

Sergeant Edward "Jack" Daniels replied, "*No sign you've been spotted, sir. I see a couple of the aliens right now. Looks like they're playing cards on a pallet of ammo.*"

"*Classic,*" said Corporal Kevin Tanzer from Jim's second squad. After a screening of an old 21st Century superhero movie, he'd voluntarily taken the handle of Taser Face. He was a tough SOB who'd obviously been in one too many fistfights. Jim thought the handle suited him.

Jim considered what they were about to do. Two platoons of CASPers, armed to the teeth, were about to slam into a bunch of civies playing war. Barring unexpected surprises, it would be a bloodbath.

<*Excellent,*> the voice snarled in delight. He shoved it down with some difficulty.

"Okay, men, we need to go easy."

"*Colonel?*" Mayer asked.

"These aren't mercs. We're not storming in on a platoon of Besquith or Tortantula." He looked at the images being relayed by the scouts. He'd never seen the Lotar until now. They reminded him a little of the SalSha, the otter-like aliens uplifted by Sansar several years ago. The Lotar lacked the long, sinewy bodies of the SalSha, and somehow the cuteness, too. Their eyes were big, with oversized irises, they had no external ears, and improbably long arms in striking opposition to rather short legs.

"We don't know how they'll respond to our attack," Jim said simply. "If they don't respond with force, we go easy on them. Allow them to surrender or run. Am I understood, Cavaliers?" Everyone acknowledged the orders. "Ten seconds to contact."

They reached the last line of buildings before the Lotar's grounded transports. As one, all 15 CASPers fired their jumpjets, vaulting over the last buildings and into the midst of the grounded transports.

Now that he was in direct combat, Jim had to concentrate on himself and not on everything else going on around him. He fired his jumpjets a pulse to cushion his landing and grounded the one-ton suit as smoothly as if he'd stepped off the last step of his stairs at home.

Two Lotar looked up from their card game in complete surprise, their huge eyes blinking as dust swirled around them. For an interminable moment, neither did anything, and Jim spoke. "Surrender." He'd already programmed his suit to translate anything he said to them into their native language, so he knew they understood. One raised its unusually long arms, and the other reached for a battle rifle propped up on the crate of ammo.

Shit, Jim thought.

The Lotar brought the rifle up with surprising speed, firing on fully automatic. The recoil rocked the Lotar, who'd apparently been unprepared for it, and the bullets worked their way up Jim's suit, sparking and ricocheting in all directions. One bouncing round took off the top of the other Lotar's head in a bloody spray of brains and bone.

Jim used one of his suit's hands to reach out and crush the front half of the gun's action. The Lotar tried to jerk the crushed weapon out of Jim's grip. Jim responded by tossing gun and alien aside in disgust.

<Kill, kill, kill them all!>

All around him, his Cavaliers were in the midst of the aliens, who appeared to be mostly support crew, pilots, and reserve troops. Surprisingly few of the aliens surrendered, their capitulation greatly complicated by the crazy, haphazard gunfire of their fighting counterparts. The Cavaliers tried to shield the ones who'd surrendered, but when Zane Voss' Mk 7 assault suit caught a handheld anti-armor rocket in the leg and went down, Jim did what he had to do.

"Neutralize anyone who doesn't lay down their weapons."

The CASPers' miniguns were designed for soft-skinned targets such as light buildings, transport ground vehicles, or lightly-armored personnel carriers. They pulped and shredded flesh and bone. The cursed voice in Jim's mind howled in delight. In a minute, it was over, ending with the majority of the Lotar dead or dying.

"*Damn fools,*" Mayer cursed as they saw what help they could provide to the wounded.

"Prepare to cover while our medics unsuit to tend the wounded."

"*Colonel,*" Sergeant Daniels commed.

"Go, Jack."

"*Might want to hold on unbuttoning anyone.*"

"Whatcha got?"

"*One of them must have called their forces. I have between 20 and 50 tanks inbound your position.*"

"Swell. Jack, I want you to swing around behind them. Keep an eye out for stragglers or infantry, they have rocket launchers, too."

"*Got it,*" Jack replied. "*Moving.*"

"Heavy inbound," he warned all the troopers with him. "What's the status on Voss?"

"*His leg's broke,*" said Private Watanabe, 1st Platoon's medic in 2nd squad. "*Suit's operational, but he's not going anywhere.*"

"Roger that. Treat him and lock his suit in place until the op is complete."

"*Understood, Colonel.*"

"*I can fight,*" Voss spoke up.

Jim could hear the pain in his voice. "I know you can, Private, but you're staying here for the rest of this. Got it?"

"*Yes, sir,*" Voss agreed. His voice held an edge of barely suppressed rebellion. Jim grinned; the kid had heart. Good.

They'd rearmed and reequipped while aboard *Bucephalus*, knowing they would be in combat against conventional armor. As such, they were armed with heavy weapons, mostly shoulder-mounted MACs and missile pods. Heavy assault was the bread and butter of the Cavaliers ever since its early days. Orbital drop had been added once the technology was implemented.

In the years since 19-year-old Jim Cartwright had taken over the Cavaliers, he'd never faced a solid opposition of tanks before. It was a unique encounter. He'd fought and defeated plenty of tanks, but not in number. Few races bothered with them. There were too many situations in the galaxy they weren't suitable for, where their heavy defenses and massive firepower became a liability. Their very bulk and weight made transport difficult. Most were too large to even be transported planetside by a conventional dropship, necessitating a large, cumbersome, and easily-targeted transport.

The landing area had 11 massive orbital transports, each modified to carry a handful of tanks. They'd brought their entire force down in a single landing, something no merc would ever do. That was either desperate or stupid.

"Set up along this line of buildings," Jim ordered, using his map of the battlespace to mark positions and send them to individual squad sergeants. "Designate individual targets. Scouts, give me the best scans you have of the tanks." A moment later the data came in. It wasn't what he was expecting.

"I've never seen that design before," Double T said.

"Me neither," Jim agreed. He cross-referenced the design against GalNet data stored in his pinplants. The design elements were all identifiable, down to the tread configuration and weapons mounts. The build, however, was unique. It appeared custom made for the Lotar, and not by them. It had all the hallmarks of the major weapons manufacturers in the Galactic Union.

"Every other trooper, target the turret rings," Jim ordered. "The rest, go for treads or targets of opportunity. *Open fire!*"

The moment the first tanks rounded cover, they were attacked. Tanks had the luxury of much thicker armor than a CASPer, and the liability of being relatively easy targets. The magnetic accelerator cannons the CASPers mounted were a late-generation design, capable of firing a synthetic diamond-tipped, tungsten steel-cased discarding sabot projected at nine times the speed of sound. The center of the slug had a core of ultra-dense uranium in most cases. They hit with tens of thousands of foot pounds of energy.

The very act of firing the weapon depleted the barrel a little, a problem 21st Century engineers had struggled with, and failed to solve prior to First Contact. Aliens long ago had solved the problem by using the magnetic fields used to accelerate the projectiles to hold them centered in the barrel, thus reducing damage to the same. Even so, every shot stripped off a little of the barrel shroud, producing a meters-long gout of plasma from the aperture. An unarmed being standing next to a barrel was in nearly as much danger as one standing in front of it.

The spectacle of 30 CASPers firing their MACs at the same time was stunning. A wall of slugs tore into the lead group of a dozen tanks, shredding them. None of the tanks mounted main energy weapons, instead opting for explosively-propelled rounds. That meant a smaller power supply, and a less expensive tank. It also meant they carried a large number of high explosives. Two of the shots penetrated the tanks' turret rings, spraying the interior with metal fragments heated almost to a plasma state. When those fragments hit and breached the magazines, the tanks cooked off spectacularly.

"*That* won't *buff out*," said Private Doug Henry, one of the troopers in Jim's squad equipped with a Mk 7 assault model. One of the two cooked-off tanks was his shot. The MAC mounted on his suit was the largest a CASPer could carry.

"*Shut up and keep shooting*," Double T growled. "*Plenty of targets*."

Too damned many, Jim thought. The follow-up tanks used their burning buddies as cover and opened fire. Where the CASPers' MAC rounds were small, 18-25 millimeters usually, and super-fast, the tank rounds were massive. They appeared to be 100 millimeters traveling at around 500 meters per second. But they were explosive penetrators. If anything, they were overkill against a CASPer.

Private Snodgrass, 2nd Platoon, 1st Squad, a new kid who'd joined out of cadre six months ago, caught a tank round square center in the chest. The explosion scattered Mk 7 parts for 100 meters in every direction.

"Move!" Lieutenant Mayer yelled at his men, and the rest fired jumpjets to clear the danger space.

More tanks pushed through the line of destroyed and disabled tanks. Some with only missing treads or secondary damage tried to bring their weapons into play, while others on fire or gutted had Lotar piling out of them.

"Leave the crews," he ordered before his men got trigger happy. The survivors of the tanks weren't bringing weapons with them; they were running for their lives. If they'd been mercs, they'd know their chance of survival after engaging an enemy would be drastically lower.

"*Second group of tanks trying to flank to the east*," the scouts reported.

"Hit them from behind," Jim ordered. "I want survivors, not charred corpses."

"*Roger that.*"

<*You're fucking weak.*>

Shut up.

<*Ha ha ha ha.*>

A half hour later, only 13 of the tanks were still operational. The Lotar had started the battle with 42, it turned out. The idiots had managed to blow the shit out of two of their own transports, taken out four of their own tanks with friendly fire, and seemed incapable of just surrendering. Jim was running low on MAC rounds and patience.

"*Why don't we just use the rockets we're carrying and finish this?*" Mayer asked him.

"Doesn't add up," Jim said.

"*We've got two KIA and three injured. Expensive bill for a near pro bono.*"

"Too expensive," he agreed. "Okay, but let's see if we can tip the balance hard enough to get them to drop the game." He switched channels. "Cavaliers Actual to *Bucephalus.*"

He waited 10 minutes. A risk that the enemy tanks could create a tactical advantage, sure. He decided it was worth it. Once the time passed, he used his open comms again.

"Calling the Lotar unit commander." Just like before, no response. "Listen, you're done, you just don't know it."

"*Our position is entrenched,*" the reply came in native Lotar.

"You read that in a combat manual?"

"*To entropy with you, Human. This isn't your fight; why are you here?*"

"Because you attacked another merc race, and they requested aid."

"*You mercenaries, so full of honor. This world belongs to us.*"

"Not from where I'm standing. Give up and we'll let you withdraw with your wounded. Limp your busted asses back home, alive. That's more than you'll get from any other merc."

"*Our gear?*"

"Forget it. Price of starting a fight you should never have tried."

"*You are making idle threats,*" the Lotar replied.

"Am I? Look up." A series of multiple sonic booms, like an artillery battery firing in rapid succession, rolled over the land. Somewhere amidst the tanks, the Lotar commander was looking up to see a platoon of CASPers dropping on their jumpjets. Only, because of the heatshields splitting into multiple parts, it would look like several more companies, not 20. Jim let the silence stretch for a few more second before speaking.

"Your move."

* * * * *

Chapter Fourteen

Yovaz System, Yovaz

"Humans?" Yeeq roared. "*Humans?*" He turned his head and speared his second in command with a glare. "They're just mercs in silly suits of armor. We have *tanks*!" His whiskers twitched in his rage.

"But we aren't mercs; we've never done this before," the second complained.

"The Lotar can do whatever we want. We're not limited like they are." Yeeq walked to the back of the command center where 50 of his most elite soldiers waited. They all had the best they could buy from the Weapons Cartel. They even had a pair of portable shield generators for improved positions. The files they'd read in the Gal-Net had all the details, how to perform an assault, a static defense, a fighting withdrawal. It was all there and so easy.

"Prepare for a counterstrike," Yeeq said, recalling the plans in the files. He called up the Tri-V image of the western part of the city. "We swing around behind where our transports landed and hit them there."

"What about their drop underway?"

"It will take them time to organize after they land. Once we are behind them, we can execute a..." He pulled up the file again. "We can execute a pincer maneuver!"

A series of flashes and an explosion of sparks from the rebar in the building wall preceded the entire wall's collapse. Everyone fell away from it in surprise as the sunlight poured in, temporarily blind-

189

ing them. When Yeeq could see again, he could make out 10 or so strange, armored figures, no more than a meter tall.

"Shoot them!" he screamed.

A couple of his elite soldiers raised their brand-new laser rifles and fired, their shots wild and uncontrolled. Even so, several hits scored. Their beams were somehow deflected off the armor in a splash of colors like a neon fan.

"Who are you?" Yeeq demanded, a feeling of dread settling in.

The little armored figures didn't answer; they raised their arms and bathed the room in pulses of coherent light. In moments, everyone was dead.

"Well, *that* was somewhat satisfying," Athena said, kicking over a Lotar with a hole burned through its head. The alien's fur was smoldering, like many others, filling the room with smoke.

Achilles and the others moved through the room, ensuring all were dead. After they were sure, Agamemnon took all the slates he could find and stowed them in his Konar. "All done," he said.

"Ajax," Achilles said, "do it."

"Yes, *Osk'ii*."

The Konar team moved back past the nearest building, verified they were clear, and Ajax triggered the explosive. The detonation obliterated the bodies, equipment, and the building. Not far away, the rest of Cartwright's CASPers were landing. Before they'd all touched the ground, Achilles and his Konar had disappeared into the ruins of the city.

"Let's find a shuttle and get back to space," Achilles said. "Then we can call our own craft and return to *Bucephalus*. Cartwright will never know we were here."

* * *

The surviving Lotar were compliant, if confused and shell-shocked. Their race appeared to be trained from a young age to follow leadership. That explained why they'd fought so hard, even when they weren't good at it, or even particularly eager to fight.

Jim, now out of his CASPer and in light combat armor and a respirator, was overseeing the enemy turning in every gun, every bullet. They'd taken all day to finish sweeping the combat zone to be sure they'd gotten them all. The Reyq had gotten the rest. He hadn't expected them to accept surrender, but they had. That spoke volumes about the Reyq, and might have been why they hadn't done well as a merc race. The only things the Lotar were allowed to keep were the clothes on their backs and their own style respirators against the toxic planetary atmosphere.

"Well done, Jimbo," Buddha said, coming over in light armor as well, and looking over the pile of small arms.

"We took too many casualties," Jim said. One of the wounded had died en route to *Bucephalus* for treatment, bringing the butcher's bill to three. The fucking Lotar didn't fight like mercs, which was a problem in and of itself. He needed to speak to their commander.

"Any is too many, as you usually say. But these parts, they're almost priceless now."

Jim nodded, unconvinced. But the blood had been shed, and the bill paid.

A small electric transport was rolling their way. It had been cleared through the Cavaliers' line. A funny looking thing, like a golfcart with an enclosed passenger area full of water. He could see three of the large eel-like aliens inside. It came abreast of him and stopped, a speaker coming to life with the same crackling language.

"Colonel Cartwright?"

"That's me," Jim said.

The larger of the Reyq at the control waved a small arm. "I am Lureli, leader of our people. I want to thank you personally and say we are sorry for your dead."

"Cost of doing business," Jim replied. "As mercs, you're painfully aware of this."

"Yes, only too much."

"This is Lieutenant Colonel Akamai Kalawai, my second in command."

"You can call me Buddha," the big man said.

"I would like to call you friends."

"We'd like that as well," Jim said. "The more we have in this crazy galaxy, the better."

"I think you are right. It would seem the guilds are falling apart."

"It does seem that way," Jim agreed. "That Lotar claimed to have possession of this world."

"They used to, years ago. Mined it with every disgusting measure you could imagine." Lureli gestured at the outside air. "This toxic mess is their fault. As the easy to find veins of precious metals and rare earths ran out, they became increasingly desperate, and used more destructive measures to extract the minerals."

"What about the rest of your people, the Reyq?"

"We are all that is left, 100,000 or so between here and on ships. Our home world was destroyed without warning by a gamma ray burster a century ago."

"Without warning?" Jim asked. "How is that possible? A gamma ray burster only moves at the speed of light. There should have been *years* of warning, plenty of time to protect the planet, or even evacuate."

"That's what we said to the Science Guild," Lureli said. "They made all manner of excuses, which ultimately made no difference to the millions of dead." Lureli shook its head, gills waving in the water.

Jim ground his teeth together. *The fucking Science Guild again. What did the Reyq know that marked them for death?* He had no doubt their death wasn't an accident. More like murder. Another merc race on the fires of some SI's darker plans? He had a lot of questions he'd like to ask the synthetic intelligence known as Minerva. The voice in the back of his mind growled ineffectual rage. He ignored it.

"Jim, have a look at these weapons."

He looked over at Corporal Paragon, who held one of the Lotar's handheld weapons. "What do you have there?"

"These are common market models," Paragon said. "Probably produced by a dozen companies in the Union."

"Okay. What's the deal?"

"They're fakes." He turned the weapon over and pointed. "I owned a pistol by this company. Looked like a good deal. I was wrong. No two alike, they're trash. Made by low-wage slaves on shitholes all over the galaxy." He opened the breach mechanism, examining the interior, then broke it down. "This? This is quality work, completely automated in a manufactory somewhere."

"So they made them look like this? Why?" Jim wondered.

"To hide who really made them."

"We didn't capture anyone in charge?"

"There was no way to tell, and they wouldn't give them up to us," Buddha said. "We thought we had a command-and-control location when we were landing, but when we checked, all we found was a blown-to-shit building." He shrugged. "I've had the techs check the tank computers. Their deep logic is locked under a hyper-encryption. It would take the most powerful computer a decade to break it."

"Maybe the Aku could do it in less," he mulled quietly.

"May we have a look?"

Jim turned to see the water in the cart draining, and the three Reyq walking out on their tails. He had to admit, it was a pretty cool thing to see how they moved. Kinda like a snake slithering in the grass, but standing upright at the same time. They were at least two meters long and could move pretty quick for a tall snake/eel.

"How long can you go without being in the water?" Buddha asked.

"It depends on the ambient humidity. Here, the limiting factor is the pollution."

"You guys good with computer tech?"

"Sort of," Lureli said.

Jim looked at the three for a moment, trying to tell them apart. Lureli looked slightly larger than the others. "Can you look at the tanks, maybe figure out how to get around the operating system?"

"I would be glad to," Lureli said.

Jim led them to one of the tanks, climbed up onto the deck, and pulled open a hatch. The Reyq slithered up behind him much easier than Jim had managed. "The main control is in the forward compartment." The three reptilians were inside in less than a second. "Nice." Jim, on the other hand, was neither slim nor slippery. For a second, he thought he'd gotten stuck, then he finally popped inside.

"These vehicles are not made for Humans," Lureli said as Jim finally made entrance.

"Yeah, I noticed." Jim examined the tank controls and brought the computer online. "We wanted to get into the deep logic behind the OS so we can find out who built these."

Lureli examined the computer for a moment, then looked at another of its number. "Meenli, can you do this?"

"Yes," the other Reyq said, and leaned forward to touch the computer with a long-fingered hand. Sparks jumped and turned into tendrils of living electricity, which arced around and over the computer.

Jim stood, open mouthed, as the computer flashed through screens like it was in a diagnostic mode, ending in the main configuration menu.

"Is this what you wanted, Colonel Cartwright?" Meenli said.

"Uh…" He was so surprised, it took him a moment to respond. "Yes, thanks!"

"No problem," the Reyq said.

The electricity stopped arcing, and Jim leaned in, typing. The answer came up immediately. "Weapons Cartel."

"Son of a bitch," he said. If the weapons had simply been purchased from the Weapons Cartel, he would have marked it down as opportunistic sales. The faked manufacturers said it was anything but.

Out of curiosity, he went into the computer log of the tank's manufacturing serial number. The one he sat in was #34-009145, one of 9,145 thus far manufactured in that year's run of tanks. *That's a lot of tanks*, he thought. *I wonder how many worlds in the galaxy have something like this going on right now? Without the Merc Guild to level the playing field, call for help, calm things down through their own version of détente, shit might be going south real fast.*

"We thank you for relieving us," Lureli said a short time later outside the tank. "You have spilt your blood for us today; we shall not forget this favor."

"Another mercenary unit, The Nightbirds, assisted as well. We couldn't have gotten through the Lotar ships in orbit without them."

"We cannot offer credits, sadly. Without mercenary contracts, our small numbers cannot generate income. Our mercenary forces are off world, waiting for a contract to be approved. We have so few, we couldn't leave any here. We thought we would be safe on this polluted planet. That was a mistake.

"What we do have is salvage. The mercs who helped you are welcome to any parts we have. For you, besides the parts you have, we offer our friendship. Call for us, and we will be there for you. The Reyq repay our debts. Always."

"I'll remember that. Hopefully this will also be the beginning of a friendly relationship with my people, the Terran Federation. We need to make alliances, not enemies."

"We would enjoy that," Lureli said.

Jim gestured to the line of operational tanks and the piles of weapons. "These are yours now; do whatever you want with them."

Hours later, the Nightbirds escorted the remaining Lotar ships to the stargate. "*They just transitioned through,*" Commander Shoji reported. "*We'll remain on station for two weeks or so, just to be sure the Lotar don't come back. The Reyq report some of their own forces should be back by then.*"

"Roger that, Commander Shoji," Jim replied. "You have the thanks of a Horseman, for what it's worth."

"*Your thanks is worth an awful lot to us, Colonel Cartwright. Safe travels.*"

Jim smiled and relaxed in his quarters as *Bucephalus* headed for the stargate as well. This hadn't been part of the plan when he'd left to visit the colonies, but the results were favorable. He made some notes on his slate before getting some sleep.

* * *

Eesius, 2nd Level Hyperspace

J'asa looked to her left and right, where eight empty plinths sat. All their former occupants were now *Nee*. All except Saleen, of course, who was dead. For as long as any records existed, nine *Tor* had led the Dusman. Led them to rule a galaxy and led them to their race's near extinction. Now, there was only one. Her.

This hadn't been part of her dream when she was in the creche. None of this had. She hadn't dreamt anything past meeting Jim Cartwright and finding the Raknar again. Being up on the plinth hadn't been part of her plan when she'd return to 2nd level hyperspace, either.

"Sometimes you just have to accept a different fate than what you expected," she said in the empty chamber. A moment later, the doors opened, and they came in. Dante, Sla'etou, Cheef, and K'raa. They looked around, and their faces and ears ran the emotional gamut for their race.

"So it's true!" Dante said, speaking first as his eyes found eight of the nine plinths unoccupied. "Did you kill them all?"

"No," J'asa said, struggling not to smile.

"Well, she is responsible for one of them dying," Seldia said.

"Tell me it was that Saleen idiot," Dante said. J'asa nodded, and he laughed. "I look forward to the story."

"Later," Sla'etou said. "Tell us what's going on."

Sla'etou had first been known to the Humans by his nickname, Sly, which she'd chosen for him when she'd been known only as Splunk. The Humans struggled with Dusman names, and it didn't serve the Humans to realize that Splunk and the others Jim had thought were called Fae were actually Dusman.

"Yes," *Ske'sa* Cheef said. She'd led the fleet against the Science Guild SI. "What's going on? Where are the *Tor?*"

"She *is* the *Tor,*" Seldia said.

"That doesn't make any sense," Sla'etou said.

J'asa explained that she wasn't the first *j'apo* in 20,000 years; there'd been another, only a century ago. How that *j'apo* had been exiled, like she had been. The prophecy of what was coming had been covered up until J'asa was born, and, once again, the prophecy was foretold in dream. Like the last time, she was eventually exiled. Only this time, her mother had fought for her. Fought and lost.

"When I met Jim Cartwright and disobeyed orders to go with him, I did what the previous *j'apo* hadn't. Of course, the order to stay on Kash-kah came from Saleen, who led the majority of the *Tor*. My mother was forced to take the *Nee*. Do it, or I was to be killed."

"Outrageous!" Sla'etou cried out.

"Outrageous, but true," Seldia said. "When my sister returned to research, Saleen thought she came to attempt to take over."

"I was only consulting the *Nee'Akee* for information," J'asa explained. "Even so, she recruited *Po'Froo* to attack and kill me."

"I have the *Po'Froo's* testimony," Cheka said. Heads turned to regard the ancient Minchantaa'Sha, who was off to one side. "J'asa offered them caste in exchange for their testimony. It is all in the *Nee'Akee* now."

"You offered *Po'Froo* caste?" Sla'etou asked in surprise. "That's dangerous."

"I didn't offer those *Po'Froo* caste, I offered *all* of them caste." All four of the new arrivals gasped.

"They are without caste for a reason," Cheef said.

"Like me? Exiled for a reason?" Cheef's mouth became a thin line. "Saleen and her faction would happily have made me *Po'Froo* if she hadn't feared it wouldn't shut me up, which it wouldn't have. I was sent to normal space to live out my life or die. She didn't care which, until this all got started. Yet, even when the factions grew, she held a narrow majority. She appointed you." She pointed at Sla'etou. "She did this, certain you'd rule on her side. Only you didn't."

"The *kroof* takes no sides; they judge. You made your case, the facts proved out. You were correct."

"The schism was complete," J'asa continued. "When I returned, it was too much, so she acted. Maybe if the *Po'Froo* had succeeded, that would have been the end of it. I don't know."

"What was she afraid of?" Cheef asked.

"That we are returning to normal space," Cheka said. "This place has its dangers, but it is safe from the rest of the galaxy…and the Kahraman."

"They cannot survive here," Seldia agreed, "but in the end, neither can we."

"We've fought a dozen major wars here, and a hundred small ones," Dante agreed. "I admit I wasn't on your side when this started. Yet you won me over, mostly."

Unlike a lot of them in normal space, he'd picked his own Human name, and used it exclusively. When J'asa had finally looked it up, she'd found it fitting. Dante had led the counterattack forces against the enemy invading Eesius during the last great war, forcing them back, at great cost in fighters and his own body. The victory had cost him an eye, part of his tail, and an arm. Despite their technology allowing for a regrowth of all the lost body parts, he'd stuck with a cybernetic arm, and no eye or tail. A curious Dusman, to be sure, and a deadly adversary.

"Well, they went too far," Seldia said.

"Giving caste to the *Po'Froo* could be considered too far," Sla'etou said. "You said four of the *Tor* took the *Nee*; that left four. It was still a majority. Yet you are here, and they are not."

"Their last act was to dissolve the *Tor* as a group," J'asa explained.

"Can they do that?" Cheef asked.

"Does it matter? They did," Cheka said.

Seldia smiled. "I said my sister was at the center of it all."

"Now you'll tell us you saw this?" Dante snorted. "You and your visions."

"My visions aren't as pronounced as my sister's," Seldia admitted. "They're harder to interpret, too. But yes, I saw she was in the center of everything as we reemerged. I didn't know how she was at the center, or how we would reemerge. It was up to her to create the future."

"They appointed me as *Tor*, as the only *Tor*," J'asa explained. "It didn't matter if I wanted it or thought it was a bad idea. This is where I am and where you are."

"So why are we here?" Cheef asked. "*Tor.*" She bowed her head in respect.

It didn't matter if they agreed with how things had shaken out or not. Dusman were raised to acknowledge caste and the status that came with it. Change was often part of the system. While it was new and involved something that had never happened before in their known history, it was the new reality.

"You're here to facilitate the next move. Cheef, I name you *ske'tor* in command of all our naval forces."

Cheef's ears went straight up in surprise. She'd been *ske'sa*, commanding the bulk of their operational forces up until now. No *ske'tor* had been named until that moment. "I accept the honor, *Tor* J'asa."

"K'raa, you were *osk'sa*, in command of all Konar on Earth. You are now *osk'tor*."

"There has never been an *Osk'tor*," K'raa said, just as surprised as Cheef.

"There's never been a single *Tor*, either."

He bowed his head. "I accept this honor as well, *Tor* J'asa."

"Dante," she began.

"You sure about this?"

"Yes. You're *Vok'tor*. Do you accept?"

"Do I have a choice?"

"I can name Ryft, if you refuse."

"To oblivion with that," he growled. "I accept, *Tor* J'asa."

"That leaves you, Sla'etou."

"You have named all your force, *Tor*," he said, indicating the new force commanders. "I was merely a *kroof*. What would you have me do? There is nothing more to arbitrate."

"I would have you stand at my side and tell me when I am doing wrong, *Tor'a*."

"I've been *kroof* my whole life," he said. "We arbitrate disputes in the Dusman. I do not know how to be *Tor*."

"There are other *kroof*, yes?" J'asa asked. He nodded. "I was born to be *j'apo*, but became *vok* instead. Tell me, what's the bigger adjustment do you think?" He didn't answer. "I need your counsel, the Dusman need your counsel, if I'm to lead us to the conclusion of this, to defeat the darkness that threatens to engulf the galaxy and us with it. I'm giving up *Vok'tor*, but I'm not giving up my Raknar."

"You must be kidding," Dante said. "No *Tor* has ever sat a Raknar."

"That we know of," J'asa countered. "I saw myself in a Raknar even before we found the first one back in normal space. Everything I feel means I stay there, in the fight. You'll lead the battles that are coming; I will lead the war. The *Tor* have always decided how we fight."

"The place of a *Tor* isn't in the front," Cheef agreed.

"It is now, *Ske'tor*. It is now. I will have *Tor'a* Sla'etou to carry forth my wishes when I am at war, and all of you to help me carry out that war."

"I accept, *Tor* J'asa," Sla'etou said, then shook his head. "The rest of the *kroof* will go crazy."

"Your type are already crazy," Dante said.

J'asa looked at K'raa. "You have one of the greatest challenges, *Osk'tor* K'raa."

"What must I do, *Tor*?"

"We cannot win with ships and Raknar. It didn't work in the last war, and we don't have 1,000 Arsenals at our disposal, we just have 3-B-E."

"There could be more," K'raa said. "There have been stories."

"Yes," J'asa said and made a dismissive gesture. "Wars are not won with stories. I've instructed 3-B-E to begin manufacturing

Konar. Going forward, 30% of its manufacturing capacity will be dedicated to Konar."

"That will make thousands a month," K'raa said.

"This is true," she agreed, "and we will need those thousands, because the *Po'Froo* have been given to the *Osk*. You will need the new Konar for your new *Osk'u*. I didn't give them anything for free; this is their chance to earn it."

"I now wonder if you've given me an honor or a nightmare," K'raa said.

"A little of both, I would think," Dante said.

"Some of the new caste will not fit the *Osk*; they might end up being *Ske*, or *Vok*," she continued. "Some will fail and return to the casteless. Yet they have a chance they've never had before."

"Because they never tried," Sla'etou said.

J'asa looked at him and nodded. "You're right, in most cases. There's something the Humans taught me; I learned it from Jim. Would you like to know what it is?" He nodded. "Everyone deserves a second chance." The assembled new military *Tor* of the Dusman considered her words. "Now, we're ready to begin my next order."

"And what is that?" Sla'etou asked.

"Begin the ordered evacuation of Eesius." They gawked at her. "We're finally descending back to normal space. It's past time for this. We're going home."

* * * * *

Chapter Fifteen

EMS *Bucephalus*, Hyperspace

Jim finished his workout and returned to his tiny cabin. The ship was in zero G while in hyperspace. Lacking a proper gravity deck, the ship's gym was equipped with the various exercise machines designed for use in a weightless environment. They were effective enough, if unwieldy to use and took longer than their terrestrial counterparts. You had to work twice as hard in space, without gravity, to get the same amount of caloric consumption.

He couldn't easily weigh himself, either. He liked to keep at least a weekly log. Every minute he'd spent planetside the last two months he'd been meeting with planetary leaders and military commanders. Dressed in a clean uniform, he went to the officer's mess for lunch.

After they'd left Yovaz, they'd gone to Chislaa, called Canopy by the Human colony. Canopy held a population of half a million, mostly agricultural, and some deep rare earth mining. Like Talus, it had been fought over and retaken, though the Golden Horde had led the operation there. Jim met with the governor and the defensive coordinator, as well as the Dusman in charge of the Raknar contingent. Just like Talus, it had a star of 14 Raknar, Konar, and the Dusman needed to operate their garrison.

Unlike Talus, they were expecting him this time, and there was a lot more pomp and circumstance. Apparently the Dusman had sent word to the other colonies to expect him. Canopy was simpler than Talus—they'd always been part of Earth's sphere of influence in the

Republic. They were happy to be in the Federation now, and considered it an improvement. After a week, they moved on.

Next up was Asyola, known as Frost, an icy planet holding a quarter million Humans. Frost was a binary system, with the inhabited planet orbing the brown dwarf of the pair. Numerous asteroids provided ample resources for a shipyard, the first off-world ship production facility operated by Humans. Like Canopy, they were a stable democracy, proud to be in the Federation, and willing to participate in the mutual defense agreement. They also had a Raknar star of 14 and the contingent of Konar. Jim was beginning to see a pattern.

"Are there Dusman on all our colonies?" he'd asked the *vok'sa* in charge.

"The ones large enough to support it and who welcomed us, yes. Your colonies have proven better recruiting grounds than Earth. We don't know why."

The people of Frost were a little less pleased to have the Dusman marching around. The miners in the outer system, though, were thrilled. The Dusman were buying any and all goods they wished to trade and paying in pure red diamonds. Jim had been wondering how they were paying for stuff, or if they were paying at all. Frost was also glad to join the Federation mutual defense pact, and were flush with credits thanks to the Dusman.

They spent three weeks on Frost, not because there was more to do, but to allow *Bucephalus'* crew and the Cavaliers' troopers shore leave. Ice fishing, skiing, and riding sailboats on ice skates called Iceriggers were fun distractions, and the crew came aboard in good spirits and well rested.

Their next stop was Paradise, a Muslim-dominated planet of only 100,000, and home to some of the more vicious fighting. After the disappearance of most of the people from New Persia, the remainder had resettled in Paradise and quickly taken over the colony's leadership. They hadn't been receptive to the Dusman, so there was no garrison there. The Humans had reasonable defenses and welcomed Jim, if a bit cooler than the other worlds had.

The planet's ruling mullah stated they were proud to be aligned with the Federation, however, they weren't interested in the mutual defense pact. They were convinced they were prepared to deal with any invaders in the future. Jim tried to tell them how wrong they were, but they weren't interested in talking about it, nor allowing any of the Cavaliers to visit the planet, outside of official meetings. Jim made a note to see if Nigel could come and talk sense into them. They left after just three days.

Their last colony stopover was Gliese 1214b, known as Valais. A world composed of 95% water, Valais produced most of the seafood imported to Earth. Ironic, since Earth was 70 percent water as well, but until recently, Earth had suffered under considerable restrictions for fishing on their own world.

Valais was garrisoned by Dusman, of course, and the normal complement of Raknar. During the Omega War, they'd had a run in with Xiq'tal. It also turned out to be where Murdock had been hanging out after returning from the dead. The old merc had recruited a bunch of his fellow retired soldiers of fortune and took care of the alien invaders before heading off to help save him on Earth.

The government of Valais wasn't well organized; they were still trying to put the pieces together after the war and uncertain what the situation was on Earth. They were equally unsure of the Dusman presence, but had been unable or unwilling to tell them no. While fishing was resuming on Earth after many decades, Jim was certain the hungry nations of Earth were interested in continued imports of seafood from Valais.

Because of the governmental confusion, Jim had to spend nearly a month helping them become better organized and working out the logistics of standing up their military, outside the Dusman presence.

Messages from Earth caught up with them while on Valais as well. The Federation leadership was pissed at him for taking off, but his progress on Talus was lauded, and he was given tacit approval after the fact to continue. Not that they had a lot of choice, since the press had gotten word of his trip as well. He sent back a status report, leaving out the incident on Yovaz. He'd brief them after returning.

When he left Valais, he also didn't tell his counterparts back on Earth about his next and last stop before returning. His goals met in the trip to the colonies, he had one more objective that needed completion.

"We arrive tomorrow?" Buddha asked, floating over to Jim with his own lunch. The prepackaged shipboard meals were boring, designed for consumption in zero G. The frown on his XO's face said he missed Earth meals.

"Yep," Jim said, taking a 'seat' next to Buddha. Various ship's officers nodded to him, and he returned the gestures. "Around 0500 ship time."

"You sure about this, Jim?"

"Yes," he said. "I made a promise, and they've done more than we could have hoped for." Buddha shrugged and ate his lunch. "It's the right thing to do."

"I'm sure your father would agree."

I hope so, Jim thought as he ate.

The next morning he was in the CIC, as usual when arriving in a potential combat zone. The ship was at Condition-3, shields and weapons standing by. None of the colonies so far had missiles they could use, so *Bucephalus* was extremely low on offensive capabilities. The Cavaliers had also used all the drop pods they'd brought with them. Jim had made a lot of operational notes for future trips, no matter what the intentions of the mission might be.

"I hope this turns out like you hoped," Captain Su told him as the clock ran down.

"Me, too," Jim said.

"Just the same, I made sure to enter the Valais stargate with a fair amount of delta-V. We made a best-case prediction on emergence vector. If our computer calculations were reasonably close, we can make for the stargate with minimal corrections." She glanced at Jim. "If necessary, of course."

"If it's suboptimal, I'll be the first to say we need to evac, Captain."

Captain Su gave him a wry smile and a nod. A second later, the helmsman gave out the count.

"Emergence in one minute."

"Very well," Su said. "Attention all hands, stand to action stations."

The final seconds counted down to zero, and they dropped out of hyperspace with the strange falling sensation. The ship was once again in the regular universe.

"Drones out," Captain Su ordered. "Helm, verify our location and plot our vector, if you will."

"Working," the helmsman reported.

"Shields are up, weapons standing by," TacCom added.

"Confirmed," Helm reported. "We're in the Golara system."

Jim watched as the Tri-V constructed an image of a system he'd visited before. The Four Horsemen had led a joint assault against this place, a staging area for Peepo's Mercenary Guild armies of occupation. A seemingly large part of her plan to enslave humanity, like the Veetanho had done with others. It hadn't quite proven to be as pivotal as they'd believed it to be.

Ultimately the Horsemen had taken the system, along with a lot of ships, resources, and even found some new recruits to their cause. Instead of a gut punch to Peepo's efforts, it was more of a tar baby, a trap intended to draw them away and bleed Earth's forces. It had also fed the Humans false intel that Earth would be vulnerable to recapture. In the end, it wasn't, and the Horsemen had been dealt a near fatal defeat at the First Battle of Earth.

"We bled in this system," Su said. "I'm not entirely happy to be back here."

"Me neither," Jim admitted, "but back we are."

Humanity had planned to hold the system. Home to a vast, rich asteroid belt, as well as a number of favorable LaGrange points (due to the trio of Jupiter-class gas giants), Golara had proven an ideal location for starship construction. The first yard was built by the Izlians more than 100,000 years ago. Dozens more had been built in the intervening time. Not even such a vast expanse of years, consuming the resources and churning out vessels, had been able to deplete even 5% of the system's riches.

As time went on, and successive wars took their toll, Golara had eventually been reduced to just four functioning yards. Then the

Great Galactic War came, and it changed hands from the Dusman to the Kahraman, then back again. By the end of the war 20,000 years ago, only two yards remained. They'd also changed hands several times, eventually ending up belonging to the Mercenary Guild itself.

It would have been an unbelievable asset to humanity, but there was zero chance they could hold it. Eventually, Peepo came to take it back, so the Horsemen did the only thing they could. They destroyed the last two functioning yards before ceding the system back to Peepo. She gained nothing but blood and ashes.

As Jim examined the Tri-V construct of the system, he could see that things hadn't remained the same. Sometime after they'd retreated and Peepo reclaimed it, the system had been reoccupied. Some of the infrastructure had been salvaged, other parts repaired, and industry returned. Someone had even moved some of the richer asteroids closer together and was using their harvested minerals to rebuild one of the yards. There were no ships under construction; there appeared to be a lot of work still to be done.

"At least the rumors are true," Captain Su said as the computer construct finished. "They're well on their way."

"I'm about to deal them a setback," Jim said. He doublechecked his pinplant records. "That asteroid, the biggest one they're working on."

"You sure about this?"

"Pretty sure," he said. *I have an ace in the hole that might work*, he thought. Along with the messages from Earth was a reply to an inquiry he'd made before leaving. Call it a missive to a higher authority, such as it was.

"*Unidentified ship, respond.*"

"This is EMS *Bucephalus*, here on business with the system administrators," Captain Su replied. "Uhm, can I ask who that is?"

"*Golara is a venture operated by the Transki Syndicate.*"

Shit, Jim thought. He'd hoped it was a small group allied together, or even an independent venture. Transki was large, maybe in the top 20 syndicates in the galaxy, possessing licenses from both the Merchants' Guild and the Trade Guild.

"*What is your business here,* Bucephalus?"

"We have a deal to offer to the operators regarding mining."

"*I'll pass along the deal, Tell me.*"

"We can only discuss it in person, at the mines. I need proof the commodity I'm interested in is present."

The comms were quiet for a time before the answer arrived. "*Very well. The administrator will meet you at the mining center; coordinates are being sent.*"

"I'm not sure if I'm glad or not," Captain Su said.

"Me neither," Jim replied, "but the die is cast. Let's see how it plays out."

* * *

Achilles looked up at Athena after the comms cut out. "I wonder what he's playing at?" he said.

"No clue," Athena answered. "I assume he's here for the Aku?"

"The turtles? Yes, I assume," Achilles said.

"Maybe they'll start a fight with us," Athena suggested, her eyes twinkling. "We haven't had any fun since Yovaz."

"*Osk'ii*, I've decrypted the message from command." Agamemnon handed Achilles the computer chip.

He slipped it into his slate and read it. "You sure of this?"

Achilles laughed and nodded. "Completely. All the codes match. She's now the only *Tor!*"

"What happened?" "What's going on?" "Tell us!" the others all demanded.

"Take it easy," Achilles said, holding up a hand. "Well, last month, J'asa returned to 2nd level hyperspace." They listened intently as he told them about the assassination attempt.

"They *didn't?*" Ajax roared, eyes wide in rage.

"They did," Achilles said. "Tried and failed."

"What happened afterward?" Athena asked.

"The *Tor* dissolved, and J'asa is now the only *Tor.*"

"She's the entire command?" Ajax asked.

"All of it," Achilles said. They stared at their *osk'ii* in stunned disbelief. "What's more, she's begun the evacuation. We're all descending to normal space."

"Then it's all true," Athena said. "We're returning to stay."

"It is," Achilles agreed. *For good or bad, whatever may come.* "Now, put all this out of your minds; Cartwright is going into a potentially dangerous situation. We need to be ready."

* * * * *

Chapter Sixteen

Transki Mining Operations, Golara System

*B*ucephalus took up a position a kilometer from the structure, which perched over the asteroid that dwarfed it. To Jim, the facility looked like a spider embracing an egg a thousand times its size. As he boarded the shuttle, Buddha was watching. "It all depends on you," he said.

"I'd rather you did this part and let me do the negotiating."

"You know I'm best at negotiating."

"Right. See you soon."

The shuttle sealed up, and soon they were en route to the facility, which had sent them a docking location while en route. It only took a few minutes for the pilot to shuttle them over. Jim was the only other person on the craft. As the pilot flew, Jim was alone with his thoughts. It seemed the longer he was in the game, the bigger the risk.

Only a few years ago, he was a kid in finishing school, dreaming about the day he'd learn the ropes, running his family's merc company. Maybe one day take over, after years of learning from his father, Thaddeus Cartwright. He never got the chance to study under his father. Thaddeus died on a mission, and Jim's mother took over the company as its steward. She was manipulated by Peepo, through the rat's operatives. Cartwright's Cavaliers was financially destroyed.

That had been the beginning of a plot to ruin the Four Horsemen, of course. Bankrupt the Cavaliers, ruin Asbaran in a series of no-win contracts, trap the Hussars and kill Alexis Cromwell, and finally trick the Horde into using a disguised bioweapon, unleashing it on Earth. One way or another, most of the plots had failed. The Cavaliers had gone bankrupt, yes, but Thaddeus had the forethought to leave behind the means for Jim to bring it back. Asbaran had been saved by Nigel Shirazi, Alexis had proven to be a far harder target than Peepo'd realized, and Sansar Enkh's Golden Horde had survived over the years by being more cunning than any adversary thought possible.

"Docking, Colonel," the pilot said.

"Thank you."

The shuttle slid into a standard Union adaptive docking bay, and was locked into place. A collar mated to the airlock door, and the shuttle's computer verified a hard dock. Jim floated over to the door and commanded it to open. The inside of the facility was on the other side, along with a pair of armed guards, both Besquith.

Swell. The person they'd spoken to had used a computer-generated voice, which didn't indicate what race they were. A half dozen races were movers within Transki, and the players changed on a regular basis, depending on internal politics. A hundred other races conducted business with them. The syndicates were nothing compared to the guilds, but that didn't mean they weren't powerful, their influence extending to all corners of the galaxy. Of all those he'd expected to run into, Besquith were not at the top of his list.

"Come with us, Human," one of them said, managing to make Human sound like a slur. The translator matrix within Jim's pinplants was quite advanced.

"Either of you two veterans of the Earth campaign?" he asked as he floated along with them.

"I fought you there," one of them said. Best described as a nightmare-influenced image of a werewolf, the Besquith's smile contained far more teeth than any race had the right to possess.

"Then you should be smart enough to show me some respect, *Pethrah*."

Both Besquith grabbed handholds, coming to a sudden stop. Jim had been sure to pronounce the word himself, not trusting their translators to render it into their language from English. It was hard to precisely word 'honorless gamma' and be sure it came out right.

"Problem?" Jim asked a second before one of the Besquith shot a hand out and grabbed Jim around the neck, pinning him against a hatch they'd been passing.

"Foolish Human, unarmed and vulnerable." The Besquith's muzzle moved to within millimeters of his nose. "You've always been far more confident than you deserve." His mouth opened, revealing the myriad of teeth and saliva. He snapped them closed, whiskers brushing Jim's cheek.

Jim didn't move, not even a fraction, except to put his hands behind him to brace against the doorway. "We earned our confidence by defeating your kind over and over again." The Besquith snarled, and Jim's hand found the door's control panel. A tiny contact on his forefinger touched the interface. A tiny smile crossed his face.

"I would enjoy eating you. There is so *much* of you."

"Funny," Jim said, "but wouldn't your boss be unhappy if you ate me before I made my pitch?"

"Perhaps," the Besquith said. "I can always eat you afterward." He pointed down the hall. "One more insult like that, and I'll deal with the aftermath with a full belly."

The other Besquith watched in either amusement or disinterest. Who could accurately decipher all the facial expressions of a were-wolf?

He was taken to a control room, likely the nerve center of the mining complex, a zero-gravity round space with a myriad of control stations, Tri-Vs, and dozens working at all of them. He saw a dozen different races. There were a lot of elSha and Jeha working at the stations; that was no surprise. A trio of Besquith, stunning in their dress, worked at the center. But in the main control position was a HecSha.

Recognizing individual aliens, regardless of the race, was always a hit or miss proposition. You grow up learning to tell your fellow Humans apart, not lizards or bipedal horses. HecSha looked a lot like dinosaurs, with relatively small distinguishing features between them. That said, Jim was pretty sure he recognized this one.

"Gob?"

"You recognize me, Cartwright? I am honored."

"You were a prisoner, turned over to the Peacemakers. You attempted *genocide* against my race, you bastard."

The huge old lizard laughed and shook his great flattened head. "Your race has some positive factors, you know. Resilience is one of them. Faith in a higher power doing what *you* think is right is not one of them."

"The evidence was overwhelming," Jim growled. "Thousands died."

"There was no definitive proof my viral agents caused those deaths, or that the virus was my own construction. We were just monitoring the primitive Humans as a Blazer team."

"Blazers are only for pre-contact civilizations."

"Maybe I was hoping you'd uplifted another race." Jim rolled his eyes. "I mean, three or four is impressive enough. Maybe you're on a roll?"

It took a moment for what the alien had said to sink in. "Wait, *three or four?* We've only uplifted the SalSha, and that was technically an accident."

"Sure, sure, I expected you to deny it." Gob shook his head and then his eyes narrowed at Jim. "Wait, are you saying you don't know about the others?"

"What others?"

"Interesting. People were wondering why none of them were spotted fighting on Earth or any of your colonies. I guess now I understand why."

"Gob, are you going to explain what you're talking about?"

The alien regarded Jim for a moment, then smiled, showing massive blunt teeth. "No, I don't think I will."

Jim inwardly fumed, mad at the lizard's lack of cooperation, and angrier at himself for letting Gob get under his skin. *Fucking asshole is probably lying, anyway.*

<Kill him, kill them all, bathe in their blood!>

For a moment, he considered it. There were a lot of Besquith around, but only four in the command center. Relieve one of his rifle, kill the other Besquith. After they were out of the way, the rest would be easy. The voice purred. *No,* he thought finally. *Bucephalus* would be at the mercy of any other ships in the system. *My Cavaliers are more important than killing these idiots.*

"You said you are offering a deal?" Gob asked. "Want to buy some materials for your little ship building project?"

He knows about that, too. Jim chewed back his anger and got back on track. "Actually, no. Tell me, how many Aku do you have here?"

Gob's eyes narrowed. "What are Aku?"

"Don't play stupid with me, Gob. You're too smart to pull it off."

Gob grunted. "What makes you think we have Aku here?"

"You aren't the only one with contacts in the galaxy, Gob."

"Whatever. We don't have any Aku here."

"Is that so." Jim pulled out a datachip.

Jim flipped it over to show the Peacemaker logo. "It's an injunction to investigate from the Peacemaker's Guild. Their fleet will be here in one week to seize any and all assets in connection with the enslavement of a race suffering from genocide."

"You're bluffing."

"Really?" Jim tossed the chip to him, spinning as it floated in zero G.

Gob caught the chip and slipped it into a reader. "There's nothing on it," Gob said, snorting. "You were bluffing."

"Well, you're right about one thing. I was bluffing about the Peacemakers. The chip was no bluff, though." The lights flickered in the command center.

Gob looked around wildly, then snatched the chip from his computer. "There can't have been anything dangerous on this chip, the computer would have detected it."

"There wasn't. Just a simple code. I put the virus into your system when those two idiots brought me here." Jim cocked his head at the Besquith by the door.

Jim hadn't been 100% certain the link on his finger had transferred the virus. Chiss had said it would; he'd seemed confident.

"Touch it to any computer and it will load itself," the Aku had told him. The chip was merely the activation code, nothing more.

"You don't have the sophistication for something like that."

"I'll admit, you're right. At least, we didn't until your little virus present was dissected. Gave us a lot of ideas. I should thank you for that." Computers went offline. The techs scrambled, not knowing what was going on.

"You'll die for this," Gob said, producing a weapon.

"Kill me, and I'll just be the first. After every computer here, every one in the system will be infected. After my ship leaves you to asphyxiate, the stargate will go, too. Anyone who comes to see what happened will be trapped. It'll take *months* for them to figure out what happened. By then, every living thing in the system will be dead; that's the downside of living on an asteroid."

"Your precious Aku will die as well."

"Better to die than live as a slave."

The Besquith looked at Gob, uncertain. More computers went offline. Calls were coming in from all over the system. The virus had spread at the speed of light. Jim grinned, and the voice cheered. Death on a massive scale.

He looked at Gob, the alien's eyes wide and teeth bared. After a second, he closed his eyes. Jim knew he was using his pinplants, probably trying to find and analyze the virus. It wouldn't be too difficult to find. Knowing the Aku, it would be a lot harder to stop. Chiss had called Gob's virus 'creative, but primitive.' Gob opened his eyes after only a minute. Some emotions weren't hard to read in most races. Gob was worried or scared.

"Your move, scumbag," Jim said.

"Kaag!"

"Yes, Gob," the big Besquith said.

"Call the mine supervisor, get all the entropy-cursed slaves up here."

"But, Gob…"

"*Just do it!*" Gob roared. The Besquith snarled, then grabbed its communicator.

"It will take at least an hour."

"You have six hours before it's irreversible. Load them directly into my docked shuttle."

"That will make it very close, Human."

"Then you better hurry. We won't broadcast the release code until the stargate is open."

"Tell them to hurry," Gob snarled at Kaag. The Besquith never stopped cursing.

Forty minutes later, Jim was floating in the lock to the shuttle. Inside were 63 confused Aku, their heads swiveling this way and that. They had no idea what was going on. He would explain *after* they were onboard *Bucephalus*. The merc ship was already accelerating toward the stargate. The shuttle would have to push hard to catch it. This, too, was part of the plan.

To Jim's surprise, Gob was there with the two Besquith. He estimated this was the most dangerous moment of the plan. The end, when Gob could decide killing him and trying to deal with the repercussions was just as good as trusting Jim.

"Cartwright," Gob said.

"Yes?"

"You better send those codes."

"I will keep my word," Jim said. "Unlike you, I keep my word."

"We won't forget this."

Jim grabbed the hatch handle. "I don't give a fuck. The Horsemen send their regards."

"Say hello to Zekta for me," Gob said as the door closed.

Who the fuck is Zekta? he wondered as they undocked. There was nothing in his pinplants on the name. He filed it away for later.

Three hours later, they'd rendezvoused with *Bucephalus*, and the stargate was opening on their approach. His mind hovered over the control that would broadcast the code to deactivate Chiss' virus.

<Don't do it.>

It isn't the HecSha and the Besquith I care about killing, he thought. *It's the innocents just working here or flying ships in later who'll be trapped and die horribly.*

<Let them die.>

"Stargate in 30 seconds, Colonel," Captain Su said.

Jim looked at the Tri-V showing the rapidly approaching stargate and sighed. The voice laughed, but he activated the transmission, sending the code to Gob.

<You are weak!>

Mercy is not for the weak.

<Revenge is better than mercy. They cannot hurt you again if they are all dead.>

Bucephalus passed through the stargate and away.

* * * * *

Chapter Seventeen

Earth Orbit, Sol System

Jim watched as Earth approached and settled in below his little window on *Bucephalus*, glad to be home at last. They were met shortly after arrival at Sol's emergence zone by an unregistered transport. Their cargo of 63 Aku were transferred to Chiss on his ship. The alien had been grateful beyond words.

"We have never experienced your like before, Jim Cartwright."

"What, someone who keeps their word?"

"Someone who risks their lives for us."

"That's what friends do for each other," Jim explained. "Take your people home now; they deserve to rest and learn they're free. I just wish we could find more of your kind. Sansar believes the rest were likely killed after the Peacemakers got involved."

"It is enough," Chiss said. "Our race can survive now."

The arrival at the Cavaliers' headquarters in Houston was more somber, as four body bags were carried down from the first *Phoenix* to land. He'd written the letters to the casualties' family members en route and transmitted them immediately upon arrival. That was always the hardest thing he ever did as a merc commander, and he hoped it never got easy.

The groundside staff were all in uniform, standing at attention next to the ship, as the injured were helped off the *Phoenix* into waiting medical transports. The KIAs were last off, and were placed into an unmarked transport. There were dozens of mortuaries in Houston who specialized in the dead from merc companies. Cartwright's had used the same one for its entire existence.

One of the body bags carefully loaded into the hearse was very small. They couldn't find many pieces of Private Snodgrass, another hazard of being a merc. Sometimes the caskets were empty, or nearly so. Once the dead were safely seen to the mortuary, Jim oversaw the rest of the Cavaliers' return to Houston. It was late in the evening before the men were released from duty to head home. When the last of them were gone, he finally headed home himself.

Splunk was still not back, and there were no messages from her. After the brief sensation of fear, there hadn't been anything else. He'd been busy most of the trip, and hadn't been able to dwell on her absence. He'd felt it most during the op on Yovaz. Now that he was home, his empty apartment made it feel all the lonelier.

The one message he'd gotten that made him smile was from Ziva. She said she was returning to Earth soon. The message was two weeks old, so she should be there soon. That was good news and made him smile as he finally climbed into bed. Tomorrow he'd report to the Federation Council.

* * *

"Minister Cartwright," the council president said, "we're pleased with the results of your tour of the colonies. Your diplomacy on Talus in particular was outstanding."

"Thank you," he said.

"Of course, the council is rather disappointed in the manner of your trip."

Jim shrugged. "I decided it was time."

"We agree," the president said. "It would have been *nice* if we could send the minister responsible for relations with the colonies along."

"The Federation is well over two years old. How long were you planning to wait?" He looked directly at the colonial relations minister as he spoke. She was an older woman with her hair up in a bun, and she looked *pissed.*

"There were matters of security," she insisted. "I've been in regular communications with all the colonies."

"Yes, they told me about your messages. Your requests for security on your proposed visits were most illuminating."

"Not everyone is a veteran mercenary," she said with a sniff.

"I would have been happy to provide security at any time you wanted, Madam Minister." He looked at the president. "My point is simple. I helped bring the Federation about with my actions, yet we're becoming known for *in*action. Is this how we're going to proceed?"

"Does the Federation want to be synonymous with the cowboy diplomacy of the 19th Century, Minister Cartwright?"

"More like merc diplomacy," Jim said. There were a lot of scowls around the room. "Do you know why Peepo invaded Earth? No? Me neither, at least not for certain. What I do know is *how* she invaded. We were weak. The easiest target imaginable. A dozen helpless colonies and a homeworld begging to be taken over. We did just about everything wrong, and *still* managed to survive, at massive loss of life."

He stood and pointed out the window. Kilometers away, across the vast expanse of the Houston Starport, the massive Raknar building was visible. "The Dusman are back. They've allied with us."

"That isn't official yet," the president reminded him.

"No, it isn't. That whole inaction thing again."

"Minister, I'm warning you."

"Warning me what, President? Warning me that I'm saying something I shouldn't? The Kahraman are out there, too. Other merc races have vendettas against us. The galaxy isn't a safe place. Winning the Omega War, or at least coming to a draw with the Peacemakers' help, didn't make us any safer. If anything, it drew a huge target on our backs. It announced to the galaxy that we're *dangerous*."

He used his pinplants to take command of the Tri-V in the room and threw up a montage of all the Raknar bases the Dusman had built on the other worlds. "All of this done without our knowledge. It was done, however, with the planetary leadership's approval. Fail to endorse the alliance with the Dusman at our own peril."

"Is that your advice?" the president asked.

"It has been from the beginning."

"You were against it when you discussed this servitor status," the foreign affairs minister reminded him.

"Absolutely," Jim agreed. "An alliance is in both our interests. We saw at our assault on Morgoth the sort of forces the Dusman have available already."

"An assault we did not approve of, and you were sanctioned for."

Jim made a dismissive gesture. He didn't give a shit about their sanction. "You've read the reports I filed, what the Science Guild was doing to the clones we've brought back. The Kahraman are a distant threat, but Minerva was the one at our feet."

"Was it wise to bring us into a conflict with a guild?" the president asked.

"Madam President, the guilds are already at war. The Horsemen acted in their own best interests, and the interest of the Federation."

"Maybe the Horsemen shouldn't be allowed to act without council approval," the minister of finance suggested. There were a couple of gasps and a hush of conversation.

"Bring it to a vote," Jim said, slapping his palm on the polished wood of the council chamber main table. "Do it, and you'll have my resignation, regardless of the outcome." He took a deep, calming breath. "It's *always* been the Four Horsemen for Earth, folks. It's seldom been Earth for the Four Horsemen. You don't control us, and you never will."

"Then what are you trying to do with the military you're building?" the finance minister asked.

"I'm trying to make it so humanity can stand on its own. You've read the report I filed about the action on Yovaz?" Heads nodded around the room. Nods, and scowls. "Don't even try to say I acted without permission. What I did, I did as a merc under merc law. My point was the facts of interplanetary conflict. Planets are arming themselves, and in some cases, already going to war with each other. Nigel is doing his best at the Mercenary Guild council, but he's only one member of dozens. The guild's inactions are bringing about uncertainty and war."

"We've read your reports on this Guild War," the president said. "We're just not sure it involves us."

"It involves us because we're a merc race. There's been no escaping that since the Iranians blew up the MinSha mercs guarding the Buma rep. It's all coming home to roost. We're not a monolithic merc race. In fact, we have nearly the lowest number of serving mercs of any race. We don't have the advantage of everyone being willing to fight. So we have to be sure those who will fight, can fight. Or the next time an alien armada shows up, they might decide it's easier to wipe us out. It's happened before and will probably happen again."

In the end, they hadn't known how to deal with what he'd said. They'd tabled it for later discussion, and Jim had gone back to his office. He spent a few more hours in his ministry office, compiling funding data and looking at the recruitment results in his absence, then returned to his office in the Cavaliers' HQ.

There he spent even more hours pouring over intel reports from his new intelligence group. Slow progress, and no results. Nothing from Minerva, not a peep. Damnit, he almost wished the psycho SI would *do* something. Now he was jumping at shadows. Too many threats lurking in the dark. He suddenly wondered if this was how ancient cavemen felt in the dark of the moonless nights.

In the end, he went home. Tomorrow he'd spend a day with the Dusman, going over Raknar pilot recruitment, and seeing how much progress had been made in the months he'd been gone. It was still good to be home…mostly. Tomorrow was another day.

* * * * *

Chapter Eighteen

J im fired his CASPer's jumpjets, rising over the low obstacle, and targeting the line of enemies. The suit instantly sent the target assessment data to his pinplants, and he responded by selecting specific targets and triggering the weapons. His arm-mounted minigun went *burrrrp!* and a stream of tungsten-tipped penetrators tore into the enemy, tearing them apart. He cut the jumpjets and plummeted 15 meters back below the building's edge, firing the jets again at the last second and flexing his knees. *Booom!* He hit the ground and used the forward leaning momentum to turn it into a run.

"Now *that* is how you execute a pop-up shot!" Double T yelled at the line of young cadre recruits as Jim turned and trotted back to the assembled group.

Jim had been watching the exercise for several hours, assessing the quality of the newest generation of CASPer drivers to sign up for a chance to be Cavaliers. When the entire class of 20 were unable to pull off even a reasonable attempt at the pop-up shot, he'd grabbed a CASPer for some suit time and demo.

When he approached the group of trainees, he popped the canopy so the trainees wouldn't be addressed by a metal machine. Those who recognized him gasped in surprise; the rest looked curious, but knew something was unusual by the other's reactions.

"When I first took to a CASPer, I could barely walk in it," Jim told them. "I was younger than all of you." He knew that because he'd approved their hiring, just like he did every Cavalier. "And in a *lot* worse shape," he said with a wry grin. Again, several of the recruits chuckled. "The pop-up shot is probably the second hardest thing you'll master, only outdone by a HALD drop."

Jim gestured at them all in their second-line Mk 7 suits. "Be sure not to blame your suits, either. Yeah, they're old and a bit worn, but so is every other Mk 7 in existence. I used one back then because that's all we had. I use it now, partly because I like them. Heavier and slower, yes, but they also have more armor and can carry more ordnance. The other reason is, I'm still a bit too big to fit comfortably in the Mk 8." He grinned and shrugged, something he couldn't do four years ago in the Mk 7. "I'd rather have elbow room than be a bit faster.

"What I'm trying to get at is, the Mk 7s are still plentiful and affordable. We have pallets of parts, and more available. Binnig made them so tough, most Mk 7s that are deadlined aren't junk; they end up being parted out. Plus Binnig started making new Mk 7 parts after the Omega War due to demand and a glut of new, unbought Mk 8s. If you don't end up making it through the Cavaliers' cadre program—" he paused and looked around the group, "—and many of you won't, odds are, you'll end up in a smaller company driving a Mk 7."

He pointed at Double T. "Listen to your training sergeants, follow the advice of the old timers, and learn as fast as you can. Trouble is coming. Trust me, I know." He didn't wait for any of the recruits to ask questions, he buttoned back up, and departed with a roar of his jumpjets.

"*Great pep talk, Boss,*" Double T said over the command channel.

"Thought they needed it. I remember how hard that maneuver was."

"*It is, but you said push these kids.*"

"I did, and still do."

"*What about that trouble?*"

"Between the SIs and this growing warfare between worlds? It's a sure bet."

"*You're the boss, Boss.*"

Jim grinned as he stuck the landing 100 meters away. He figured since he was already suited up, he'd get some trigger time in. He headed to the range to expend some ammo. The Cavaliers had spent a lot of credits on the range facilities over the years, buying up abandoned malls, housing areas, and even old, disused oil refineries. If the aliens' arrival had done one thing good for the planet, it had pushed it off burning carbon-based fuel for power.

Fusion really changed the game. The only ones who saw that coming had been the Arabs, and their response was to bomb the UN while they tried to negotiate with the aliens. Of course, that didn't work out well either, since Iran ceased to exist under the gentle ministrations of the MinSha.

Jim finished a combat run in the mall, then did a quick spin through the industrial section before calling it quits. The kids were still doing drills in the high-density residential target zone. Double T was taking the opportunity to incorporate their experience with the tanks from Yovaz. Made sense. He could still remember the number of tanks from the Weapons Cartel. Thousands, at least.

As he worked his way back to the armory, he reflected on other lessons they could incorporate, also considering how non-merc combat might influence their deployments. The "Rules of War" the mercs operated under didn't apply to individual races in many ways. As in, the primary method of enforcement involved sanctions from the Mercenary Guild Council. If you weren't a merc, you wouldn't care about being fined by a governing body with no authority over you.

Now if you went over the top and nuked your enemy from orbit, employed bioweapons, or went all genocidal, the Peacemakers were likely to get involved. Likely, but not guaranteed. After all, the Aku were nearly extinct before the Peacemakers got fully involved, and, even then, their efforts were lackluster at best.

Jim walked his suit into the main armory and backed it into a support harness. Once engaged, the computers began running diagnostics, automatically locked all the weapons, and opened his cockpit. As he waited for the power-down sequence, he remembered the discussion after they'd finished the battle at Morgoth. The discussion about the SIs in general, in relation to what they'd learned about Minerva, suggested there were probably many more of them around.

Have they been running the show all along? Jim wondered. Nigel would certainly be on the lookout in the Mercenary Guild, going forward. His former girlfriend, Adrianne, had even hinted they had an SI captive at their secretive Section 51 headquarters.

"Say hello to Zekta."

Gob's words as they were leaving Golara came to mind as he was showering adjacent to the armory. He hadn't thought about the Hec-Sha's words since they'd picked up the Aku. They'd been a handful to care for on the ride back to Earth. Being newly freed slaves, it wasn't really their fault. But he'd been thinking about how the

Peacemakers had just quit after they'd saved the tiny core population on the Aku homeworld.

A search of the word, or name, on the Aethernet had found no matches. He was still going over it in his mind again, and again later in his office. That evening Ziva showed up, and he completely forgot about Gob, the Aku, and whatever Zekta was.

* * * * *

Chapter Nineteen

Cartwright's Cavaliers' Headquarters, Houston, Terran Federation, Earth, Sol System

"Well, you look like you did something fun last night," Buddha said as he walked into the office. Of course Jim's XO had found out about him and Ziva as soon as it happened. He wasn't surprised, either.

"Ziva and I had a fight," he admitted.

"Oh, that's bad, Jimbo. Everything okay?"

"Yeah, we went to Knuckle Sandwich and got in a bar fight."

Buddha stopped, hand on the office door handle, eyes blinking. "I'm sorry, did you say a *bar fight?*"

Jim did his best, but in the end, he laughed. "Yeah." He explained that they'd been at his place, and then he got all crazy and accused her of walking out on him. Well, she hadn't planned any sort of thing, so they'd yelled at each other, and she left. He'd gotten pissed, broke a coffee table, and then Fssik had shown up to tell him he was an idiot.

"When a Depik says you're an idiot…"

"Yeah," Jim said. "I know." He finished his story about how he'd gone to the bar, apologized, and they'd spent the evening drinking and dancing.

"Sounds innocent enough."

"It was. You know about Knuckle Sandwich?"

"Heard of it. A lot of the starport people work there. Tough place, after hours."

"And we were there until after hours." Buddha nodded his head. "It was all good until some meathead grabbed Ziva."

"From what I've heard about her, she's been trained by the Depik, right?" Jim nodded. "So I'm sure she could take care of herself."

"She can, but I kinda lost it."

"What, you punch the guy?"

"And his friend, and a few strangers. Ziva might have cut someone's hamstring…"

"Holy fuck!"

Jim chuckled, remembering the orgy of violence, then grinned bigger when he remembered the other aftermath at home. He shook himself out of the recollection and grinned shyly. "It's not as bad as it sounds."

"I hope not," Buddha said seriously. "Especially considering the way you were smiling when you talked about it."

"Was I? I didn't realize." He tried to make himself more serious. "Sorry, it's just been fun having her back and everything." Buddha looked at him suspiciously, but Jim just stared back. "So, what's up?"

He and Buddha spent several hours going over the budget for C Company, which was almost to readiness status. Then he went over the Federation TO&E, or Table of Organization & Equipment, for the basic Heavy Mobile Infantry company—what the Federation was calling their CASPer-equipped soldiers. The finance minister was going into cardiac arrest over the budget.

Back in the early 21st Century, it cost around half a million to train and equip a basic infantryman, or about 5,000 credits. A single

CASPer Mk 8, even at the discount the Federation Military was expecting, ran 350,000 credits. Add another 50,000 for training and basic equipment brought it to a 400,000-credit bill. Jim had wanted at least a full battalion of HMI. Following the standard established by Human mercs of 10 per squad, two squads per platoon, two platoons per company, and two companies per battalion, that added up to 80 soldiers. A cool 32 million credits.

Ongoing training, maintenance of the suits, salaries of staff, and support staff, meant another 3-5 million a year, ongoing. He'd proposed a force disposition within 10 years of two brigades, with those structured as holding five battalions each. Eight hundred CASPer-trained and equipped soldiers represented an investment of 320 million credits.

There were enough credits in his budget to go forward with the first company, and Jim had been forming the training programs as well as personnel. Tapping the current body of retired mercs was helping. Many of them had been caught helpless when Peepo invaded. Telling them they could help make sure something like that never happened again was an incentive. Offering at least a partial refund on previous credits paid in taxes was an even bigger incentive.

He was in his Federation office the next day when the final budget numbers came in from contractors. That included acquiring former US military property for the base. He thought Fort Hood was a good location. Fitting, actually. With the manufactory Alexis had loaned them, F11 from the Aku, and the quickly growing asteroid mining operation providing raw materials, they had the makings of a real military.

"Five years," he said aloud. "We just need five years to get ourselves to the point we can defend ourselves." *What about the Dusman?* a voice in the back of his mind said. "Yeah, what about them?" he asked the empty office.

He started getting official messages from the colonies he'd visited. They included budget proposals, outlines of military development, and requests for advice. For the first time, he actually felt like he was doing the job they'd hired him to do.

Talus reported the first two classes had begun basic training. The instructors were from a core of experienced mercs, and some from the government's previous 'secret police.' They'd all been carefully screened, and the Dusman were monitoring all activity around them. One was arrested two days after training started. He'd been caught trying to recruit for a new "Council" like the old one.

Governor Allen was staying true to his word, holding anyone caught trying to revive the old regime and conducting detailed investigations. *Legal* investigations; no kangaroo courts. The arrest of the instructor had resulted in the rounding up of another two dozen co-conspirators. Those found guilty weren't executed, but put to work in the burgeoning asteroid mining efforts. Jim nodded in approval; that was progress for Talus.

The other colonies showed small progress as well. Of course, they were much smaller than Talus, with a proportionately smaller pool of talent to draw from. Any progress was good progress was the position he was taking as he drafted a report to the Federation Council.

Jim had made some inquiries to the Federation Intelligence Service. It was further along than his own, but still not fully up and running. These things took time. He'd asked Sansar to help, but she hadn't been able to yet. No reason was given. He wondered if something big was up and it was drawing all her attention. Seemed possible.

* * *

J im had been finding even the mind-numbing number crunching at the ministry office tolerable lately. Having a lovely woman at home most nights helped a lot. It was a week after the events at Knuckle Sandwich before he began to worry about it. There'd been a bit on the news that night. One of the punks had suffered brain damage. He wasn't worried about the asshole; he was worried because the startown PD had opened an investigation.

He went out to inspect the Raknar complex to take his mind off the incident. He found it partly abandoned. There were only a couple dozen Dusman doing technical work on the Raknars and Humans moving equipment, doing maintenance, or storing newly arrived materials. None of the senior Dusman were present, in particular Dante, who seemed to spend his every waking moment in and around the Raknar.

The trainee Humans were housed in a barracks near the Raknar, and they were occupied watching Tri-Vs of operational instructions. Jim and Splunk had filmed some of them just after the Omega War; others had been recorded by the Dusman with an eye toward teaching their Human pilots. He asked around about when the last time was that anyone had seen Dante or the senior *vok'aka*, or trainers.

"A little over two months ago," was the answer. The trainees had been informed an important operation was underway and to continue studying until the trainers returned.

He talked to a few of them, especially the ones recruited after he'd left on his colony visit tour, and then returned to his Cavaliers' office. Jim sat at his desk, staring at his office computer long into the night, worrying what might be going on, and afraid of the answer.

He left and returned home. Just after he got there, he got a call from Lieutenant Johnson.

"Colonel, I wanted to report on some actionable intel."

"What's up?"

"*Well, we have several reports that indicated known provocateurs are operating in Austin.*"

"We've been aware of that for some time. They're likely trouble-makers from the US. Sansar had a report on them just last month. I read it while I was off world."

"*That's true, Colonel. However, those reports were correlated with this. A local Austin police unit found a parked car with laser weapons in the trunk. They looked like they were salvage from the occupation, except when they were evaluated, they were all found in perfect working order.*"

Jim had been about to get annoyed at being bothered over another report, until the last. Lieutenant Norman H. Johnson, III had been picked because he was recommended by Sansar, an intelligence professional with decades of experience. Adding the part about the lasers sealed the deal.

"What did you do about it?"

"*I sent the only asset I had available. Ziva.*"

Shit. "What's her op?"

"*She's investigating the provocateurs and following up with the weapons claims.*"

"Okay," he said. "When she reports in, ping me. *Immediately.*"

"*Yes, Colonel.*" Johnson paused. "*Should I not have sent her, Colonel? I was under the impression you had confidence in her and that she's been trained by Depik?*"

"No, you did fine. Thanks for calling me."

He didn't get to sleep until late.

* * * * *

Chapter Twenty

Eesius, 2nd Level Hyperspace

"Newest scout reports, *Tor.*"

J'asa took them without comment, feeding the chip into her workstation and examining it. "Has *Vok'tor* Dante seen this?"

"Yes, *Tor.*"

"Very well," she said and stared at the data. They'd been working for two months to prepare, and the enemy had started an offensive right on time, unfortunately. The tactical assessment said it was no worse an offensive than the last three, but with forces greatly reduced, and the exodus due to begin, their attack had the potential for disaster.

The alarm sounded, preempting her opportunity to plan a cohesive response. She checked her slate. The attack was underway. "Fuck."

"Sorry, *Tor?*" the aid asked.

"A Human word," she said and waved him away, then grabbed her comms unit. "*Vok'tor* Dante?"

"*I'm on it,* Tor," Dante replied immediately. "*We're scrambling two stars of interceptors.*"

"No, don't. Launch all available drones."

"*Tor, there are only 200 left here; the rest have all been taken down already. We won't be able to recover any of them.*"

"And if the interceptors aren't enough, we'll be overrun, and we'll lose all the interceptor pilots. The drones can be replaced; the pilots cannot. Do as you are ordered."

"*As you order,* Tor."

She had to smile at the sneer in Dante's voice. He didn't really care what caste she was now, or her position within that caste. He never changed.

"We have to move up the schedule," she said to herself. She looked once more at the scout data, then shook her head. *No, we cannot delay, not even in the face of this offensive.* They couldn't afford a series of defensive actions that would cost them forces they couldn't afford to lose. She cursed for a moment. English, as a language, lacked many of the deeper nuances of her own, not the least was empathic elements. It was effective for invectives and cursing, though.

She contacted her assistant. "Everything is moved from the habitation domes to the transports?"

"*Yes,*" Sla'etou confirmed.

J'asa nodded. The creches and the most vulnerable of their people were already gone. Most of what was left was infrastructure, Eesius itself. What was a structure? Not its people, surely. She was letting the attachment to a thing affect her decisions. That was a waste of time and effort. They were never going to hold it when the majority of her forces were below.

"Very well, I've made my decision. Have the last essential modules forcefully detached and towed to the largest transport. All personnel, fall back to the final transport. We're leaving the rest."

"*As you say,* Tor. *Some will be disappointed.*"

"Their disappointment will be tempered by what awaits us on the other side."

All the preparation and careful planning disintegrated as thousands of Dusman exploded into action. Forces raced to temporary defensive positions in case the drones failed. J'asa moved to her personal ship and watched as the drone bays in Eesius were emptied. The scouts were on their way back in as the drones formed up and accelerated in the 2nd level hyperspace medium. In moments, they passed each other, and the sickle-shaped enemy fighters came flashing in.

Explosions filled the strange space, drones and fighters sparred in ways impossible in normal space. Near instant deceleration followed by a turn that would have inflicted thousands of Gs on their pilots. Lasers, missiles, and mesons lashed at each other. Some of the enemy fighters flashed and died, and more of the drones were destroyed.

There was nothing for J'asa to do personally except listen to the reports of the logistics teams and watch the distant battle unfold. The drones had been programmed to hold nothing back, unlike before. She prayed to whatever might be listening that the enemy wouldn't see it as a desperate move. *Think we have more drones in reserve, please.* Twenty minutes passed, an hour since the alarm had been raised. Shuttles flew from Eesius to the ships in a constant stream.

She didn't need anyone else to analyze the situation; it was clear there wouldn't be enough time. Half the drones were gone, but only a quarter of the enemy fighters. Once they'd reduced the drone force enough, she knew their ships would follow.

J'asa was moments from ordering a halt to the evacuation when the enemy fighters suddenly turned away. In all their eons of waring, the enemy had never quite got the hang of dealing with a bluff. The drones didn't pursue, but returned to their ready positions, as if it were just another counterattack.

The announcement of "All Ready" came sooner than she'd hoped it would. In the intervening time since she'd been named *Tor*, the people had come to accept the change, if not fully understanding why. Many had been excited by a *j'apo's* coming without realizing the implications. Now the excitement was building, along with an undertone of fear. Momentum had a way of overcoming trepidation and uncertainty.

"The *Nee'Akee* has been attached to the rest of the ships," announced the *akl'a*, or master shipbuilder. It was the last major component to be evacuated.

"The Arsenal is ready as well?" J'asa asked. Of all the parts she was concerned about—thousands of Dusman, equipment, supplies, and a million other things—the Arsenal was probably the most crucial. An artifact of their power from 20,000 years ago, it was absolutely key to anything she hoped to do, and likely to their very survival.

The *akl'a* looked at her and sighed.

"You're not confident."

"No, *Tor*, I am not. Moving the Arsenal here was a move of pure desperation. We have no way of knowing if it was damaged in the process. It is far too vast, far too old, and much of it a mystery for us to even be sure of what we're seeing."

More mysteries of lost knowledge, she lamented. The *akl'a* and her predecessors had spent centuries combing through the *Nee'Akee* for every tiny bit of knowledge on the Arsenal that could be harvested. It wasn't much. It made her feel like a primitive animal that had discovered a spaceship. It also made her angry at the former *Tor* for ignoring the priority of relearning what had been lost in the Betrayal.

"Send the Arsenal first," she decided. The *akl'a* looked dubious. "This way, if the effort fails, we're still here and can maybe find another way. It's better than nothing."

"Understood, *Tor*."

Minutes later, the countdown was concluded. J'asa watched through a live Tri-V feed as the Arsenal flashed, a rainbow discharge of every color imaginable, then its multi-kilometer-long bulk was gone. She let her breath out in a whoosh.

"*K'apo* in normal space confirms the Arsenal has arrived safely."

"Quickly," she said, "before the enemy can respond, all others go!"

The dozens of ships and transports flashed similar rainbow ripples and disappeared in quick order. J'asa's command *Ogleesius*-class battlecruiser was the last to vanish. For the first time in untold thousands of years, there were no Dusman in 2nd level hyperspace. The artificial construct they'd called Eesius after the long-passed architect of their race's survival was a now a collection of empty shells. Lights still shone where power sources hadn't been removed, or couldn't be, to keep life support working until the end of the evacuation. But nobody was there to see them. Until the enemy arrived.

They moved in slowly, carefully poking through the remnants left behind. Many times the Dusman had tricked them. It took many hours for the enemy to become convinced this wasn't yet another deception. Eventually the abandoned base was occupied, examined, studied. They knew where their enemy had gone, the invader that had so long thwarted their efforts. They just couldn't pursue the Dusman. At least, not yet.

* * * * *

Chapter Twenty-One

The *Phoenix*-class dropship touched down on the runway and taxied toward the terminal. Jim relaxed in the only occupied seat. He found it funny, even after so many life-and-death situations he'd found himself in, that he still got nervous dropping from orbit in a dropship. If he was in his Raknar or a CASPer, it would be no big deal. Maybe he'd talk with Ziva about it; she was so understanding.

As the dropship parked and the rear cargo ramp cycled down, the already humid Houston afternoon air swirled in. Spring came early and didn't stay long before giving up to summer. He remembered spending half his life playing indoors at the family mansion. Maybe one day it would go up for sale again and he could buy it back. The estate was the only real thing left from his father's era he wished he had back.

The dropship pilot trotted back to check on him. "You okay, Colonel?"

Jim chuckled. "Not my first drop, son," he said. The pilot, probably a couple years older than he was, looked flustered. Jim held up a hand. "It's okay. You're new, right?"

"Two weeks ago," he admitted. "Been training dirtside, came up as soon as *Bucephalus* arrived back home."

Jim nodded. He knew they'd hired a lot of starship crew in preparation for the ships soon to roll out of the manufactory. This man was one of them. "It was a good flight, Lieutenant," he said to placate him. The man nodded his thanks. "Orders showed you were to station here at the base for a few days for training?" The pilot nodded again. "Good. Get your bird turned around, in case we need you."

"Something brewing, sir?"

"I don't know," Jim admitted as he shouldered his rucksack and walked down the ramp. A hypersonic *craaack* made him look around. Another ship was coming around on final. It fired breaking engines, so he knew it was an orbital craft. A second later, he could discern the smooth lines and curved wings. *Dusman*, he thought.

The Dusman shuttle landed and taxied off the main runway, directly to the Raknar/Dusman facility. As Jim walked toward his offices, he saw it park, the ramp drop, and a 10-member team of Konar trot out and into the building.

"Hmm," he said, shrugged, and headed into his office.

He was still trying to catch up a week after getting home. Of course, there were hundreds of hours of undone work. He was still going over various reports and communiques from the Federation. One of the first things he did upon his return was make sure there was no mention of the Aku, either from the trip back with the ones he'd emancipated, or the ones already in the system. Not a word, no sightings, nothing. *As long as it stays that way.*

This flight to orbit had been to oversee starship progress and 'inspecting' the first orbital defense platform. It wasn't much more than a hub and framework that would become rings in a few years, but what it was right then was almost 1,000 good paying jobs for Federation citizens.

Inspections were a huge waste of time—except when he found problems, which he did more often than not. Frankly, he was quickly losing his patience with the job, especially when it took him away from Ziva for several days. Of course, she was still in Austin. Her reports looked worrisome. He was considering recalling her and handing it over to the Federation Intelligence Service. If something was going hot, he didn't want to risk his own people.

As it was getting later, he watched the soda on his desk rattle in the glass, and he craned his neck. The Raknar base was two kilometers away, but he could see a trio of the 30-meter-tall behemoths lumbering along. They had a slight amount of grace, which meant the trainees were learning. *I should be there with them,* he thought. His next Raknar session was four days away. The Dusman had returned, finally. No explanation, just returned. But Splunk hadn't shown up yet.

As the end of his day approached, and he'd switched to ministry business, dictating his inspection report, he found himself composing his resignation. Jim had agreed to be the minister of war when they'd drafted him for a term of not more than five years. He'd only been doing it two. That didn't change his feelings.

Though he was due to leave for the day, he brought his office's main Tri-V online and examined the timetables. The colony military training was on schedule on Talus, and not far off with the others. If he moved this there, and that over here...He grumbled and played with the schedules. Another year, maybe less, and the process would have a momentum all its own. Be hard to fuck it up.

"At that point, why am I here?" He sighed. Then he wrote an email to Sansar. *"Please give me a list of possible replacements for minister of war. Thanks."* and sent it off. There. He'd taken the first step.

His office door opened, and a Dusman in their customary dark-red uniform, a holstered pistol, an eyepatch, and a cybernetic arm came in.

"Hi, Dante," Jim greeted him. "What do you need?"

The Dusman walked over and hopped up on his desk, just like Splunk would have. He never expected one of them to talk to him from the floor. Even sitting, Jim towered over the aliens, who were only 70 centimeters tall on a good day. Their upright posture didn't emphasize height, either.

"Trainee report, *Osk'ka*," he said and handed him a standard Union slate.

He took it and examined the numbers. "Only another five?" he asked, looking up.

"Correct," Dante said. "The number of false positives is increasing."

The recruiting program used a carefully concealed test to evaluate possible candidates. Jim had gotten the minister of education to slip the test into the end of the Voluntary Offworld Assessments—or VOWs—by explaining it as a proposed expansion. They'd extended it to older people as well, by offering retakes to anyone under 50 years old.

"Why, do you think?" Jim asked Dante.

"I think someone figured out your fake tests," the Dusman said.

"That's a big help," he replied peevishly. The Dusman shrugged. Dante wasn't one of Jim's friends in the Dusman, mainly because his faction of the race had been in favor of remaining in 2nd Level hyperspace, where most of their kind had stayed since the end of the Great Galactic War 20,000 years ago. He was a good trainer and warrior, but he followed Jim's leadership only grudgingly.

"I'll take it under advisement," Jim said.

The Dusman nodded, started to leave, then paused.

"Something else?"

"J'asa will be back soon," he said.

Jim never had gotten used to Splunk's real name. The ranks were hard enough. "Good."

"Yes, she has been busy."

"What's going on?" Jim asked finally.

"What do you mean?"

"I'm just a Human, but even I can tell you guys are up to something. Too many of you were missing for a long time while I was gone. Splunk, I mean J'asa, has never been absent this long without explanation. Dusman ships, transports—*big* transports—coming and going. And it's not the colony Raknar project. It's something else. Tell me."

Dante's single eye examined him for a long moment, his ears curling slightly in a sign of amusement. "You know, I don't think much of Humans in general."

"No shit?" Jim replied, not in the mood to duel with the grizzled old alien.

"I think your race is reckless, prone to snap judgments based on emotions, and often gets into shit so deep you can't breathe without getting a mouthful."

"It's pretty apparent what you think of us, *Vok'sa*," Jim said, using Dante's official rank. To his surprise, Dante looked upset at hearing the rank. No, not upset, offended? *Wait, what's going on now?*

"I said that about your race, Jim Cartwright," Dante said after he'd composed himself. "You and a few others, on the other hand, show potential. J'asa will explain everything when she gets back, probably tomorrow." Without another word, the Dusman jumped off his desk and left.

"Glad to see you, too," Jim said, adding, "fucker," after the door was closed.

While there was more work, he decided it was time to go home and get some sleep. He wanted to check out the new Raknar recruits tomorrow. He'd just stood up when his phone buzzed. "Shit," he said, and pressed the button. "Colonel Cartwright."

"*Colonel, it's Lieutenant Johnson in intel.*"

He felt cold rush through his guts. "Lieutenant, what's happening?"

"*Riot underway in Austin. Not spontaneous. It's bad, and Ziva's in the middle of it.*"

* * *

Athena shook Achilles awake in their little observation room hidden behind Jim Cartwright's office. "What's happening?" he asked.

"We don't know. He got a call and ran out."

Achilles rolled out of the hammock he'd been snoozing in. The space was barely sufficient for the watch team of two, so they shared a hammock. Considering he and Athena had mated a couple times, it wasn't a bad deal. His race didn't have nearly the hang-ups over reproduction the Humans did, thank the infinite.

He pulled on his dark red duty uniform and was at the computer in only a few moments. Athena had already cued up the recording for him.

"Colonel, it's Lieutenant Johnson in Intel."

"Lieutenant, what's happening?" Cartwright's voice was clear and easy to understand. The other person was the one running the Cavaliers' new intelligence agency. They were headquartered in an old underground bunker. The problem for the Dusman was that they'd been unable to penetrate its systems. The other Human, Sansar Enkh, had helped set it up. Her computer experts were infuriatingly efficient. Digging a tunnel 50 meters down without the Humans noticing wasn't practical.

"Riot underway in Austin," the Human deep underground said. *"Not spontaneous. It's bad, and Ziva's in the middle of it."*

"What does he mean by 'not spontaneous?'" Achilles asked Athena.

Athena made a face and tapped on her slate as Achilles watched the recording play out, with Cartwright closing the call and heading to the elevator, traveling down to the Intel bunker.

"I'm not finding anything significant about the word," Athena said, indexing the Human English language against their own. "Most reliable translation is instant. No instant protest? This makes no sense."

Achilles made an angry face and thought. The Human female, Ziva, was Cartwright's newest mate. He had been vigorously mating with her every chance he got. Humans managed to turn a biological function into an hours long gluttony of emotions and sensual experiences. He honestly didn't get it.

"Anything more from him?" he asked.

"Nothing yet," Athena confirmed. "I have all assets monitoring for anything out of their secure area."

Achilles idly scratch an ear, considering the implications. The Humans' propensity to complain about everything, which they called protests, was a major societal issue he believed servitorship could have helped relieve. They spent far too much time worrying about what to do, or what someone else was doing, instead of doing what *needed* to be done. While he pondered, Athena contacted the resident expert on Human psychology, the *k'apo* stationed at the Raknar installation nearby. By the way Athena's eyes were rolling up in her head, it was clear the *k'apo* was giving her a lengthy description on Human behavior. J'asa's sister, Seldia, was almost normal compared to many of her fellow *k'apo*.

He guessed talking across the universe must have a destabilizing effect on their mental condition. *K'apo* only occurred in 1 out of 10,000 births. They were immediately noticed due to their strange coloring, a metallic-looking tint in their fur. Even if it wasn't for this, they would have been quickly spotted in their creche just by their behavior. Regardless, he's always considered it odd that the foremost xenologists in their society were all *k'apo*. *Maybe the strange understand the strange?*

Finally, Athena ended her conversation; whether she'd gotten everything she wanted or not, Achilles didn't know. "The *k'apo* says that a spontaneous protest is of less concern to Human authorities than a non-spontaneous protest. A non-spontaneous protest, something she called a 'riot,' is usually the prelude to an armed attack of some kind."

"Damn," Achilles said and grabbed his own comm. He pressed the control for base command. "*Vok'ka*, this is *Osk'ii* Achilles. We have a potential deployment situation. No, not Raknar. There may be an armed action imminent elsewhere in this sub-nation. Index city called Austin. My Konar team needs ready transport there. Time? Within the hour. Affirmative. Out." He turned off the comms and turned to Athena. "Have the team ready to deploy."

"Word already sent." She gave him a smile full of sharp teeth. "Been weeks since I killed anything."

"Remember, this is likely a Human-on-Human conflict, so we have to be judicious about *who* we kill."

"Me?" she asked, the grin getting bigger. "I'm always judicious about killing."

* * * * *

Chapter Twenty-Two

Insertion Shuttle, Descending Over Austin, Terran
Federation, Earth, Sol System

"*The big Human can move fast when females are involved,*" J'op said as the shuttle finished its parabolic trajectory, throwing the occupants into freefall.

"*There's more than his female,*" Athena said. "*This appears to be an anti-Federation organized insurrection.*"

"*Who cares about their Federation?*" Hector asked. "*They'll all eventually serve us anyway.*"

"It matters because it's a stabilizing force with the Humans," Achilles explained. "I thought you'd all studied Human history. Absent a strong, controlling central authority, they immediately begin killing each other to see who's in charge."

"*This is what a non-caste society looks like,*" Agamemnon added. "*Much of their lives are taken up by a search for power.*"

"We're not immune to that," Achilles interjected. "Have you already forgotten what happened to Tor J'asa?"

"*We have not forgotten,*" Ajax said. "*It makes us all look bad.*"

That was something they could all agree with. Achilles hoped the Humans didn't find out about what had transpired to put J'asa in charge.

"*On course for deployment,*" the *ske'a* told them. "*Time on target, eight minutes.*"

"Understood," Achilles said. "Prepare for deployment."

The clock ticked down, and the *ske'a* opened the rear doors right on time. The 10 Konar dove out of the back into the twilight over Austin. Achilles thought the city was like any other Human city. Too large, too spread out, and too brightly lit. The Humans seemed almost afraid of the night. Dusman preferred less light, rather than more. Their large eyes were well suited for the dark.

Inside their Konar, the light was kept to a minimum. Tiny superadvanced Tri-Vs projected images directly into their eyes, making it feel to the operators as if they were standing outside, wearing nothing. The suits' limbs, jumpjets, and weapons responded to subtle physical cues from the operators, who themselves were trained in suit operation from the moment they left their creche. Their *J'Zha* was among the toughest and longest there was.

The Konar dropped like darts from 50 kilometers, quickly breaking the sound barrier, barely feeling anything inside their suits. Their adaptive armor formed a more aerodynamic shape, allowing their speed to far exceed what would have been normal for a humanoid object their size. Achilles watched the air speed pass Mach 3, then decrease again as the air got thicker.

"*Cavaliers have begun their drop,*" he was notified via comms. A *Feesius*-class had altered its orbit to provide a high vantage point on the basic operation.

"Acknowledged," he replied. Meanwhile, their Konar were busily mapping data as quickly as their sensors could receive it. This wasn't like Yovaz, though. That had been a small, mostly abandoned industrial target. This city called Austin had a population of millions, and most of them seemed to be on the streets at the moment.

"Narrow scans to potential targets," he informed his team. "Energy signature sufficient for weapons, explosions, fires, and any weapons fire." The rest acknowledged. The previously slow to assemble map leaped forward in complexity.

Three areas of the city were experiencing the most protesting, or rioting, whatever the Humans chose to call it. It was too soon to see where Cartwright was jumping. If he picked wrong, he would be many kilometers away from his charge. They were below 20 km; he had to make up his mind fast.

"The female," he suddenly said. "Cartwright's mate."

"*What about her?*" Athena asked.

"Her status here was part of the message. Cartwright isn't supposed to get personally involved in a battle for the Human government. I think her presence here is his reason for disobeying those orders. Locate her."

Agamemnon went to work, coordinating with the *Feesius* in orbit. Achilles watched as the altimeter spiraled down toward zero. They were below 15 kilometers when the answer arrived.

"*Got the female,* Osk'ii," Agamemnon said, and a spot lit up on the map, the furthest combat zone from where they were falling.

"Entropy, it figures," he said. "Team, alter flight profile immediately!"

They converted from drop profile to landing and came in quietly as a team, landing on the roof of a building. Achilles didn't know the structure's purpose, only that it was big enough. "Verify the perimeter," he ordered, "then let's get eyes on Cartwright. He should be dropping in any time." Nearby, a rooftop lit up with gunfire directed skyward. Achilles smiled; he had his first target.

* * *

chilles and his team leapfrogged over three buildings, saving power on their suits. Unlike the Human CAS-Pers, the Konar didn't use fuel to fire rockets, they used power to drive super-efficient micro turbines. That allowed the *Osk* more flexibility by balancing power against need. They wouldn't run out of fuel at a critical moment, as long as they still had power. Konar could also recharge from almost any power source in a pinch. Their only limitation on endurance was the operator's physical survival and potential life support.

If their jets had a downside over the Humans' jumpjets, it was response speed and noise. The jumpjets were quick in response because there were no jet components that needed to spin up, and while the jumpjets were rockets, they were actually quieter, because the rocket chambers were inside the suit's armor.

As Achilles' team cleared the second roof en route to their target, the enemy manning the antiaircraft guns heard the scream of the Konar jump turbines, even over the hammering of the guns. *Entropy*, he cursed as he took evasive action. A laser deflected off his shoulder, and others flashed out at the rest of his squad. He'd wanted to keep it neat and quiet, engage the gunners at close range so nobody knew they'd been there. That option was gone.

"Take them out," he said, and all 10 Konar opened fire with their lasers, even as they angled in for a landing.

The Humans manning the guns had partial cover, and used it to effect. Achilles saw several cut down, though more were still active. Two of them, through plan or luck, both concentrated fire on Paris. The Konar armor was effective at defending against lasers because of its control over reflective armor plating. When hit by two lasers at once, though, it was easily overwhelmed. Paris' Konar was penetrated, center mass. Achilles watched him die in an instant.

The rest of the team landed and killed the remaining Humans in hand to hand. Nobody liked losing a team member, so yeah, they took it out on the Humans. Achilles swept the rooftop to be sure none of the enemy remained, noticing Athena with a Human head in her hands. Paris had been a friend of hers.

"Check on Cartwright," Achilles ordered. Most of the team was looking at Paris' Konar lying on the rooftop amidst the Human bodies and silent antiaircraft guns. "Dusman, snap out of it!" he roared at them. "We're *Osk*, we're at the edge of the blade when we ride in a Raknar or when we deploy as commandos. Look at him," he pointed at the dead *osk*. "He's not the first; he won't be the last. We could all die the next time we go into battle. Don't forget it." He smacked an armored fist into Agamemnon's side. *Claang!* "Where is Cartwright?"

"*Checking,*" came the terse reply. "*Got him.*" He pointed. "*Two kilometers, on foot now, moving.*"

Achilles looked down at the dead and pointed. "Place a charge. We can't afford to take him with us, and we can't let the suit be found."

Athena plucked a charge from her suit's side and clicked it over Paris' suit's main power battery, then activated it. "*Ready,*" she said. "*J'pa take you, my friend,*" she whispered, and they leaped off the roof toward Cartwright's position. Behind them, the charge went off, detonating the Konar's power supply, and destroying most of the rooftop. Any Humans investigating would find little evidence of Paris beyond some melted metals. That would be the only monument to Paris.

* * *

"Keep moving," Jim ordered over the squad net. His team had been streaming through the city streets, moving fast to reach their objective. Buddha in 2nd Platoon had finished securing the antiaircraft, noting that one of the locations near Jim's landing point had been blown to pieces.

"Probably the crap guns they were using," Buddha said.

Jim didn't have time to ponder it. They'd wasted a busload of people with weapons, including a mortar, furthering the theory that this was a carefully planned attack. The problem was, the streets contained hundreds of people, and there was no easy way to tell whose side they were on. CASPers weren't designed to engage in non-lethal combat. Some of the other squads had a smattering of the closest thing the Cavaliers had in their arsenal: a sort of shotgun loaded with taser submunitions. They weren't lethal, usually.

If anyone on the streets acted aggressively, the Cavaliers had orders to use non-lethal measures unless said aggressor employed weapons capable of injuring a CASPer driver. If some idiot popped a couple 9mm rounds at a passing Cavalier, they were ignored or ate a taser round. The threat of a thrown Molotov, grenade, or anything larger than .50 caliber got the minigun.

Two blocks from their objective, they came upon the smoldering wreckage of three garbage trucks. Jim slowed his loping gait to look curiously at them. The closest leaked diesel and blood, in equal amounts.

"The fuck happened here?" Voss wondered. He had been a little stiff, recovering from the broken leg on Yovaz, but the surgeon had cleared him for duty.

"Someone else on the playing field, if I had to guess," Double T said.

"*Objective in sight*," said Private Glendale, the squad member equipped with the Mk 8 scout variant.

Jim glanced at the mess one last time, then filed it away for later consideration. "First Platoon, Second Squad, in position for possible backup?" Sergeant 'Tap' confirmed they were ready. "Roger that; we're beginning our assault."

* * * * *

Chapter Twenty-Three

"Sweep east so Cartwright doesn't see us," Achilles ordered. His appreciation of the Humans and their oversized Konar had grown in the last hour. They mounted an impressive amount of firepower, and they could *move* when they wanted to. His team was straining to keep up while watching for threats at the same time.

"*We're being spotted,*" Agamemnon warned.

"*And our batteries are running down,*" Ajax added.

We don't have time to recharge, either, Achilles thought. Surely there must be a colorful human curse word for this situation. "Update on Cartwright's location?"

"*They just shot up a bus full of enemies,*" Agamemnon said as he received a direct downlink from the *Feesius* in orbit. "*They are 1,200 meters ahead of us.*"

"We need to jump ahead of them," Achilles said. "Can you infer their objective from their path?"

"*I am pretty certain,*" Agamemnon said.

"Then let's move."

They screamed into the air, angling low and fast to cover distance quickly. Agamemnon's data feed showed Achilles exactly where Cartwright was, allowing them to make excellent time. His Konar said its battery was down to 45%. It also showed all the other members of his team, the highest being 61%, and the lowest 41%. Overall they had less than an hour of combat effectiveness remaining.

They landed amidst a tornado of stirred dust and garbage in an alley well ahead of Cartwright's line of advance. Their batteries were further reduced in capacity. He was about to instruct Agamemnon to plot a course through the alleyways to the target when a door burst open, and a trio of heavily-armed Humans rushed out. The Humans instantly came to a stop when they saw the nine Konar standing in the center of the alley, all of which turned to face them.

One of the Humans screamed something unintelligible, while another raised a pistol and fired at Achilles point blank. The bullet bounced off with a *zhiing*, doing no damage. Achilles' response was instantaneous, punching out with an augmented fist. The impact caved in the Human's sternum and launched him back through the door he'd just emerged from, screaming as he flew. The other two yelled, eyes wide in terror, and tried to raise weapons. Achilles' team cut them down before either could pull a trigger.

"*So I guess that qualifies as a hostile Human?*" Hera asked, amusement in her voice.

"*Who cares, as long as they're dead?*" Athena mumbled, kicking one of the corpses, just to be sure.

Agamemnon jumped through the door after the one Achilles had punched. They heard a laser fire, and he emerged a second later holding a device. "*He had a radio.*"

"Did he get off some comms?" Achilles asked.

"*Yes, that's why I went in after him, I picked up the radio frequency spike. The Human was in terrible shape, I was surprised he could speak. Maybe he didn't, I don't know. Only picked up his radio working, not what he sent.*"

Achilles turned in place, examining their position. Just running into a trio of heavily armed Humans made no sense. "Agamemnon, have the *Feesius* check for high-energy signatures."

"*Checking.*"

"Everyone, high alert," Achilles said, setting his sensor suite for constant spherical scan.

"*Confirmed, three high energy signatures, 200 meters over there.*"

"Move!" Achilles said, and they ran down the alley.

Like all the alleys in Human cities, it was filthy, full of garbage bins and refuse. The Humans cared little for their residences, it seemed. They were forced to run around everything from abandoned ground vehicles to discarded appliances. Their power was low, and the distance short, so Achilles kept them on the ground.

They raced across a narrow street, running at full speed. He caught a glimpse of CASPers in the distance. Checking his map, he saw they were Cartwright and his squad. Achilles hissed in anger; the energy signatures were adjacent to his charge's path. He pushed his speed as fast as he could, his breath coming in great gasps.

They rounded a final corner and found three huge vehicles sitting in the street, side by side, taking up the whole avenue. It only took a second to see that each was heavily modified from its original purpose. A plasma cutter had removed and rewelded great chunks of heavy steel. Primitive but powerful crew-served lasers were mounted behind improvised gun carriages, and the majority of the open rear of each vehicle was crammed with dozens of armed Humans. Dozens more were pouring out of the adjacent buildings and forming up to join. It was an ambush ready to spring.

"Hit them hard!" Achilles yelled, skidding halfway across the street as he scrubbed momentum. Huge sparks were thrown up by the alloy metal in his Konar's boots. He triggered his flight system, which took half a second to spin up before launching him into the air. Others in his squad with more power to spare fired up their own jets before stopping, turning their forward momentum into angular momentum, and rocketing at the trucks.

This wasn't like the previous attacks, where the Humans had been clueless and unsuspecting. As Agamemnon had said, the Human had gotten a communication out. Some of the Humans manning their cobbled-together APC were watching in all directions, and as soon as Achilles skidded around the corner, they opened fire. Assault rifles of Human design unleashed a stream of armor-piercing bullets. Well, armor-piercing to anything but Dusman tech, anyway.

The air was filled with bullets and a couple laser beams as the Konar flew into the storm. *Osk* were never timid in the face of fire. Any who were, were quickly removed from the *J'Zha* and assigned elsewhere.

The bullets whizzing at them were compounded when they bounced off the formidable Konar armor. In a second, the entire roadway was a crazy shooting gallery full of ricocheting bullets and lasers. Athena, always the one to exercise restraint, sprayed pulse laser fire from her left arm into the APC on the left, and tossed a bomb inside with her right as she went over. The bomb went off, and sent bodies flying like pinwheels through the air.

The exchange was fast and brutal, just the way an *osk* liked it. Once they were closer, Achilles and Ajax pushed the output on their arm lasers to maximum and used them like swords, slashing directly into the backs of the other two APCs. At that power level, each beam cut through five or more people at a time. Great gouts of blood flew into the air from the clean, brutal lasers.

One of his lasers must have hit a power source, because the middle APC went up like a volcano. The blast hit Achilles right in the face, sending him spinning backward and into a building.

"*Osk'ii*, are you awake?"

Achilles realized he'd been unconscious and immediately checked his diagnostics. His Konar was beaten up pretty badly. It was Athena leaning over him. "I'd be fine if you hadn't dropped a bomb in my target."

"*Nice try; that was you guys setting that one off.*"

He sat up and had the armor check his physical condition. Bruises and maybe a minor concussion. He triggered some painkillers and got to his feet. "Situation?"

"*They're all dead, vehicles destroyed. You were the only casualty.*"

"I am not a casualty," he insisted.

"*Damn, I was hoping for a promotion,*" Athena said.

"Sorry to disappoint you." He looked at the remains of the APCs, a charnel house of blood, hydrocarbon fuel (which the Humans still used), and burning debris.

"*Cartwright inbound, less than a minute,*" Agamemnon said.

"Clear the zone," he said and reviewed their power situation. It was bad. He now had the highest level, at 21%, with Athena the lowest at 11%. They quickly got off the street, breaking into an abandoned store, or maybe it was a city service building. Achilles didn't know or care, they just needed to be out of view when Cartwright went by.

He already considered the 'don't be spotted' part of their operation a glaring failure. The least he could do was keep out of sight of *Tor* J'asa's Human pet. "Are there any power sources here?"

"*In the basement,*" Agamemnon said, indicating some stairs. The door stood open, which should have been his first warning.

He pointed at Hector and the door, sending Hector down the stairs. "Maximum caution," he warned. "We don't need another fight like that, or we'll be on foot."

The Konar had small arms stored in their structure, and the light armor each of the *osk* wore in the suits would serve them well. However, without the mobility and firepower of the Konar, they were less than useless in any situation the Human CASPers might find difficult to deal with.

Hector moved quietly down the stairs, the other eight surviving members of the team behind him. Where the Konar excelled over the CASPers was stealth. When your armor was only slightly more than a meter tall and weighed just 200 kilograms, you could go places and do it quieter than the lumbering half-ton of steel the Humans used. The Dusman electric muscle fibers were also far superior, requiring less power and being nearly silent. All of his team had taken some damage, though, which meant the armor segments squeaked and sometimes grated against each other. He'd sent Hector because his armor was in the best shape.

"*You gotta see this,*" Hector almost whispered over their comms. The team came to a stop at the bottom landing of the stairs, about 10 meters below ground. Hector was standing at the edge of a door, leaning in just far enough so his suit's sensors were functioning at maximum efficiency.

Achilles could already see second hand from Hector's suit; he wanted to see himself. He stepped past Hector to examine the basement. "What in the depths of oblivion is this?" he hissed.

"*I have no idea,*" Hector said.

"Agamemnon, have you ever seen anything like this?"

The team moved carefully into the basement room, lasers charged and ready, watching every corner for movement. In the center was a console, with all manner of computers attached to it. A handle protruded from the top. Attached to the console were data and power cables that led to four pods, each a little over a meter tall, mounted to each of the basement's four walls.

"*Nothing specifically like this, no,*" Agamemnon said.

"Is it a weapon?" Achilles asked.

"*No,*" Agamemnon said, "*that much is certain.*" With a series of hissing snaps, his armor unlocked and split, allowing him to walk free of it. He removed a mobile sensor unit from the arm and walked around, sweeping the sensor over each piece of equipment. The rest increased their vigilance to protect him out of his armor. "*Some things are easier outside a Konar,*" he said.

"I wasn't going questioning your tactics, *Osk'i,*" Achilles said.

"*He's cuter outside his Konar anyway,*" Hera said. The team shared a chuckle. It only took a minute for Agamemnon to finish his scans.

"*These are life support units,*" he said, pointing to the four pods. "*They're being powered and controlled by this console. There's a micro-fusion reactor nearby.*" He bent and scanned the connections on the main pedestal. "*Power here,*" he said, and the team immediately hooked up.

"How long before Cartwright reaches his main objective?" Achilles asked Agamemnon, who was climbing back into his Konar.

"*Checking,*" he said. "*He's reached his objective!*"

"We're out of time," Achilles said. "Get what power you can; be prepared to move in two minutes."

They had their power tethers hooked up, drawing energy as quickly as the coupling would allow. Agamemnon reinitialized his sensors and continued scanning the equipment. Achilles was about to order them to disconnect when Agamemnon suddenly called out.

"*There are life signs in these pods!*"

"What?" Achilles said, moving next to his technology specialist.

Agamemnon was closely examining the pod's controls. After a moment, he touched one, and it slid open to reveal an opSha. "*Like I said.*"

Achilles looked closely at the alien, who was unconscious. Tubing connected it to the pod in several places, and cables were hooked to both its pinplant external links. He leaned in closely. The opSha, a simian species like Humans, had only vestigial eyes. Instead, they used echolocation to comprehend their surroundings. Even so, their eyes functioned, with lids that opened and closed, indicating wakefulness. This one's eyes were open.

"They're alive, right?"

"*Yes, or I wouldn't have sensed them on my instruments.*"

"Can you do a brain scan? Is there activity?" Achilles leaned in and touched the opSha's face with his suit's finger. It didn't respond; the eyes remained open.

"*Not a very detailed one,*" Agamemnon said, and moved a hand over the alien's head, sensors in the glove relaying information for him to study. "*No sign of brain activity.*"

"*Why keep a dead person alive?*" Ajax wondered, looking at the other pods. "*What about those?*"

"*Three of the four are occupied, all inactive like this one.*"

"We don't have time," Achilles said. "Everybody, get ready to go."

"Osk'ii," Agamemnon said.

Achilles turned to see Agamemnon scanning the central console. "*Do you know what this is?*"

"Obviously not, but what difference does it make? Our primary charge is—"

"*Is of no importance against this!*"

Achilles was taken aback. "Do you know what you're saying?"

Agamemnon reached out and touched a control on the console. The handle rose, revealing it to be attached to an armored case locked down via a complicated array. He scanned the case and sent the results to Achilles.

"Oh," Achilles said. "*Feesius,* this is *Osk'ii* Achilles. I have a situation here."

* * * * *

Chapter Twenty-Four

Austin Texas, Terran Federation, Earth, Sol System

"Go!" Jim said, and fired the last of his jumpjuice. The Mk 7 CASPer roared over the edge of the abandoned apartment building's roof and across the alley. He crashed through the wall of the target building shoulder first, exploding through steel, concrete, and glass into an empty office. The rest of his squad arrived similarly. Heavy weapons fire exploded outside, aimed at the roof they'd just vacated. Jim grinned. *Suckers.*

The squad split up, half heading up to neutralize those on the roof, the rest heading down the stairs. Jim took them four at a time, his CASPer an extension of his body; the two were one. The voice was mumbling about blood, and he was in the mood to give it. He didn't notice how far ahead of his squad he'd raced, or the instrument measuring electromagnetic radiation spiking just behind him.

He hit the bottom basement landing less than a minute after they'd made their entrance, surprising six armed men in camo. He tore through them without hesitation. He didn't bother with weapons, just used the suit like a metal meatgrinder. He reached the basement door and decided to enter the same way he had above, blasting through the door and skidding to a stop in the midst of six CASPers. Only they couldn't be his squad, they were behind him, not ahead.

"Hey, boys, what's up?"

275

An opSha standing behind them laughed. "Worked like a charm."

Jim examined the CASPers, still activating, and realized he'd fucked up. "I thought it was Peepo's former allies, up to their old tricks. I was wrong, wasn't I?"

"Minerva sends its regards." The opSha closed its eyes and commanded the CASPer with pinplants.

Jim was impressed; remote controlling a squad of CASPers was no mean feat. Harder than the time he had destroying them. The voice cried for the robots' destruction, then their master's blood. He was fine with giving it what it wanted for a change.

He used the <slow> augment first to move faster than the opSha expected, defeating two of the enemy, then switched to <boost> to use increased strength to tear through the rest. Not without a payment, though. CASPers weren't designed to fight their own number in close quarters battle. Each one he defeated cost him damage; every single one.

The opSha fled once it was clear Jim would best his toys. When Jim wrecked the last of them, he stumbled after the alien, his suit barely functional. The strength-enhancing nanites had run their course. All that was left was rage and determination.

Then he was outside, searching. The opSha jumped on his nearly wrecked CASPer from above, wiggling its little body *inside* his suit with him. It tried and failed to access his pinplants, and that's when the knife came out. The rest was blood and hell.

"As you Humans like to say, to hell with you."

"You first." Jim spat blood and tore its neck out with his teeth. He staggered and fell, the suit hitting the concrete with a thunderous crash. *Huh. It doesn't really hurt.*

* * *

Dusman Shuttle, Descending over Austin Texas, Terran Federation, Earth, Sol System

"There's a lot of fighting underway, *Tor*," the pilot said. "Are you certain about this?"

"Very," J'asa said. "ETA?"

"Twenty minutes."

She nodded and went into the rear of the shuttle. Ten *osk* were there, armored up and ready for action. They immediately saluted, fist to chest, as she entered.

"*Tor*," the *Osk'tor* K'raa said. "We're ready. But are you sure?" He indicated the 11th Konar locked into a cradle, it's access open.

"As positive as I was when the *ske'o* questioned my orders," she said sternly.

"I was not questioning your orders, *Tor*, just your *training*."

J'asa smirked. "I was *vok* before I was *Tor*. If I can handle a Raknar—"

"With all due respect, honored leader, a Konar is not a Raknar. Aside from being an armored system, there isn't much more in common."

"Then it's good I have the *osk'tor* with me."

She couldn't see K'raa's face, so she couldn't see if he was smiling or scowling. It didn't matter, she guessed.

"*Tor*, I have a relayed comm from the *osk* team escorting Cartwright."

"Put them through to my personal comm," she said. "This is *Tor* J'asa. Achilles?"

"*Yes,* Tor."

"What is Jim's status?"

"He's engaged with what he believed to be insurgents. He's wrong. Look what we just found."

An image appeared in the tiny Tri-V built into the comm unit. The metallic case, it's construction, the interface for its connection to the pedestal. Then the image changed to the pod with an opSha inside. Her blood went cold at the sight.

"Is that case..." she trailed off.

"Agamemnon believes it is."

"What do you think?"

"I agree."

"Fuck," she cursed.

"I see you appreciate English cursing as much as I do."

"It's more effective at conveying emotions than Dusman."

"Report from the Eesius *watching the battle says Cartwright is fighting right now,"* the pilot said.

"Tor," Achilles said, *"we can be there in less than a minute, but we'll have to leave this behind."*

J'asa stared at the bulkhead. She could feel Jim fighting, his concern, his rage, the strange bloodlust he felt now in battle. She jerked slightly at some injury. She'd never made a more difficult decision.

"Ske'o," she addressed the pilot, "redirect to the coordinates provided by *Osk'ii* Achilles."

"Yes, Tor."

Pain. It tore through her body. *Jim!* She screamed and fell to the deck, striking her head. When she could focus again, K'raa was there, turning her over. Jim was dying, she knew it, and she would die with him. "I'll order the *ske'o* to return to your ship."

"NO!" she snapped, a searing pain in her chest. Her vision swam, and she looked at the chest plate of K'raa's Konar. "Listen to me and

follow my orders," she said. "No matter what happens, rendezvous with Achilles; secure what he's found. Do you understand? Only once it's secured do you go for Cartwright. No matter what."

"Yes, *Tor*, but why?"

She nodded her head, struggling to breathe, her vision dimming. "Just…do…it." The pain took her away.

* * *

J im floated in a featureless void, weightless and unafraid. If this was death, it wasn't so bad. He could sense his life stretching out behind him, but stopping where he floated. He thought back and found many moments of pain, more of happiness, and a few of joy.

There was Splunk, J'asa, a flickering sensation he couldn't touch, yet could always feel. The connection was strange, alien, reassuring, though it was also tied to his body in a strange way. A way that he knew if it broke, so would he.

Another connection was Ziva. This one pulsed and glowed. It had started as a fond thread; now it was white hot and essential. It had the potential to become even more. This frightened and excited him at the same time.

A myriad of other connections surrounded him like the many moons of Jupiter. Friends and associates who'd colored his life so fully. Buddha, Rick Culper, Double T, Captain Su, and so many more. He realized they were a web holding him up, supporting him, and making it possible to do what he had to do. *Life is so beautifully complicated,* he thought in wonder.

The severed connections were painful. His father, the oldest and longest cut of them all. Dad was just out of reach, now nothing more than a dim memory. His mother, with mixed feelings of loss and betrayal. Captain Winslow, struck down in battle while saving so many. Hargrave. He shied away from that one; it hurt too much.

Then the dark connections, the ones he was tied to despite his wishes. Amazingly, Peepo was there, though she was dead. Despite the severed line, she still affected his actions, and would for many more years.

Adayn. That wasn't really her name, yet he still thought of her that way. The connection was strong and malevolent. "Love/hate" was the term. Deceiver was another. And yet she'd saved him, and given him the nanites that had not only helped him escape Peepo, but had saved his life many times since.

These were the threads of his being, and they were slipping away. It would be so incredibly easy to let them go. Despite the tenuousness of the future, he felt like it didn't matter. "Haven't I done enough?" he asked the void. "Haven't I bled enough, cried enough, fought enough, or died enough?"

There was no one to answer him, yet he knew the answer. No, of course it wasn't enough. Not only did he have more to give, he wanted to *live*. He pulled on the connections to bring himself back to them, to strengthen the bindings of his soul. For a moment, he could see back along his life as clear as a winter's night sky.

But wait, why did it seem to blur past a point several years earlier? *That's strange*, he thought, but then he ascended into the light and forgot all about it.

* * *

The insistent beeping of machines and the glare of brilliant surgical lights stabbed into his eyes. He tried to move his hands to block them, his mind full of cotton.

"He's regaining consciousness!" someone yelled.

"You're goddamned right I am," he wanted to say, but there was a tube down his throat. For a fleeting second, he saw surprised men and women in masks looking down at him, bloody instruments in their hands, and he realized his chest was open. *Oh*, he thought, *that's what my lungs look like?*

"Putting him back under," another voice said.

He wanted to complain and tell them it was fine, but then he sank back into the inky black depths of unconsciousness.

* * *

"She's coming around."

J'asa blinked at the bright white lights. A pair of *coo*, healers dressed in red robes, had her hooked up to a dizzying array of instruments. "Is he alive?" she asked.

"Of course he is," a gruff voiced answered. She turned her head and saw Dante standing by the bed, a scowl on his face. "You think you'd be alive if he wasn't? You know how this works, you fool."

"You're speaking to the *Tor*," one of the *coo* said.

"I'm speaking to a fool," he said again.

J'asa snorted and sat up. Of course she was fine. She hadn't nearly died because of her injuries, but because of Jim's. "How bad is he?" she asked Dante.

"You should be worried about yourself, *Tor*." The one speaking was *coo'i*, an expert healer, then. "Your brain activity was dangerously affected. We've never studied the effect of these *Akee* bondings. All we have are records from the *Nee'Akee*. There's almost nothing there; it's never been indexed. You could have died."

"But I didn't," she snapped. "Can I get out of this cursed bed?"

"I wouldn't recommend it."

"That wasn't the question the *Tor* asked," Dante said sharply.

"Other than strain, you have no lasting effects."

"Good," J'asa said and got up. Then she looked around. The medical bay was on a ship, but they were under gravity. She looked at Dante. "Where the fuck am I?"

He laughed. "You're in the medical bay of a *Feesius* grounded in Austin. The city officials shit themselves when the ship set down."

"I bet they did. Where's Jim?"

"St. David's Medical Center."

"Take me to him."

He gestured at her uniform. She donned it, picked up her belt with sidearm, and followed him out. Behind him, the *coo* were busy gathering up their instruments and equipment. A pair of Human *coo*, doctors they were called, were looking in with resentment at the intrusion on their space. J'asa stopped and pointed at them.

"See that they are compensated for our use of the facility."

"I will," Dante said, and fell in behind them. "You need to know about Cartwright."

"First, tell me about Achilles. Did they secure the prize?"

"They did. It's at the Houston Raknar base."

"Good, now what about Jim?"

Dante sighed and explained it. It was more complicated than she'd feared.

* * *

The next time Jim awoke, he was in a recovery room, and the wooziness was quickly wearing off. A nurse was checking his vitals, and a doctor stood nearby with a slate, making notes. He turned his head and saw Ziva as well, her Depik perched on a shoulder. Her face was sunken, eyes exhausted. He'd never forget the expression on her face.

"It was really lucky you were there, Ms. Alcuin," the Human doctor said. "Even so, I'm surprised he held on long enough to let your nanites work. Jim Cartwright, you're a tough bastard!"

"Thanks, Doc," Jim croaked. The nurse stuck a straw in his mouth, and he drank some cool water. It helped.

A Depik jumped up onto the foot of his bed and stared at him. "I know you wish to be up and moving, Jim Cartwright, but you will displease me, our Ziva, and therefore Fssik, as well as your Dusman friend if you push too hard. Do you understand this?"

"Have we met, Hunter?" Jim asked.

"I am Esthik, formerly of Night Wind Clan, now Hunter of Hurts for Clan Tamir. Welcome to our negotiation."

"I'm not really in a position to negotiate right now," Jim said.

"I'm glad to hear you joking," Ziva said, stepping forward so Jim could see her better. She navigated her way around several "Get Well Soon" balloon bouquets and walked up to the side of the bed. Then she took his hand and threaded her fingers through his. "Esthik is our best healer. I called him for you."

Jim noticed the Human doctor frowning slightly, but didn't say anything more. Splunk was sitting on the end of the bed, watching him with her huge blue-on-blue eyes. She wore her dark red uniform and an expression of sadness.

"Yes," Esthik said. "We are all here to see that you heal properly, Jim Cartwright. As I said, you will displease a number of deadly beings if you do not. Do we understand one another?"

"Never annoy a Healer," Fssik said from his perch on Ziva's shoulder. "A proverb of my old clan."

"Wise saying," Splunk said. She was regarding him for some reason. Jim wondered what was happening. Something about her felt...different. Eventually, she moved over and snuggled down next to his uninjured side. "Best listen to killer kitty healer, Jim."

"Fine..." Jim sighed. "I won't push it. Thanks for coming. I'll be good. But—can you give me a minute? I want to talk to Ziva about something."

Splunk laughed. "Her kitty won't leave her, and I won't leave you alone with two of them, Jim. Don't be dumb."

Ziva drew breath to retort, but Fssik got there first.

"They need to talk, Dusman," he said. "If we want them to breed, we need to let that happen. We can wait outside as soon as the Healer is finished."

"And I am finished," Esthik said. "You may not overexert yourself, Jim Cartwright. Sex will have to wait a few days, just so you're aware."

"Good lord, Esthik, okay." There was a chuckle in his voice, but he cringed as he laughed. The pain moved down his side and legs in a shudder, catching him by surprise.

Splunk scowled at Ziva, then at Esthik and Fssik both. "Fine," she said. She patted Jim's face softly. "Be good. I'll be right outside." Then she turned her back and jumped down, heading for the door. Esthik gave Ziva a slow blink before following.

"Be careful with him, my Human," Fssik said as he leaped down from the shelf above the door. Ziva rolled her eyes and laughed, though her face flamed in mortification.

"I love you, Hunter," she said. "Now get the fuck out."

Fssik slow blinked and exited, closing the door behind him.

"Well," Ziva said, drawing in a deep breath. "It seems like they know what they want."

"Yeah," Jim said, shifting a little in his bed. It was difficult, no matter what he did; it hurt or caused a shot of pain.

"Are you okay? Comfortable?"

"Yeah," he said. "It's just...is that what you want, Ziva? You want kids?"

Ziva paused, taking her time before speaking with great care. "I do," she said finally. "I've always thought that I'd like kids, but now...with everything going on in the clan. I'm starting to think I should get on that sooner rather than later. And the truth—" she cut herself off, her fingers tightening on Jim's.

"What?" he asked, his roughened voice strangely gentle.

"The truth, Jim, is that when I saw you there, knife in your chest...I couldn't breathe. I couldn't move for fear of losing you. And then I knew that if I *didn't* move, I *would* lose you! We're not safe people, you and me. The things we do...we do for a damn good reason, but no one would ever accuse us of being safe. So maybe having kids wouldn't be fair to them. But then I think about my mom, and this incredible legacy she left behind. And my clan, my family. The Cavaliers are like that for you. They're your clan, and your legacy, and..."

Ziva trailed off, then let out a gusty sigh. She looked down at Jim and pushed a bit of hair back from his face. Then she leaned down and brushed her lips against his.

"We both have families that need us, and if we're gone, they need a part of us to remain. Yes, Jim, I want to have kids. Specifically, I want to have _your_ kids. Let's make some babies. Let's tie Cartwright's Cavaliers to Clan Tamir with ties of siblinghood. Let's leave our families stronger when we're gone."

Jim stared up at her, his eyes dark. Ziva's eyes darted around his face, searching, pleading in their desire to know what he was thinking. He didn't speak. Instead, his lips twitched upward in a tiny smile that melted her soul. Then he nodded.

Ziva smiled back before leaning in for another kiss.

* * *

J'asa stood on the table outside the hospital room and wondered what was transpiring inside. Jim felt…different. He'd even noticed her change in caste and status. She'd underestimated his abilities once again. Her own body still felt out of sorts after the shock of his near death. She tried to imagine the _vok_ of old, and what they'd gone through. Tried and failed.

Dante was still pretty pissed, both at Achilles and her, too. He felt Achilles' team should have stuck to the plan. J'asa refused to allow them to be punished for following _her_ orders. It was a good thing Dante was under her command, because she was quite sure Dante would have killed Achilles.

In the time she'd been gone, Jim had gone from friendship to lover with the female Ziva. She was partnered with a Depik, too, which made matters even more complicated. The damned Depik were not only formidable killers, they also had a severely overdeveloped opinion of themselves as well. It would have been so much better if Peepo had finished them off. It was too late now. Far too difficult to cleanse the Depik, with the Humans intertwining in their affairs.

If Jim did produce children with Ziva, it wouldn't be a bad thing. It might even make Jim a little easier to control, a little less wild. She hadn't had time to go to Ja'kuapa. Her ascension to *Tor* had put all that off. Now she was occupied with getting her people settled and the assignment of all the *Po'Froo*. Setting up the Arsenal to work at full power, and, and, and. She sighed.

"You are a troubled being," Esthik said from his perch on a table, licking the back of a hand and using it to wash his face.

"You have no idea, Depik," she replied.

"Are you going to tell him you are the Dusman's leader or not?"

J'asa managed to not gape at the Depik, though only just. The damned feline smiled.

"Yes, we can sense your castes. Our connection to quintessence extends our senses far beyond making ourselves invisible or feeling enemies. I can also sense your fear of the future, though I do not understand why."

"Then you should be glad of your ignorance," she replied. "Yes, I'll tell him. Soon enough for that. He deserves some happiness."

"He doesn't know the extent of his injuries yet," the Depik healer said.

"They told me they're still evaluating him," J'asa said. "I'm going to have our *coo*, our healers, check him as well."

"He'll know soon," Esthik pointed out. "Even the Human medicine will eventually spot the damage to his spinal cord."

"The nanites didn't catch it?" Fssik asked.

"I understand he has a built-in nanite healer, something we've never seen before. I fear the shot Ziva gave him interfered with his own, which were specifically tailored for Humans," Esthik explained.

J'asa shook her head, not speaking for a long moment. "For now, let him enjoy the female," she said eventually.

"My Ziva is just as happy with him as he is with her," Fssik said from a perch in the corner of the hallway. "I guess this makes us family, Dusman?"

"Don't push your luck," J'asa said and hopped down to go looking for some food. She wasn't sure, but she could swear the damned cats were laughing at her behind her back.

* * * * *

Epilogue

The hospital room door opened, and a small crowd pushed in. The doctor, who'd only just recovered looked horrified, holding up her hands to try to stem the flow.

"Now, now!" she barked. "I said a *few* visitors, not the whole damned waiting room!"

"There is nothing to worry about," Esthik said. "This wasn't a surgery, but a normal event in life. The visiting will do them both good."

The doctor threw up her hands in exasperation and pushed her way out of the room.

"Way to go, Jimbo!" Buddha said, pumping Jim's hand vigorously.

"I didn't do anything, she did it all," Jim said, moving to shake Buddha's hand with a whine of servos.

"That's not how it works," Captain Su said, smiling. "Are you doing okay, dear?" she asked Ziva.

"Of course, just a little sore."

"Well, let's see him!" Buddha said, and the group of well-wishers voiced their agreement.

Ziva, sitting up in bed, gently reached down and moved the blanket a bit to expose the baby. His skin was still splotchy, like all newborns, but his eyes were bright as he looked around the room. A hand came free, waving uncontrollably. Jim reached down, and the tiny digits encircled his index finger. Applause broke out, and the baby started but didn't cry.

"He is a fine kit," Fssik said from the hospital headboard, looking down and smiling at the baby.

Splunk sat on the room's coffee table a few meters away, watching without comment, though her ears were curled upward in a sign of approval.

"You settled on a name?" Buddha asked.

"We've chosen Thaddeus," Ziva said. Heads nodded in understanding.

"I think there've been enough Jims in the Cartwright line," Jim said.

Ziva smiled up at him, reaching over to pat his behind, and accidentally patting the metal support. "Are you okay?" She looked up at him. Double T was breaking out some beers he'd smuggled in. He pretended not to notice.

"Don't worry about me," he said. "It's better today." She smiled and looked back at Thaddeus, so she didn't see the hard set to Jim's jaw. He used his pinplants to adjust the cybernetic leg braces. It was a struggle to be on his feet more than an hour before the pain became too great. It was like a feedback loop most times, out of control. A couple oxycontin with his orange juice that morning had made sure he'd make it this far. Now they were wearing off. He ground his teeth and ignored it. The words of the specialist last month came back to him.

"The damage to your spinal cord was a near thing, Mr. Cartwright. Considering the same blade took a chunk out of your descending aorta, and you survived, most people would consider themselves lucky. You have 50% use of your legs, normal bowel and sexual function, you've taken well to the bionic leg supports, and have had a steady increase in function."

"I'm a goddamned merc, doc," he'd complained. "You're the best orthopedic specialist on the planet."

"I am, and the damage was partially healed by nanites. But the same healing also interfered with the natural healing process. We've come a long way since the aliens came along, but we can't replace or jump the spine yet. Your external bionic walking aids are the best we can do."

If the Depik and Dusman doctors hadn't said basically the same thing, he would have given into the ever-disgruntled voice and punched the doctor in the throat. The birth of his son was the high point of the last year. Maybe he'd feel better if Minerva had made another attempt on his life. The lack of anything made him feel worse. It was as if the SI had decided he was no longer a threat.

The guys had cigars out now. The Depik doctor shook his head, but the Human doctor just about lost her shit.

Jim had almost quit, turned the Cavaliers over to Buddha and ran them from the office. When he told Buddha, his XO had sent in Lieutenant Mayer.

"You quitting, Colonel?"

"What do you want, Lieutenant?"

"For you to reconsider. I've fought with you, watched men die with you. Figured I had the measure of your soul. Didn't pick you for a quitter."

"What was that?"

Mayer reached down and pulled up his uniform trousers to reveal metal legs. "Gonna make an excuse now, sir?" Jim frowned. "I was 22 when I lost my legs in that spacesuit accident. You still have yours. Don't give up. I know you can do it." That was six months ago, after he'd mostly healed. He was still in charge and still minister of war. Life goes on.

While the visitors popped beers and lit cigars to the doctor's loud complaints, Ziva hummed a tune to their child. Jim dearly wished she'd chosen something other than "Cat's in the Cradle."

# # # # #

About Mark Wandrey

Living life as a full-time RV traveler with his wife Joy, Mark Wandrey is a bestselling author who has been creating new worlds since he was old enough to write. A four-time Dragon Award finalist, Mark has written dozens of books and short stories, and is working on more all the time. A prolific world builder, he created the wildly popular Four Horsemen Universe as well as the space opera Earth Song series, and Turning Point, a zombie apocalypse series. His favorite medium is military sci-fi, but he is always up to a new challenge.

Find his books on Amazon at https://www.amazon.com/Mark-Wandrey/e/B00914T11A/

Sign up on his mailing list and get free stuff and updates! http://www.worldmaker.us/news-flash-sign-up-page/

* * * * *

About Kacey Ezell

Kacey Ezell is an active duty USAF instructor pilot with 3000+ hours in the UH-1N Huey and Mi-171 helicopters. When not teaching young pilots to beat the air into submission, she writes sci-fi/fantasy/horror/noir/alternate history fiction. She is a two-time Dragon Award Finalist for Best Alternate History. She's contributed to multiple Baen anthologies and has twice been selected for inclusion in the Year's Best Military and Adventure Science Fiction compilation. In 2018, her story "Family Over Blood" won the Year's Best Military and Adventure Science Fiction Readers' Choice Award. In addition to writing for Baen Books and Blackstone Publishing, she has published several novels and short stories with independent publisher Chris Kennedy Publishing. She is married with two daughters. You can find out more and join her mailing list at www.kaceyezell.net.

* * * * *

For More Information:

For a suggested reading order to the 4HU, go to:

https://chriskennedypublishing.com/the-four-horsemen-
books/4hu-suggested-reading-order/

* * * * *

For a listing of all the Four Horsemen books, go to:

https://chriskennedypublishing.com/the-four-horsemen-books/

* * * * *

Do you have what it takes to be a Merc?

Take your VOWs and join the Merc Guild on Facebook!

Meet us at: https://www.facebook.com/groups/536506813392912/

* * * * *

Did you like this book?
Please write a review!

* * * * *

The following is an

Excerpt from Book One of the Lunar Free State:

The Moon and Beyond

John E. Siers

Available from Theogony Books

eBook and Paperback

Excerpt from "The Moon and Beyond:"

"So, what have we got?" The chief had no patience for inter-agency squabbles.

The FBI man turned to him with a scowl. "We've got some abandoned buildings, a lot of abandoned stuff—none of which has anything to do with spaceships—and about a hundred and sixty scientists, maintenance people, and dependents left behind, all of whom claim they knew nothing at all about what was really going on until today. Oh, yeah, and we have some stripped computer hardware with all memory and processor sections removed. I mean physically taken out, not a chip left, nothing for the techies to work with. And not a scrap of paper around that will give us any more information...at least, not that we've found so far. My people are still looking."

"What about that underground complex on the other side of the hill?"

"That place is wiped out. It looks like somebody set off a *nuke* in there. The concrete walls are partly fused! The floor is still too hot to walk on. Our people say they aren't sure how you could even *do* something like that. They're working on it, but I doubt they're going to find anything."

"What about our man inside, the guy who set up the computer tap?"

"Not a trace, chief," one of the NSA men said. "Either he managed to keep his cover and stayed with them, or they're holding him prisoner, or else..." The agent shrugged.

"You think they terminated him?" The chief lifted an eyebrow. "A bunch of rocket scientists?"

"Wouldn't put it past them. Look at what Homeland Security ran into. Those motion-sensing chain guns are *nasty*, and the area between the inner and outer perimeter fence is mined! Of course, they posted warning signs, even marked the fire zones for the guns. Nobody would have gotten hurt if the troops had taken the signs seriously."

The Homeland Security colonel favored the NSA man with an icy look. "That's bullshit. How did we know they weren't bluffing? You'd feel pretty stupid if we'd played it safe and then found out there were no defenses, just a bunch of signs!"

"Forget it!" snarled the chief. "Their whole purpose was to delay us, and it worked. What about the Air Force?"

"It might as well have been a UFO sighting as far as they're concerned. Two of their F-25s went after that spaceship, or whatever it was we saw leaving. The damned thing went straight up, over eighty thousand meters per minute, they say. That's nearly Mach Two, in a *vertical climb*. No aircraft in *anybody's* arsenal can sustain a climb like that. Thirty seconds after they picked it up, it was well above their service ceiling and still accelerating. Ordinary ground radar couldn't find it, but NORAD *thinks* they might have caught a short glimpse with one of their satellite-watch systems, a hundred miles up and still going."

"So where did they go?"

"Well, chief, if we believe what those leftover scientists are telling us, I guess they went to the Moon."

* * * * *

Get "The Moon and Beyond" here:
https://www.amazon.com/dp/B097QMN7PJ.

Find out more about John E. Siers at:
https://chriskennedypublishing.com.

* * * * *

The following is an

Excerpt from Book One of Abner Fortis, ISMC:

Cherry Drop

———————————————

P.A. Piatt

Available from Theogony Books

eBook and Paperback

Excerpt from "Cherry Drop:"

"Here they come!"

A low, throbbing buzz rose from the trees and the undergrowth shook. Thousands of bugs exploded out of the jungle, and Fortis' breath caught in his throat. The insects tumbled over each other in a rolling, skittering mass that engulfed everything in its path.

The Space Marines didn't need an order to open fire. Rifles cracked and the grenade launcher thumped over and over as they tried to stem the tide of bugs. Grenades tore holes in the ranks of the bugs and well-aimed rifle fire dropped many more. Still, the bugs advanced.

Hawkins' voice boomed in Fortis' ear. "LT, fall back behind the fighting position, clear the way for the heavy weapons."

Fortis looked over his shoulder and saw the fighting holes bristling with Marines who couldn't fire for fear of hitting their own comrades. He thumped Thorsen on the shoulder.

"Fall back!" he ordered. "Take up positions behind the fighting holes."

Thorsen stopped firing and moved among the other Marines, relaying Fortis' order. One by one, the Marines stopped firing and made for the rear. As the gunfire slacked off, the bugs closed ranks and continued forward.

After the last Marine had fallen back, Fortis motioned to Thorsen.

"Let's go!"

Thorsen turned and let out a blood-chilling scream. A bug had approached unnoticed and buried its stinger deep in Thorsen's calf. The stricken Marine fell to the ground and began to convulse as the neurotoxin entered his bloodstream.

"Holy shit!" Fortis drew his kukri, ran over, and chopped at the insect stinger. The injured bug made a high-pitched shrieking noise, which Fortis cut short with another stroke of his knife.

Viscous, black goo oozed from the hole in Thorsen's armor and his convulsions ceased.

"*Get the hell out of there!*"

Hawkins was shouting in his ear, and Abner looked up. The line of bugs was ten meters away. For a split second he almost turned and ran, but the urge vanished as quickly as it appeared. He grabbed Thorsen under the arms and dragged the injured Marine along with him, pursued by the inexorable tide of gaping pincers and dripping stingers.

Fortis pulled Thorsen as fast as he could, straining with all his might against the substantial Pada-Pada gravity. Thorsen convulsed and slipped from Abner's grip and the young officer fell backward. When he sat up, he saw the bugs were almost on them.

* * * * *

Get "Cherry Drop" now at:
https://www.amazon.com/dp/B09B14VBK2

Find out more about P.A. Piatt at:
https://chriskennedypublishing.com

* * * * *

Made in the USA
Monee, IL
26 October 2021